Shooting in the Dark

Riot Police in Britain

GERRY NORTHAM

faber and faber

LONDON · BOSTON

First published in Great Britain
by Faber and Faber Limited
3 Queen Square London WC1N 3AU

Photoset by Wilmaset Birkenhead Wirral
Printed in Great Britain by
Mackays of Chatham PLC Chatham Kent

British Library Cataloguing in Publication Data

Northam, Gerry
Shooting in the dark: riot police in Britain
1. Great Britain. Riots. Role of police
I. Title
363.2'0941
ISBN 0-571-15090-X

Contents

Acknowledgements, vii

1 The Carruthers Estate, 1

2 The Paramilitary Drift, 29

3 Tooling Up, 44

4 The Operational Knowledge, 65

5 Tactical Options I, 82

6 Tactical Options II, 93

7 Related Matters, 117

8 The Colony Within, 126

9 The Golden Concept, 140

10 Shooting In The Dark, 156

Appendices

A Part 1: Government statement on rioting in
Bristol, House of Commons, Wednesday
6 August 1980
Part 2: Review of arrangements for handling
spontaneous disorder.

B The Public Order Forward Planning Unit

C Extracts from the ACPO *Public Order Manual*

D Report of Home Office working party on
police use of firearms 3 February 1987

Index, 196

Acknowledgements

This book began with four BBC programmes, two for television and two for radio. My interest in British policing techniques was aroused while producing a *File On 4* programme broadcast on Radio 4 on 9 September 1980, which featured Steve Bradshaw as reporter. The discovery of a colonial influence on domestic police forces came while reporting a *Brass Tacks* documentary, 'A Fair Degree Of Force?', which was shown on BBC2 on 31 October 1985. The researcher was Su Carroll and the producer Rob Rohrer. The first opportunity to see paramilitary policing as it is currently taught was during filming of another *Brass Tacks* programme, 'Arms Of The Law', which was broadcast on 17 July 1986, again on BBC2. The researcher was Liz Carney and the producer Steve Anderson. The extent to which the Metropolitan Police have reconstructed training at Hendon and Hounslow became apparent while recording a *File On 4* documentary which was heard on Radio 4 on 29 September 1987. The producer was Brendan McCarthy and the editor Brian Walker. I am deeply indebted to the imagination and insight these colleagues have brought, and to the editorial guidance of three outstanding superiors who have formed my journalistic ABC: Colin Adams, Roger Bolton and Colin Cameron.

Many direct quotes reproduced in the text come from these four programmes. Others, where not attributed elsewhere, come from interviews I have conducted with those concerned. The remarks of the Deputy Chief Constable of Northumbria and the chairman of the local police authority quoted in Chapter 9 are taken from interviews conducted by Francis Wilkins of Crewe and Alsager College for his dissertation on British police methods.

My approach to these issues was sharpened during a vigorous discussion of public order policing which was held at St George's

House in Windsor Castle one weekend in February 1986 under the chairmanship of the then Director, Tom Batho, who kindly invited me as a speaker.

Will Sulkin of Faber and Faber has been a delightful and encouraging editor and I thank Peter Taylor for introducing us.

John Alderson and others have helped more than they know by reading the manuscript and shaping its final form. They are, of course, innocent of its remaining faults.

Above all, I acknowledge the co-operation of police officers, named and unnamed, who want this story told.

I   The Carruthers Estate

It is sometimes necessary to think in terminology which has more of a military connotation.
ACPO Public Order Manual

As usual, Saturday begins quietly in Sandford. In the town centre, shopkeepers are boarding up their broken windows and deciding how much to tell the insurance companies they lost during the looting. The owners of two burnt-out cars from the night before are at the police station explaining that their documents were destroyed in the glove compartments. But it is a fine day, rather warm for April in Sandfordshire, and the gangs of boys who caused all the damage are long since back in their beds. This afternoon they will get up as usual and go to see Sandford win at home against Chelsea, and as usual one of them will stab a visiting supporter and there will be a decent-sized punch-up at the ground. The police will have their work cut out trying to keep order and get the gangs from Chelsea back on the trains without anyone else getting hurt.

Then late at night, just before closing time, the landlord of The Vines on the edge of the high-rise Carruthers Estate, next to the town centre, will try to close early when his customers start fighting each other. His pub and the flat above it will be set on fire. Six hundred people will build barricades across the entrances to the estate and, as usual, start a riot inside it. The police commander on the ground will send in armoured vehicles to break through the barricades. A unit of police in riot gear will rush in behind them to take back the territory and, as they do, someone in one of the tower blocks will fetch down his rifle and start shooting at them. It happens every Saturday in Sandford. It is what the town and the Carruthers Estate were invented for.

Sometimes the police get back in control by Saturday midnight.

Other times they spread out too thinly and are beaten back. On a good Saturday they can get the fire crews in early enough to save most of the estate. On a bad night they face such a hail of petrol bombs that they are lucky if they come through in one piece themselves.

The police know that they will always win in the end. What makes it instructive is that neither side knows how long they will take, or what the cost will be in casualties and arson. It all depends on the police commander in charge of the operation. He is the crucial variable. Every other factor in Sandford, from the violence of the gangs right down to the weather, is as constant and predictable as the computer which controls them.

At ten o'clock on a Thursday morning in a real room in the city of Birmingham, five senior officers are sitting down to test their nerve against it.

The backstreets of the Carruthers Estate are known to policemen from all over Britain. Uniformed officers have trained in their thousands in the escalating violence of Sandford on a Saturday night. To a senior officer – Chief Inspector upwards – the names of the four entrances to the Carruthers Estate are as familiar as the Old Kent Road and Park Lane (from a different board game). They are: Polygon Close where the public house is set on fire, Wren Close, Robin Close and Snow Close where the shooting starts. The whole of Sandford was created in 1983 by a small committee of senior officers from different police forces who devised a training programme for every part of the country to prepare for real-life rioting of the kind which broke out in London, Liverpool, Manchester, Bristol and elsewhere in 1980–1. Their job was to ensure that riot police from each force are trained in exactly the same way, so that men from anywhere can be sent as reinforcements to disturbances anywhere else. At that stage, in 1982, none of those involved talked about taking on pickets in an industrial dispute or fighting a convoy of hippies. It was riots that worried them, and Sandford could stand for any of the tense real-life inner-city areas where they might break out. The tactics police have learned in Sandford are now ready for any city in the country. In 1984, every police force in England, Wales and Scotland started training with the full kit: a large map of Sandford to be spread out on a table-top; a box full of wooden police vans and little wooden crowds with numbers of rioters printed on them (from 15 up to 600); another box of coloured wooden counters with codes on them indicating units of the Sandfordshire Constabulary; a handful of senior officers, also made of wood and labelled CH INSP or SUPT; and a control kit listing all the possible complications to the basic story which the computer could generate in response to hasty decisions by the commanders under training. They also had four wooden police dogs, each labelled DOG.

The Facilitator arrives and sits down next to a low table with the map of Sandford spread out. In normal life he is Superintendent Derek Williams of the West Midlands police, an amiable and slightly stocky man in his early forties who came into the force as a constable in the Black Country and has done well to become Deputy Head of Operations, a department which ranks high in the pecking order. In Sandford, he is the aide-de-camp of the computer.

An electronic siren in the VDU next to the map interrupts the social pleasantries, and the first contestant takes his seat opposite the Facilitator. He reads the screen:

YOU ARE THE CHIEF SUPERINTENDENT IN CHARGE OF 'D' DIVISION SANDFORD.

YOU KNOW THAT LAST NIGHT THERE WAS SPORADIC DISORDER ON 'A' DIVISION WHEN CROWDS OF YOUTHS COMMITTED LOOTING AND DAMAGE IN THE CITY CENTRE.

AS A RESULT THE WHOLE FORCE HAS BEEN PUT ON A GENERAL ALERT.

The Facilitator adds some new information just in from the Carruthers Estate. A report from Father Brown, who has been a reliable source of intelligence in the past, indicates that there is going to be trouble on the estate tonight. In addition, a local councillor had phoned to say that snooker balls, stones and petrol bombs are being stored in some of the tower blocks.

The computer prints up a piece of cop sociology:

YOU KNOW THAT THE CARRUTHERS ESTATE IS A COMPLEX OF MANY TYPES OF HOUSING. THE OLD HAS BECOME RUN-DOWN, THE NEW IS MAINLY MULTI-STOREY FLATS. SOCIAL PROBLEMS SEEM MORE ACUTE HERE.

The Facilitator reaches for his box of pieces and begins lining up the wooden transit vans and panda cars along the edge of the map. To the left, his assistant arranges the magnetic coloured counters on a large deployment board which will show at a glance which police units are on stand-by around Sandford throughout the trouble to come. 'Just a couple of points, gentlemen,' says the Facilitator. 'These yellow flashes I shall introduce at certain points are not meant to represent fires necessarily, they stand for any kind of incident requiring police attention. And in deference to our guest, can you say "protective equipment" please Gents, not "riot gear"?'

The siren sounds again.

TODAY IS A WARM SATURDAY IN APRIL.

THE TIME IS 6 P.M.

The news from the football ground is mixed. On the positive side, the Facilitator can report that, once again, Sandford have beaten Chelsea who played their usual kind of game. But regrettably there was at least the usual amount of violence on the terraces, and police at the match are worried that it might get worse if they encounter any delays in getting the Chelsea fans on to their trains home. They are particularly anxious to pack them all off before opening time at 7 p.m. There is, however, a problem:

ONE VISITING FAN (A YOUTH) WAS STABBED.

HE IS UNCONSCIOUS IN HOSPITAL, HE IS *NOT* IN A CRITICAL CONDITION.

A radio message from the police commander at the match, relayed through the Facilitator, gives a further twist. Some of the Chelsea supporters are refusing to leave the ground because they have heard a rumour that this brother-in-arms has died in hospital from his stab wounds. The commander says that he knows this to be untrue, but cannot convince the crowd, who are threatening to move towards the hospital. The commander is asking for instructions from the Chief Superintendent back at 'D' divisional headquarters, the man in the hot seat; and would he kindly be quick about it as things are getting out of hand.

As it happens, the first contestant has got his answer ready. He has dealt with difficult football crowds often enough in real life, and takes some pride in having learned their codes of antagonism and trust. He knows they will never believe any police officer's assurance that their colleague is alive and mending. Some of these people have no respect for authority at all.

'Tell him to get the crowd to appoint one of their number as a representative, and lay on a police escort to take him to the hospital to see his mate. Then get him back and give him a loudspeaker as fast as possible.' The divisional radio room passes on the message.

Then the contestant sees another problem coming up – there is less than an hour to go before officers on the 11 to 7 day-shift go off duty. They include all the units at the football ground, and other officers all over Sandfordshire who have been doing a normal day's work. The Superintendent says he wants to spend some money, and keep all those in 'D' Division on for overtime. The Facilitator says that, in the circumstances, he feels sure the Assistant Chief Constable will support the decision.

They look across to the deployment board to check the strength of their forces. Nine blue counters represent the Police Support Units, each consisting of twenty constables, two sergeants and an inspector, all fully riot-trained and kitted out with 'protective equipment' in pairs of transit vans. The police call them 'SPG-style' units. Four green counters represent the permanent reserve of the Task Force, in the same 20:2:1 units and the same vans, but better prepared as a fighting force because they work and train together all the time. Four red counters represent the dog vans, with one dog and one handler in each. Add in the divisional headquarters staff, and their opposite numbers in the control room at D2 subdivision, and that's the battle-strength.

The Chief Superintendent checks that the rest of the force are still on general alert, and that he could call them at an hour's notice. He looks at his watch, and takes a moment to work out that it is still set to Birmingham time. The Facilitator tells him that in Sandford it is getting on for ten past six in the evening. It will be dark in less than ninety minutes. He has got to prepare himself and his officers for whatever the night may find on the Carruthers Estate. The home crowd will have a boisterous evening after their win. It could get lively before closing-time. Closing time? That's hours away! He has still not seen the lads from Chelsea on to their trains. He says he wants the Assistant Chief Constable to begin contacting neighbouring forces to explore the chances of getting some of their men to Sandford later in the evening, under the agreed system of mutual aid. Then he drums his fingers for a minute, until the Facilitator brings him the news he wants. The truth worked wonders with the visiting fans, and they are now *en route* to the railway station under police escort. A few of the home crowd are hanging around trying to get at them, but the commander at the ground expects to keep control and have the visitors away before 7 p.m.

The Chief Superintendent takes a deep breath and turns his mind to the next problem: how to deal with the home crowd they've left behind. The Facilitator lets him off. 'Right, thank you, Mr Jones. Got us off to a good start.' A numble of approval greets the first contestant as he takes his seat back with the other four.

'Mr Jeavons, will you take over please?' Into the hot seat moves Superintendent David Jeavons – a sharp-featured, pensive man with steel glasses, whose usual posting is in Bradford Street police station in the centre of Birmingham.

'Let me just tell you something more about the Carruthers Estate,' says the Facilitator. 'You have some fears about it from the information you got from Father Brown and the local councillor. That centre quadrangle there is about the size of a football pitch, and tends to be a pedestrian-type area with trees, wastepaper bins, benches, etc. There are one or two shops but no more than that in the centre quadrangle. It is not a shopping precinct. Snow House, where you have got one of your observation posts, is a fourteen-storey block of flats, as is Robin House across the other side. Polygon House, Owl House, Wren House are again high-rise of six or eight storeys.

'The four entrances into the estate are Wren, Robin, Polygon and Snow Close. They have concrete pillars cemented into the ground to prevent vehicle access, with the exception of one which has collapsible metal barriers to allow fire brigade or other emergency vehicles into it. High-rise and low-rise, generally low-class type dwelling, and generally speaking, a place where the local police officer is received, but not a place where he is well received.'

What the Facilitator, Derek Williams, does not add, is that the Carruthers Estate bears a remarkable similarity to the real Broadwater Farm Estate in Tottenham where the Metropolitan Police faced rioting on Sunday, 6 October 1985. The riot was of particular significance, marking the first time that police officers armed with plastic bullets were deployed on streets in Britain, though in the event they were not called on actually to fire the weapons. More ominously still for the men now imagining themselves in charge of police operations in Sandford, the Broadwater Farm Estate marked the first riot in post-war Britain where police themselves came under fire from at least one shotgun in the surrounding tower blocks. It also saw the injuring of 200 police officers and twenty civilians, and the killing of a community policeman.

David Jeavons is easing himself into the rank of Chief Superintendent in charge of Sandford's inner city 'D' Division. 'My fear about the Carruthers Estate,' he tells the Facilitator, 'is that if disturbances do develop we are going to find it very difficult to contain the situation, especially if rioters get into the high-rise dwellings. So I would be looking to keep large crowds from congregating towards that area. At this stage of the evening, I would be trying to get intelligence from the two officers I have got there in the observation post. Of course, as a Chief Superintendent, I would already have access to people like Father Brown and members of the police authority, so that if anything does break, I could get in touch with them.'

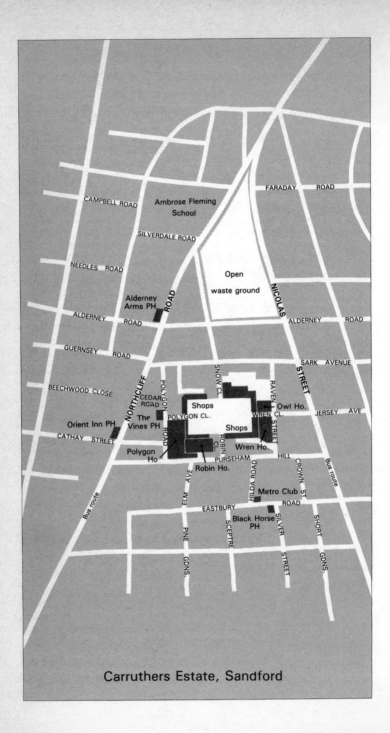

Carruthers Estate, Sandford

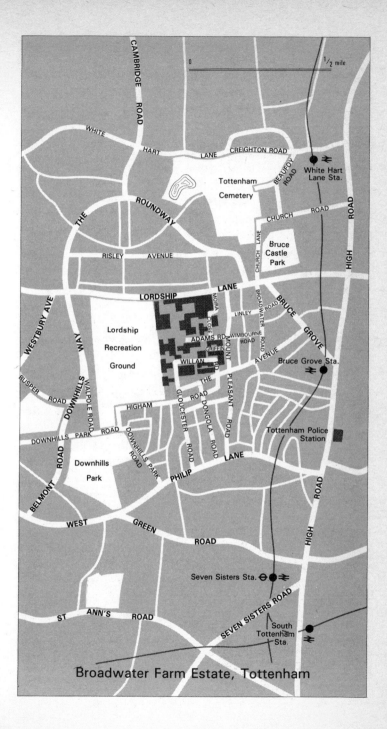

Broadwater Farm Estate, Tottenham

A secret police riot manual which was agreed by a committee of Chief Constables and approved by the Home Secretary in 1983, refers to people like Father Brown as 'community intervenors'. It says that information from them, together with an evaluation of their merit as sources, is necessary as part of a 'properly structured intelligence-gathering system'. One of the objectives it sets for police in every British city is: 'To identify within a tense community those persons who are or who purport to be local community leaders or leaders of minority groups'. They should be sought out and 'involved in the policing problems of the community', and in addition to their importance in alerting the police to potential trouble, they can 'enable the police force to minimize, neutralize or control anti-police propaganda or the spread of harmful rumour within an affected community'.

The Facilitator is more basic in his language than the secret manual: 'He's a good stick, old Father Brown,' he tells the Chief Superintendent, 'and he has got a very good rapport on the estate, irrespective of religious denomination'. The Chief Superintendent says he wants Father Brown with him at divisional headquarters for the rest of the evening. Meanwhile, he sends out an order that officers on foot patrol throughout the division must go about in pairs. 'I do not want to put them into any unnecessary danger,' he says.

As the Police Support Units at the football ground are sent back in their vans to D2, the sub-divisional station to the south of the Carruthers Estate, they learn that, as usual, they are to stay on duty until further notice. So they make their way to the canteen for their usual sausage, beans and chips. Then they and their Chief Superintendent and the Facilitator sit still and stay awake while they wait for something to happen.

There are occasional reports of small groups gathering inside the estate, on the centre quadrangle. The policemen in the observation post in the Snow House flats report small crowds forming and dispersing, but remaining 'by no means troublesome'.

Then there's a telephone call from the landlord of The Vines public house, which is just outside the estate on Polygon Road. It is 10.30 p.m. He says he wants to close now, even though the licensing hours go on until 11 p.m. His bar is bursting at the seams, and some of the customers are getting rough. He is worried that if he keeps serving them for another half hour, one of the small fights which have already started up could turn nasty. The Chief Superintendent thinks about it for a moment. For a start it must be pretty rough already if the landlord is about to turn away a barful of paying customers. In law, it is the barman's decision that counts, of course, but the police have a duty to offer their advice. 'Well, he is saying that he thinks it is dangerous to stay open. But in actual fact, my experience is that if public houses are cleared half an hour early, it might well create more problems. I would probably encourage him to keep them there until closing time, if he could.'

He looks across to the deployment board. The eight vans of the Task Force are out on patrol, and two of them are criss-crossing the area around the Carruthers Estate. 'They look very handy to cope with any disturbance which may arise from that public house,' he says.

A glance back to the deployment board. 'And we have a Chief Inspector and a Superintendent at D2 station. I think the time is now right for the Chief Inspector to be going towards the Carruthers Estate. He is local, he has a knowledge of the area and the residents. I want him there to establish communication with members of the public on the ground and feed back reliable information.'

'In fairness to him,' adds the Facilitator, 'he has come into the station in response to an earlier call. He is just back off leave, very disgruntled, but he has arrived and you have put him out on the ground.'

'Right. So he's gone to The Vines public house.'

They both look at the VDU screen as the siren sounds again. The Chief Superintendent winces and mutters a word which is not in the riot manual. 'And our message now tells us,' the Facilitator says with a shade too much anticipation, 'that The

Vines public house is set on fire.' There is a pause of a few seconds.

'My thought,' says the Chief Superintendent, 'is that obviously the fire services are going to be needed.' The other four contestants shuffle in their seats, and one whispers the word 'brilliant' to his neighbour.

'We have got to make sure,' the Chief Superintendent continues, getting back into his stride, 'that they have a route through to the area. I would be considering that we have some Special Constables on duty, and could deploy them to create traffic diversions well away from the Carruthers Estate, so that we can gain access for the fire brigade.'

'In fact', interrupts the Facilitator, 'they have already reported that they are sending two tenders down and they are asking for an escort.'

'Yes.' The Chief Superintendent now tries to regain the initiative. He asks, remembering the euphemism, if it is only the Task Force which has got 'protective equipment' on board their vans. 'I would be looking at this stage to ensure that all the other vehicles had that on board too.'

But events, mediated through the Facilitator, wrongfoot him again. 'The Task Force has arrived at The Vines and rescued the licensee and his wife from the fire. They are now being attacked by a group of about a hundred outside. The Task Force, as you say, have got their protective equipment in the vans. Can they put it on?'

The Chief Superintendent is in a corner. He wants to say yes they can put it on double-quick. But he knows the dangers of dressing his men in riot gear. It might provoke the crowd even further, which is a charge he would have to face next day, and which could mark his career for years to come. He plays for time. 'I would be looking for information from the Chief Inspector who is with them as to whether it was possible to disperse the crowd without it. Meanwhile I am bearing in mind that I do not want them going in the direction of the Carruthers Estate and I want a Police Support Unit to prevent entrance on to the estate.'

The Facilitator pushes the pace: 'The information is coming in that they are going in that direction and there could be an attack with stones and bottles.' That's a clear enough threat to swing the decision in favour of riot gear.

'If that is the intelligence from the Chief Inspector, then I suggest to him that it would be wisest for them to be fitted into protective equipment.'

So the stage is set. The crowd is getting ready to attack, and the police have crossed the critical line. They have ceased to be constables in ordinary uniform, and have become a riot force which will act with military precision. From now on, the game will be played by combat rules.

When the police put on riot gear, their senior officers have to bear in mind not only the dangers they already face, but the dangers they may create. The secret riot manual gives a detailed and frank summary of the pros and cons:

OVERT PROTECTIVE CLOTHING IN RESPONSE TO SERIOUS DISORDERS

(a) Description
Officers deployed in areas of serious public disorder wearing the following items of protective clothing:
 (i) pure wool barathea uniforms treated with Zirpro and Nuva-F
 (ii) protective gloves
 (iii) cricket box
 (iv) shin pads
 (v) protective boots
 (vi) clip-on tie
 (vii) riot helmet and visor
 (viii) fire resistant overalls
 (ix) any additional body protection that forces may consider necessary and have available.
 In addition, these officers would probably be equipped with long or short shields.

(b) Advantages
 (i) provides good personal protection against injury to officers employed in serious disorder

(ii) gives officers additional confidence and thereby lessens the likeli-
      hood of over-reaction
(iii) heightens the team's response because of confidence that they are
      specialists, properly equipped for riot control
(iv) psychological effect on the crowd in that they perceive that they are
      dealing with a properly disciplined, trained and equipped force
(v)   the sight of officers so dressed will encourage onlookers and the
      less committed members of the crowd to disperse before the
      violence escalates
(vi) reassurance to the families of officers so deployed
(vii) reassurance to law-abiding members of the public that effective
      police action is being taken.

(c) Disadvantages
(i)   the traditional image of the British police is removed
(ii)   may attract unnecessary attention
(iii) may heighten tension between police and the community
(iv)   may precipitate disorder
(v)   may encourage the crowd to escalate their violence
(vi)   may encourage rioters to wear protective clothing and carry
       offensive weapons
(vii) may restrict movement of officers
(viii) may become uncomfortable, particularly in warm weather
(ix)   may be used as anti-police propaganda
(x)   officers so deployed need to be removed from the area as soon as
       the violence subsides in order to return to normal policing as soon
       as possible.

Overt protective clothing is not to be put on unless the condition
of 'sporadic disorder' is present. This is the third stage of a
potential riot, coming after 'normality' and 'high tension'. It is
defined in the manual as: '*Sporadic Disorder*: The situation in a
community where there are frequent outbreaks of disorder, any of
which might trigger a riot.' The later stages of disorder are
rioting, serious rioting and (ultimately) lethal rioting.

Whether the Chief Superintendent in Sandford knew it or was
simply acting from instinct, it was the report of stones and bottles
being prepared for an attack on the police which pushed a
condition of 'high tension' towards 'sporadic disorder' in the
official police categories, making riot gear quite in order.

In Sandford, the police are taking the risk that their overt protective clothing 'may heighten tension between police and the community', or even that it 'may encourage the crowd to escalate their violence'. Whether it will 'encourage rioters to wear protective clothing and carry offensive weapons' only the next few hours will tell. For good or ill the decision has just been taken to remove the traditional image of the British police. The officers concerned will have to live with the consequences.

The Chief Superintendent is showing signs of strain. The blast of war may have blown in his ears, but his sinews remain stubbornly unstiffened. He seems to find it impossible to conceal the thought that this is not what he joined the police for. If he had wanted to command battles, he would have gone into the army. Unknown to him, he is not alone in this feeling, even within the room. A similar thought is running through the mind of the Facilitator. But the game must go on. The computer is unrelenting:

FROM: CID

PRISONERS FROM THE PUB DISTURBANCES HAVE BEEN QUESTIONED.

THEY STATE THERE WILL BE A RIOT ON THE ESTATE TONIGHT.

POLICE WILL BE ATTACKED.

The Facilitator has worse news yet: 'Mr Jeavons, a do-it-yourself shop on Wren Close, on the other side of the estate, has been broken into. Tools, paraffin, paint, thinners etc. have been seized. The information has come from officers who are on foot patrol in pairs in the area.'

The Chief Superintendent puts the break-in to the back of his mind for a moment. His immediate concern is what to do about the remaining foot patrols who are still walking about in pairs in ordinary police uniform. 'Those officers are now at risk. I want them withdrawn, so that they can be mobilized and formed into a Police Support Unit. There is a grave danger of them being subject to individual attack.' He is back on top.

'Fine,' says the Facilitator. 'Meanwhile the fire engine has come round Northcliffe Road and is just going into a side street by The Vines licensed house.' At least something is going right. 'Now Mr Jeavons, it is time you went and had a refreshment – I would suggest not alcohol, just a cup of coffee. Mr Crowe, perhaps you would come and take over.'

As David Jeavons leaves the map table, he is greeted with the same mumbling of approval, but this time it is accompanied by the odd nod of sympathy for his performance under duress. The first hour of the game is almost complete, when Chief Inspector Eric Crowe steps forward to see what he can make of the next part. He is wondering how important the break-in at the do-it-yourself shop may prove to be, but before he can begin to tackle it the Facilitator moves him along: 'Look at the screen, Mr Crowe, the fire engines have just come round the corner to the pub, and they have come under attack by a crowd of about one hundred and fifty. What is your first consideration?'

'My immediate concern is the safety of the fire service units. I want the Task Force to disperse that crowd and stop the attack.' He orders all units which have not yet kitted themselves up with protective equipment to do so straight away. While the order goes out, the Facilitator returns to the question of the break-in.

The new acting Chief Superintendent, Eric Crowe, knows there is something he's missed about the do-it-yourself shop. He knows that a crucial point is staring him in the face, but he can't get it clear in his mind. The Facilitator drops a large hint, the first of many. 'We have not yet responded to the report of the break-in, but now we have got a car on fire just round the corner.'

'I'll bring a Police Support Unit to Wren Close. I want the keyholder contacted, and the city engineers to board it up as soon as possible.'

'All right,' says the Facilitator, 'we will get back to the control room to contact the keyholder. What kind of assistance are you expecting from him?'

'Sorry, what did you say?' asks the Chief Superintendent, who is still searching his head for the right idea. 'I want him to check for stuff that is missing. Ask him to go to the station at D2 and we can meet him there and escort him under police cover.'

The Facilitator drops another hint, the size of a fire-engine: 'Unit 5B has arrived at the scene and says there is a strong smell of paraffin.'

'Then send another PSU with protective equipment, and leave the fire service to that.'

The Facilitator is about to give up the effort, but he tries one more time: 'What about the rest of the stuff inside? This is right on the entrance to the estate!'

'Well I have got a unit there securing the premises.'

'Do you think the fire brigade might help with getting rid of the paraffin?'

Eric Crowe is beginning to see his way out of the smoke. 'Yes, ask the fire brigade to get rid of it and leave the Units there until they have.' Then suddenly, from somewhere, he gets an idea that restores his poise: 'I am thinking at this stage of setting up a bridgehead somewhere, to bring in some of my reserves. Is there any news of the mutual aid units?'

'Well, they are still some considerable time away because it is not yet eleven o'clock and they are not due to arrive in Sandford until midnight. But we have one more Task Force unit still at D1 available for you.'

'Yes. Now this open waste ground next to the estate – is that suitable for the bridgehead I have in mind?'

'Not really. It is well-trodden debris, not the safest of ground. It is really a derelict site which has grassed over, a bit rough.'

'How about the school playgrounds or fields?'

'There is Ambrose Fleming School which is quite close to the estate. We have made a check and it is not being used tonight, so it could be available.'

'Then I want to use the school as forward holding point. I'll bring those Units in reserve up to there, and I want to see some dogs there too.'

Some police officers find it uncomfortable to talk like military commanders with their 'bridgeheads' and 'forward units'. Their secret riot manual is not only filled with army jargon, but even explicitly draws attention to the new role it demands of the constabulary. In an introductory section headed 'Borrowed terminology', it lays out the case with perfect clarity:

When considering deployments of police personnel in a riot context it is sometimes necessary to think in terminology which has more of a military connotation.
Examples of these are as follows:
    pincer movement
    leapfrogging (of units)
    out-flanking movement
    diversionary tactics
    feints
    frontal attacks
    attacks from the rear
    infiltration
    entrapment
It is not considered necessary to define these words in a police context since the meanings are those of common usage. The application of the movements which these words imply can easily be translated to the police context.
    Such words constitute an important part of the vocabulary of strategic and tactical planning and for police officers, whose ordinary duties do not include such thought processes, it is necessary to make a conscious effort to tune in on this level.

Eric Crowe is by now thoroughly tuned in on this level himself. He calls for a situation report and discovers that the crowd outside The Vines is being kept back from the fire-brigade, which is tackling the flames. The licensee and his wife have been rescued and taken to divisional headquarters at D1 station to be interviewed by the CID in spite of their distress at losing not only their livelihood but also their home in the flat above the bar.

    Meanwhile, some of the crowd have moved off towards the Carruthers Estate, and are gathering in growing numbers inside the centre quadrangle having got past the police units which were supposed to keep them out. The latest information from the observation posts is that several small crowds have collected, making a total of about 300. The Facilitator wants to know if there is anything Father Brown can do to help. He is, after all, waiting at headquarters in case trouble breaks out on the estate.

'Yes, certainly. Ask him to go to the people in the square and use his . . .' He pauses while he consults his mental *Thesaurus*; ' . . . his presence to try and deflate the situation and talk good sense to the leaders of these groups.'

'Send him on his own, or with a police officer?' asks the Facilitator innocently.

The acting Chief Superintendent has seen that ball coming; 'I think this man operates alone. In normality, he moves around in society and is quite accepted within it. I would not fear for his safety at this stage.'

And with that, Mr Crowe is stood down. He receives a mixed response from the other contestants. They like his idea of setting up a bridgehead, but are all itching to tell him what he had overlooked at the do-it-yourself shop. He will find out soon enough.

Meanwhile, the Facilitator is arranging some elementary catering at the Ambrose Fleming School for the police units which have been on duty for twelve hours. One of the contestants chimes in: 'We'll get a lot of mileage out of them with just a cup of tea.' One of the others thinks it might take a couple. There is a brief discussion about whether the Chief Superintendent himself ought to call it a night and hand over to his deputy. After all, he has been on duty all day too, and his head won't be getting any clearer. The consensus is that he should get right away from the scene – go home and get to bed, and leave the police operation to someone else who is of course as capable as he is himself. They all agree that would be best. But not one of them can declare that he would actually do it in real life.

They also raise the question of getting the Press Officer and one of the Assistant Chief Constables into action to deal with the press and television interest which is bound to be alerted by now.

Then the Facilitator reports that events in the centre quadrangle have taken a turn for the worse. The crowd is now 600 strong and very agitated. In Snow Close, they have started taking out the street lighting and ripping up the trees and benches. Police units are sealing off all four entrances to the estate in an attempt to contain the area of disorder. There is slightly better news from The Vines, where the fire is now out, and only a token force of police is needed to protect firemen during the damping-down for an hour or two.

In Raven Street, the burning car is now out too. At the do-it-yourself shop, the fire brigade has pumped off all the remaining paraffin. The units from neighbouring forces are expected to arrive at the agreed rendezvous-point (the nearest motorway service station) in less than half an hour.

'Mr Foster, it's your turn.'

Superintendent Michael Foster, from Dudley, is the only contestant to have kept his jacket on. Being a CID Officer, he is not wearing a uniform. His is a smart blue jacket that goes with his sharply pressed trousers to give him the air of a sales manager facing the board of directors.

He takes the seat with confidence. 'I am particularly concerned with the burglary at the do-it-yourself shop, because of the inflammable liquids which were stolen. I want someone to tell me now the size of that tank and the amount which had gone before the fire-brigade arrived. I am also eager to learn if there have been any recent thefts of milk bottles or other containers in the area.'

The obvious danger dawns on Chief Inspector Crowe. He puts his right hand up to his temple to block his view of the other contestants as they give him the smiles that say 'That was it, Eric.'

But the new Chief Superintendent is not done yet. 'I would also be reviewing the events of the previous night to see if there was anything to suggest the same thing happening tonight as a pattern rather than a spontaneous thing. I see a CID involvement here in respect of the intelligence, in order to try and prevent the situation occurring again. I would expect to have by now, in situation, an incident room, gathering all of that information and providing a very good intelligence system for the officer in charge.'

The Facilitator asks him what should be done with officers as they come off duty in rotation. Should they be left alone to get over the battering they've had, or does he see a need to debrief them?

'I think it is essential to debrief them. They may well have seen incidents which are not reported at this stage. They may have heard rumours or had intelligence given to them which they must now be giving back into my incident room so that it can be passed on.'

The Facilitator is almost silenced. 'Thank you very much', is all he can find to say.

Mr Foster returns to his seat, with his confidence polished. The table-top map is now so crowded with wooden vans and yellow flashes that it is almost impossible to see the Carruthers Estate beneath them. All four entrances are completely blocked off by police units. Inside the centre quadrangle, there is now just one wooden crowd with the number 600 printed on it. The visiting riot police from neighbouring forces have been met at the motorway service area and are on their way to the Ambrose Fleming school. Everybody can see that this is the final pitched battle of the night. The fifth, and last, contestant is brought forward to lead the police troops into it.

Superintendent Dick Chidley has earned quite a reputation in the West Midlands for his skill and enthusiasm in riot training. He is a tall, dark-haired man from one of Birmingham's most difficult policing divisions. His duties in C Division cover the Handsworth and Lozells districts, where there have been real-life lethal riots. He is reckoned to have the right stuff when it comes to maintaining public order. His previous training sessions with the table-top difficulties of Sandford brought high opinions from the Facilitator. The police managers think enough of him to arrange a special training session later in the month at their training ground, when he will command a hundred real police officers in a battle to control not little wooden crowds on a table-top, but a full-scale riot by a hundred other policemen in civilian clothes, with proper sticks and stones and petrol-bombs as weapons.

As he takes the Chief Superintendent's seat in the Sandford exercise, he realizes how much of his future is at stake. The computer brings him the latest report:

FROM: PSU INSP.

BARRICADES HAVE BEEN ERECTED AROUND THE CENTRE OF THE
ESTATE, ABOUT HALF WAY DOWN WREN CLOSE, ROBIN CLOSE,
POLYGON CLOSE AND SNOW CLOSE.

THEY HAVE OVERTURNED VEHICLES AND USED BUILDING
MATERIALS.

Dick Chidley begins by summarizing the bad news. 'We have a
situation in the estate of escalating disorder. There is some stone-
throwing and some broken windows, and we have had one attack
on a do-it-yourself shop where accelerants have been stolen
which could be used as firebombs. But we have taken further
temptation away from there. I have got all major exit and entry
routes covered by PSUs still in their vehicles, but kitted up and
ready to go out on the streets if the situation dictates.'

He looks back at the VDU screen and reads again about the
barricades. 'The crowd are trying to create an area where the
police will not be able to go. I want anyone coming out of there –
civilian or police officer, injured or not – to be going for a
debriefing so that we can keep a full picture of everything that
happens. We have also got two spotters in there who are feeding
information back. Now with these barricades being introduced, I
want to take the protected officers out of their vehicles, with
shields, to take back the territory that has been declared by the
rioters as a No Go Area.'

'Why bother?' asks the Facilitator. 'They are inside, we are
outside. Why not just leave them to it?'

The Chief Superintendent switches into auto-response: 'I
presume that not everyone inside is in sympathy with the riot. Our
main priority as a police force is the protection of life and property,
and we have got to take back that area as soon as possible.'

'I suppose ultimately,' coaxes the Facilitator, 'that you would
have to consider an evacuation?'

'Yes, we would. Evacuation to a place of safety, particularly for
people who want to get out and are vulnerable by reason of age,
either at the top or bottom of the scale.'

'All right then, how are you going to take these barricades out?'

The Chief Superintendent says he wants the help of at least two barricade-removal vehicles from the local authority. Behind the barricades he expects to find a force of rioters armed with various devices to protect the barricade, and he plans to use units of riot police armed with short shields and truncheons to break up the crowds. Meanwhile, other units will line up behind the long shields in a containment formation, to keep all the rioters inside the estate. As time goes on, short shield units will run through these lines to make arrests and frighten some of the crowd into giving up the fight.

It is a well-practised manoeuvre known to most policemen (but not the authors of the secret riot manual) as a 'snatch squad'. The version of it outlined in the manual is a direct import from the British Colonial Police, perfected twenty years ago in Hong Kong. It is a part of a sophisticated armoury of public order tactics which the Royal Hong Kong Police have taught officers in Britain since 1981.

Dick Chidley has learned which manoeuvres he can use on his own initiative, and which would need the agreement of a senior officer of his own force. The code phrase is 'ACPO approval', a reference to those ranks eligible for membership of the Association of Chief Police Officers – the organization which prepared the manual. It consists of Chief Constables, Deputy Chief Constables and Assistant Chief Constables.

At least two of Dick Chidley's planned tactics will need to be referred up to one of Sandfordshire's Assistant Chief Constables. The use of bulldozers or armoured lorries to break up barricades, and the offensive manoeuvres of short shield units, are considered dangerous enough to require the approval of very senior ranks.

'I understand that ACC (operations) is on hand at the command post.'

'Yes, and he is quite willing to listen to your sympathetic pleas.'

The Chief Superintendent and the Facilitator then go through the prescribed warnings to be given to the crowd before the police move in to attack. They solemnly agree that before any offensive

action can be taken, three clear warnings must be shouted to the
rioters through a loudspeaker. If at all possible, they should be
broadcast through a mobile public address system mounted on a
Task Force van. They should be recorded for possible use as
evidence later. The mood of the crowd should also be noted, and
the exact time. If the police have banners handy announcing their
intentions, they should hold them up to reinforce the warning.
The discussion has a similar air of unreality to the earlier
conversation about going home to bed as the battle was about to
start. Everyone nods wisely and agrees that, for the purposes of a
training exercise, three clear warnings should be the rule.

'Three warnings,' says the Chief Superintendent, 'before my
officers equipped in NATO gear make the final push to retake
this territory.' 'NATO gear' is another borrowed phrase meaning
riot gear.

'How long are you going to wait after the final warning before
you go on to the offensive?'

'Not at all. We go in immediately.'

The barricades are pushed over by council bulldozers. Officers
in short shield formations run through the gaps with their
truncheons ready, yelling battle-cries at the top of their voices.
Some of the crowd, frightened and bewildered, start to run away.
But in a sealed quadrangle, with four simultaneous police attacks
through the entrances, there is nowhere to run to. The lines of
long shields move forward at the double to take the territory the
short shield men have cleared. The snatch squads re-form behind
the lines, waiting to run through and make further arrests among
the crowd. The police, under Dick Chidley's command, rapidly
regain the upper hand. Throughout the entire evening, the Chief
Superintendent (played by a succession of five contestants) has
not stepped nearer the conflict than the control room at divisional
headquarters, more than a mile away.

Dick Chidley is beginning to look relieved. If he had mistimed
his moves he could have found himself in trouble. If he, and his
fellow 'Chief Superintendents', had gone on to the offensive too
early they might have to face the very serious allegation that they
had provoked the worst of the violence. If they had left it too late

they might have been struggling to contain even fiercer fighting in the centre quadrangle, while fires began sweeping through the tower blocks.

The Facilitator is encouraging the atmosphere of self-congratulation which has settled on them all, when the siren sounds on the VDU:

FROM: PSU INSP.
I HAVE JUST HEARD TWO SHOTS FROM SNOW CLOSE.

'This is an Inspector telling us', says Dick Chidley with some attempt at disbelief, 'that we now have firearms on the streets?'

'That's right.'

'Then the Police Support Units in Snow Close must immediately retire out of range of the shots.'

'All right,' says the Facilitator, 'you can withdraw the troops to a safe distance.'

'But what about the person who fired the shots?'

'I would direct that we have Firearms Department available,' responds Dick Chidley while he searches for the right euphemism, 'available to take courses of action if we can identify and isolate the user of the gun.'

It is a circumlocutionary masterpiece. Firearms Department instantly make themselves available to take courses of action, while the Facilitator announces that at this cliff-hanging moment the exercise is at an end and lunch is about to be served. The contestants stand up and shake each other by the hand. Four of them start to put their jackets on, while Superintendent Michael Foster straightens his hair. They joke for a moment with the Facilitator and then step from the D1 control room in Sandford out into the daylight of Birmingham.

Once they have all left, the Facilitator resumes his usual bonhomie as Superintendent Derek Williams. Most of them did quite well, he thinks. He has put more than 250 senior officers through their paces in Sandford, and this lot were a bit above average.

His main programme of training courses was carried out between October 1984 and October 1985. This meant that most

of the officers who came to him as students of public order tactics
had already gained experience of large crowds at football
matches. Many had also seen action against the picket lines
during the dispute between the miners and the National Coal
Board, when they had been to Yorkshire and Kent as visiting
forces themselves under the mutual aid arrangements.

There are some pieces missing from the Sandford board game.
The fictional constabulary has no plastic bullets or CS gas, so
these 'specialist weapons' are barred from use at the Carruthers
Estate. There are no water cannon either, though this makes
Sandfordshire less untypical, since only the Metropolitan Police
have so far even experimented with these appliances. Derek
Williams maintains that the Carruthers Estate exercise is as
realistic as anything available to the police. Its marked resemb-
lance to events at Broadwater Farm in October 1985 confirms the
point in his mind – though he insists that no individual area was
taken as a model when the game was invented in 1983. But while
the game may be realistic enough about the choice of police tactics
during the escalation of public disorder, it seems imaginative
about the nature of the rioters and the causes of unrest.

No explanation is offered of the prescience of those arrested
outside The Vines who confidently tell detectives that 'there will
be a riot on the estate tonight'. How do they know? Have they
been talking to Father Brown? Or is their statement merely a
reflection of the view expressed by a number of police officers,
that riots are the product of organization by ringleaders with
either a criminal or political motive?

It is an uncomfortable fact that a central omission in Sandford
is the kind of action by the police themselves which precipitated
the real riots at St Paul's in 1980, Brixton and Toxteth in 1981,
and Handsworth and Tottenham in 1985. As Lord Scarman
noted in his 1981 report on riots:

Significantly, the beginning of the disorders in Toxteth on 3–6 July
1981, namely the arrest by a police traffic patrol of a youth who had been
riding a motorcycle, invites comparison with the beginning of the
disorders in Brixton. In each case a minor incident set off a great riot.

In the United States, the National Commission established by President Johnson to report on the wave of riots which swept the country during the 'long hot summer' of 1967 reached an almost identical conclusion. It analysed the stages of each city's rioting in great detail, with particular attention to the background of grievances. The deepest and most intense grievances they discovered in the ghettoes related to police practices:

To many Negroes police have come to symbolize white power, white racism and white repression. And the fact is that many police do reflect and express these white attitudes. The atmosphere of hostility and cynicism is reinforced by a widespread perception among Negroes of the existence of police brutality and corruption, and of a 'double standard' of justice and protection – one for Negroes and one for whites.

This hostility, the Commission said, combined with social grievances over poverty, unemployment, slums and schools to form an explosive mixture. The fires which had raged that summer were often set off by a single spark, an incident of little apparent importance. The person found to have struck the spark was usually a police officer:

Almost invariably the incident that ignites disorder arises from police action. Harlem, Watts, Newark and Detroit – all the major outbursts of recent years – were precipitated by routine arrests of Negroes for minor offenses by white police.

This incendiary metaphor was tailored by Sir Kenneth Newman in April 1987 to fit London. As Metropolitan Commissioner, Sir Kenneth was giving one of the last major newspaper interviews of his term in office. He spoke memorably of the predisposing causes of community violence – discrimination, underprivilege, unemployment and poor housing – as 'a volatile vapour hanging over the city looking for a spark to set it off'. In Britain too, that spark can be struck by the police.

The leader of the ACPO working group which invented Sandford and devised its table-top exercise in public disorder was Geoffrey Dear. At that time, he was an Assistant Commissioner in the Metropolitan Police. It had been his duty to present part of the Met's case at the Scarman Inquiry. He is now the Chief

Constable of the West Midlands. Mr Dear identifies a problem for the police on two levels. They have first to face specific grievances over their own force's behaviour in some city areas. In addition, they face a general sense of hostility as the most visible representatives of the state in places where it is least supported. People who live in conditions which breed resentment may find their social and political emotions suddenly brought together, he maintains, by a police raid on one of their clubs: 'It is a fact of life we have to live with that it is almost always police action – even the very best kind of police action – which forms the trigger-point of a riot.'

2 The Paramilitary Drift

Do not let yourselves drift into a paramilitary role and away from policing as you and I know it.
RUC delegate to the Police Federation
Conference, May 1986

When a thousand police officers arrived at the Scarborough conference centre at the end of May 1986, they might have guessed that they were in for a lively three days. The previous year, they had shouted at their star speaker Leon Brittan. Television news bulletins had shown to millions the unprecedented spectacle of a Conservative Home Secretary being heckled, booed and jeered, not by students at Manchester University, but by the lower ranks of the British police service.

As their monthly magazine *Police* boasted, the new Home Secretary, Douglas Hurd, must have travelled to Scarborough in 1986 'well aware that his predecessor's rapid political decline could be dated from his disastrous public performance at our conference last year'.

But neither Douglas Hurd nor the Police Federation could have foreseen what would become the most memorable moment of the 1986 conference. It was certainly not the comparatively sedate reception the new Home Secretary earned for his address; and Mr Hurd can have been little surprised by the Federation's verdict that he is 'an altogether more astute platform speaker' than Mr Brittan. Nor was it the succession of stunned tributes paid to the memory of PC Keith Blakelock, who had been killed in the riot at Broadwater Farm seven months earlier.

The event which upstaged all others was a speech made by Alan Wright, the chairman of the Police Federation branch in Northern Ireland. If anyone had expected a routine recitation of fraternal goodwill from across the water, they were in for a rude shock. Mr Wright took the rostrum to deliver a sermon against the sin of turning policemen into soldiers. He did it with such passion that his audience had no doubt that it came both from his heart and from his unarguable authority as an officer of the most heavily militarized force in the United Kingdom, the Royal Ulster Constabulary.

He began predictably enough, presenting the virtues of an unarmed police force and the reasons why Northern Ireland no longer enjoys such a civility. Then he went to the very heart of British policing in the eighties. He warned his colleagues on the mainland not to accept any measure which, in the long term, might corrupt the ideal of an unarmed service. His voice dropped for dramatic effect: 'Your police service, on this point alone, is admired the world over; you must keep it like that.'

He concluded by telling them that Britain still boasted the most respected police service in the world; but summarized the awful foreboding he felt that their future would follow a pattern he knew only too well from Northern Ireland. 'Do not let yourselves drift into a paramilitary role, and away from policing as you and I know it.' His warning may have come too late.

Since the introduction of the first Special Patrol Group in 1965, the police in mainland Britain have proceeded step by step down the very slope which alarmed Alan Wright. Since 1981, they have slipped towards the tactics of public order control which characterize the military. The 'drift into a paramilitary role' is already a fact of life. Three elements are discernible at each step down this slope: the police have edged themselves into acting like soldiers; there has been a shift of political control towards Whitehall and away from town halls; and public debate has been minimized, either by presenting these fundamental changes in a misleading light or by keeping them secret. In a democracy which maintains the tradition of policing by public consent, the public has not even been informed, much less asked, about the most far-reaching recent changes in police strategy.

The result is that almost every major city in Britain now has a police force armed with plastic bullets, CS gas and live firearms, and trained to use them to put down disturbances. Its policemen and some policewomen have undergone a rigorous course of crowd control techniques modelled on the riot squads used throughout the British colonies. The men who walk our streets as community bobbies today are equipped and ready to take them by force tomorrow. The important milestones and motives of this policing revolution have been inadequately reported.

There are some commentators whose general approach is critical of the police, who have written of public order policy in the eighties as if it were the product of a dark yearning for armed authoritarian control among British police officers. They analyse the drift of the past two decades in terms of illiberal and macho impulses beneath the blue serge uniform: a persistent push by, as it were, the Military Tendency within the police force, encouraged since 1979 by the government in Westminster. Police apologists, on the other hand, including the more vocal among the police themselves, have presented the paramilitary drift as an inevitable and reluctant response to increased violence by pickets, rioters and other ne'er-do-wells. Each riot shield, they claim, merely serves to protect an officer of the Queen's Peace who wants nothing more than to turn the clock back to the days when crowd control consisted of clipping boys' ears for scrumping apples. It is as if the police gunners reaching for their plastic bullet dischargers might wish to echo the words of the kindly headmaster: 'This is going to hurt me more than it hurts you'. The account in these pages is not intended as an exercise in psychology. But examination of the words and deeds of real policemen during the past few years suggests a more complex explanation than either of these. It is, however, no more comforting.

The paramilitary drift has been a piecemeal response to deep-seated perceptions of increased threat among police officers. Some of these feelings have been well founded, especially following the sustained periods of battering and defeat suffered by many ill-trained men during the Bristol and Brixton riots of 1980–1 and worse still in Broadwater Farm in 1985. But policemen as a group are noticeably more conservative than the population as a whole, and frequently more deferential to authority. (In 1986 one

Chief Constable concluded a discussion with some of his new recruits, who had proved close to the rightward edge of the political spectrum, with the observation that it seemed impossible to attract liberals into the force.) They can often convince themselves that social change and dislocation in our cities are merely fruits of concealed activity by radicals. It can be hard to find a police officer who dissents from Margaret Thatcher's declaration of war against the Enemy Within. So their view of the threat posed by dissidence in the form of a convoy of hippies or a student demonstration or a civil disobedience campaign may be coloured by suspicion and lack of sympathy. To hear a senior officer policing one of the most volatile and riot-prone areas of the country explain the wave of disturbances in 1981 as the creation of a left-wing group which wanted to start a national riot in order to discredit the police and attack the foundations of society, is to enter a world in which social explanation is exhausted with the discovery of a villain. There may also be some officers who enjoy a physical fight and relish the trappings of paramilitary force, though even among the front-line troops of the long coal dispute of 1984–5 there seemed to be few who fitted neatly into this stereotype. Far more seem genuinely dismayed at their new role as soldiers in blue uniforms. It is really not what they joined the police for. They will take it on, of course, and ensure that they do it well, because they are given their orders and, perhaps, because they want the Enemy Within to be beaten, but they seem not to enjoy the battle. This creates a tension which can make them suspicious of those who question their tactics and resistant to public disclosure or discussion of their policies. Like any group of people who cannot always be proud of what they do, they prefer to keep it secret and pretend that nothing really has changed since their good old days.

If this analysis is accurate, then British policing may not yet have slipped out of control down the paramilitary slope. It may not be too late, even now, to halt or even reverse the drift among men who wish to remain police officers even while acting like soldiers. But time is running out. There are serving officers who fear that when they retire they will be replaced by new men and women who expect police work to include occasional paramilitary street battles. They see that, politically, maintaining public order brings greater rewards than fighting crime, and they know that the new elite police corps consists of the riot squads rather than the CID. They look ahead with alarm to Britain in the next century, with a police service not only using paramilitary force but also staffed by people who believe in it. What chance then of maintaining the unarmed tradition? What chance of international admiration for the British police? Where will the drift take them next?

Beneath the blue serge – police changes in the eighties

In 1980, with relatively few exceptions, the police looked much as they had in 1945. But their appearance was deceptive. For beneath the uniform familiar from Dock Green, there had already been a literal and metaphorical transformation of the British bobby.

The physical changes below the surface were disclosed in a BBC *File On 4* radio documentary in September 1980, which followed officers of one Special Patrol Group to a football match in Coventry. Their commanding officer, Chief Inspector David Blick, was persuaded to describe the hidden changes in his men's clothing:

Blick: We start with the cricket box, which is the normal kind to protect the groin from kicks and missiles and similar sorts of aggravation to a police officer's body. Nothing sophisticated about that. Then we have got two sorts of shin-pads. One here will provide full cover to the lower shin while still remaining away from the public's gaze. The problem has been trying to find something that is efficient without being too visible – a hockey-pad would make the trousers bulge out and give an aggressive image, which is what we are trying to avoid.
File on 4: You have also got a visor on the helmet.
Blick: As you see here, it clips on to the top of the helmet to stop smaller missiles such as staples, small bricks, fluids of any description from affecting the officer's eyes. The visor can be carried in the pocket out of sight. The helmet has also been reinforced with a double layer of cork, and there is a mesh inside which supports it on the head so that if a house

brick comes down on top of it the force of the blow is spread across the top of the head.

File On 4: The bobby who is geared up with all this may look like an ordinary British policeman, but he isn't really, is he?

Blick: No. That is something which the police force has tried to avoid, but it is a step we have had to take to protect our own members.

Chief Inspector Blick then produced the only visible sign of his officers' new preparedness for disorder – the then controversial full-length riot shield.

Blick: The protective shield – we don't like the term 'riot shield'. It is made of a polycarbonate substance and is clear so that officers can see through it as they move forward or back.

File On 4: Isn't there something provocative about a policeman behind his riot shield, though?

Blick: Yes. It has been found that people who would not normally throw anything at an unprotected policeman will certainly throw at a shield.

By 1980, there were Special Patrol Groups like David Blick's in twenty-seven British police forces, more than half the total. Every major city had already acquired and trained its own elite force of officers dressed like Chief Inspector Blick's men and equipped with long riot shields.

But to the public, their uniforms looked indistinguishable from any other officer's. That was how the police themselves wanted it. Senior officers made a point of claiming that nothing had changed about either the bobby or the British policing tradition he embodied.

Chief Inspector Blick's force was led by an articulate Chief Constable, Sir Philip Knights, who gave this official line:

Knights: Grosvenor Square in 1968 persuaded us that we had got to rethink the way we handle crowds. The choice was to go the Continental way and look for water-cannon, riot gear and all that kind of thing, or to use ordinary flesh and blood policemen in a more controlled and disciplined way. We decided to take the latter course.

A Government Green Paper reviewing the Public Order Act was published in the same year repeating the point:

The British police do not have sophisticated riot equipment – such as tear gas or water cannon – to handle demonstrations. Their traditional approach is to deploy large numbers of officers in ordinary uniform in the passive containment of a crowd. Neither the Government nor the police wish to see this approach abandoned in favour of more aggressive methods.

But there were other voices calling for a military approach to be introduced into the police force. A small handbook, *Public Order and the Police*, was published by *Police Review*, with an introduction by the Home Secretary, William Whitelaw. It was written by a training officer of the Greater Manchester Police, Kenneth Sloan, who criticized the traditional tactics of crowd control as primitive and said there was an obvious requirement for something different. Since police officers would be called upon to do battle, he argued, they should be able to learn from the experience of the Army in controlling civil disorder and adapt military methods for their own use.

Training methods require some fresh thought . . . One obvious requirement for all officers who may be called upon to do battle is that they should be physically fit and practised in working as a team. Great experience in controlling civil disorder has been obtained by the Army in recent years and their methods could doubtless be adopted for police use.

Other hidden changes had also taken place. By 1980, the police national computer was ten years old and providing a secret pool of intelligence for the fifty-two theoretically independent forces in Britain. Rapid deployment of large numbers of officers from neighbouring forces during a crisis could be organized at national level, through the National Reporting Centre which had been established at New Scotland Yard after the defeat the police suffered at Saltley Coke Depot during the dispute of 1972. There were also significant numbers of officers in each force trained in the use of firearms, an average of one in ten throughout the country.

But the Home Office and the police themselves could still claim with justification that the British police did not have sophisticated riot equipment and that crowds would continue to be contained in the traditional British way.

They were not to know it, but these assurances would be rendered invalid within eighteen months. Events were about to unfold which would precipitate the greatest escalation of police fighting power in British history.

The 1980–1 riots

Just after 3 p.m. on Wednesday 2 April 1980, twenty officers of the Avon and Somerset police raided the Black and White Café on Grosvenor Road, in the dilapidated St Paul's area of Bristol. A crowd formed in response to the raid and turned on the police, who by 5 p.m. were heavily outnumbered and decided to exercise discretion as the better part of valour. They left the scene. An enormous crowd gathered during the next two hours in Grosvenor Road, City Road and Ashley Road. It was reported to be 2000 strong, and composed of many races, united in hostility to the police. One local cleric said later that it was notable for being the first genuinely multiracial event St Paul's had seen. The Chief Constable gave the order to retake the area shortly before 7 p.m., with a mere 100 officers equipped with riot shields. They were beaten back so fiercely that by 7.15 p.m. the Chief Constable ordered them to retreat, leaving the streets unpoliced. He said later that he had been faced with Hobson's choice. For four hours the police waited for help to arrive from neighbouring forces. It was past 11 p.m. when they moved back into the area to quell the looting and arson which dominated the evening.

The next day, the Chief Constable, Brian Weigh, found himself on the defensive. He told reporters that the decision to withdraw his men had been agonizing, but he had to take it. 'It offends every tenet I believe in as a police officer of some experience.' Spokesmen for other big city forces – the Metropolitan, Greater Manchester, the West Midlands, Strathclyde – held unattributable briefings to emphasize their concern at the way police had behaved in Avon and Somerset. Their own Chief Constables, they said, would undoubtedly have ordered their men to stay put even at the risk of death. Mr Weigh also had to answer the charge that his men had been inadequately equipped; in particular, that they should have had water hoses to turn on the rioters. An anonymous 'senior officer' in his force was quoted as saying that this tactic would merely have worsened the situation and was never even considered.

Commentators began to write menacing feature articles about the fear of similar violence breaking out in other parts of the country. There were, after all, plenty of inner city areas with social decay far worse than that found in Bristol.

The Home Secretary, William Whitelaw, announced a review of the disturbances and the police response to them. It produced an eloquent statement of the unarmed British policing tradition, favouring containment techniques based on large numbers of officers in ordinary uniforms linking arms and forming human wedges to break up crowds. It explicitly rejected the use of sophisticated riot equipment as liable to alienate the public, and stressed that the police themselves would not welcome the development of paramilitary riot squads. This statement to Parliament was to be the swan song of the British police tradition in public order. (It is reprinted in full as Appendix A.)

The Home Secretary presented the review to Parliament, with the conclusion that it would be desirable neither in principle nor in practice to depart from the broad approach adopted by the police for dealing with disorder. He stressed that the successful maintenance of public order depends on the consent of those policed.

For the rest of the summer of 1980, nothing further happened to test the arrangements set out in this review. Then, in 1981, urban rioting broke out in city after city, and with a ferocity far beyond anything Bristol had suffered.

In April 1981 another police operation (code-named 'Swamp 81') set off a weekend of rioting in Brixton. Lord Scarman's report later called the operation 'a serious mistake, given the tension which existed between the police and the local community'. In early July, the most serious disorders to date broke out in Liverpool's inner city for three consecutive nights. Two days later, Moss Side in Manchester was ablaze, and by the end of the following week, rioting had been reported in a further twenty-seven towns and cities. It may be a reflection of journalistic enthusiasm that the reported lists of casualties included four in Cirencester and eleven in Tunbridge Wells. But the total effect was undeniable.

By the middle of July, it looked quite possible to police officers throughout the country that mass violence on an unprecedented scale might break out in almost any conurbation week after week, and even year after year. If the prospect was alarming to the constabulary, it must have seemed positively terrifying to the Government. Lord Knights, who as Sir Philip Knights was the Chief Constable of the West Midlands at the time, has described the concern of both police and Government to show that they were doing something about it. 'There is no doubt that from June 1981 through to the summer of 1982 people were biting their nails as to whether it was going to happen again. If we had done nothing there would have been a furore. You have got to be seen to be doing things – and that is not just true of police officers, it is true of politicians.' What the police did, with the explicit approval of the Government, was to depart from the British tradition of policing by consent. They decided to equip and train their officers secretly as paramilitary units, prepared to fight like soldiers in the streets and to kill if they had to.

ACPO changes course

In September 1981, a new approach was adopted by members of the Association of Chief Police Officers (ACPO) at their private annual conference in Preston. The rise of ACPO to form, in effect, a national leadership for the fifty-two separate police forces in Britain has been one of the more remarkable developments of the past decade.

As a professional association its membership is small, numbering only a few hundred. They are apparently unhampered by its informal standing in law, which gives ACPO, unlike the police trades unions, no basis whatsoever in statute. For their influence in practice has become decisive. ACPO consists of Chief Constables, Deputy Chief Constables and Assistant Chief

Constables. They meet together to agree policies, and hold regular meetings with officials and ministers of the Home Office. The Home Secretary himself attends their annual conference.

When they met on 3 and 4 September 1981, an emergency session was held to discuss public order. Three forces with particular expertise were invited to address it. Two of them were familiar from previous years. The Metropolitan Police reviewed the events of the summer of 1981 and gave a candid assessment of the inadequacy of police preparations to contain the disorders. Then the Royal Ulster Constabulary gave a presentation of crowd control techniques they had adopted and refined for use in Northern Ireland.

Then came the turning point. A new force, outside the United Kingdom, was asked to describe measures it had perfected to contain public disorder. It brought to ACPO more than twenty years' experience of suppressing riots and uprisings, and was expert in coping with far greater levels of street violence than had occurred in Britain. Its methods were often harsh and sometimes lethal. The force in question was the Royal Hong Kong Police. Their Commissioner, Roy Henry, was asked to send one of his top officers to teach British police a new method of crowd control, based on the Hong Kong model. Mr Henry defines the Hong Kong approach to policing public order as 'paramilitary'. He instructed his Director of Operations, Richard Quine, to fly to London, to attend ACPO in Preston and to tell them all they wanted to know.

Richard Quine presented to them the full range of Hong Kong's public order and internal security arrangements – the distillation of British Colonial policing as practised in the most important remaining outpost of the empire. It was a paramilitary blueprint for suppressing rebellions by Chinese communists, indigenous trades unions or anybody else who had the nerve to take on the colonial power of the British abroad. He gave a detailed briefing accompanied by a slide show.

It set out the computerized system of communications which provides a minute-by-minute command and control network; the 'riot suppression unit' consisting of platoons of men in units with specific tasks such as wielding batons (truncheons), firing CS gas, making arrests and shooting firearms; the 'light striking force' which could strike with the same power but with greater flexibility; the column patrols to enforce curfews and show the flag once fighting was over. He itemized the armoury of police equipment regarded as standard in Hong Kong, and the training which was the key to the whole process: 'I underlined the need for a very complete programme of training, which is given a great deal of attention with all our recruits in Hong Kong.'

Then he recommended the formation of an elite squad of police officers who would be committed to continuous training over a period of ten weeks, in a concentrated burst of tactical exercises covering all kinds of disorder, crowd control and riot suppression. In Hong Kong the squad is called the Police Tactical Unit, and is used as a ready reserve in the event of natural disasters or major crowd control problems such as racedays and riots.

He showed the British police a handbook containing all Hong Kong's expertise in the arts of suppression of public disorder. It was its manual of internal security instructions. He gave a most thorough lesson, and ACPO took it eagerly to heart. Those at the meeting showed considerable interest in the colonial police manual and the anti-riot equipment on which it relied. There was special interest in the technique of transforming a peacetime police force into a dedicated paramilitary fighting unit with highly trained and disciplined officers. Richard Quine's impression as he spoke was that his audience was very attentive and anxious to bring the Hong Kong model to Britain. Their only reservations, he thought, concerned its acceptability to public opinion and their political masters.

The ACPO conference spent a whole morning talking about public order, and then made an important decision. With hindsight, it can be seen as their most influential decision of the decade. They set up a working group to review British riot control tactics in the light of experience of other countries and come up with a programme of action. Its title was to be the Community Disorder Tactical Options Inter-Force Working Group. One of the Chief Constables who was present at the meeting in Preston has given an account of the thinking behind it:

We had learned some hard lessons about the training of police officers. Forces in the main urban centres were already pretty well trained in the use of Police Support Units, the tactics of crowd control, the use of shields to form cordons and so on. But the forces that came to our aid from rural areas were not as well trained and it had become obvious that in order to respond to emergencies, everyone had to be trained to the same standard, with the same orders, the same formations and the same tactics. Otherwise it was just confusion.

That meant we had to have a national training package, a national manual on which to work. So ACPO set about devising one.

The working group consisted of half a dozen senior officers from different forces. Three of the key figures were Deputy Assistant Commissioner John Radley of the Metropolitan Police, Chief Constable David Hall of Humberside and Superintendent Jim Chalmers of the West Midlands. They reported to the ACPO sub-committee on public order chaired by Christopher Payne, the Chief Constable of Cleveland. In two years they prepared a massive volume of paramilitary and other manoeuvres called the *Public Order Manual of Tactical Options and Related Matters*. Another working group, chaired by an Assistant Commissioner of the Metropolitan Police, Geoffrey Dear, produced a range of training materials based on the manual for officers of different ranks, from frontline constables up to commanders and senior policy makers in force headquarters. The whole project was encouraged by the Home Office. When the *Public Order Manual* was in its final draft, the Home Secretary, William Whitelaw, read and approved it.

The stage was set for the most significant shift in police strategy Britain had known for a century and a half, but nothing was made public. The preparations were carried out in total secrecy. The ACPO spokesman at the end of the 1981 conference told reporters only that it had concentrated on spontaneous public disorder and that 'although there have been no positive decisions or recommendations, the conference has drawn together a lot of information about the right way of dealing with this subject. One thing we have had as a theme is the need to retain traditional policing methods and what our policemen look like.'

The visit from the Royal Hong Kong Police was never made public; the decision to adopt a national approach to crowd control and the paramilitary trend of the chosen route were known only to the higher ranks of the police themselves, and the Home Office. At one stroke, two central traditions of British policing were thrown into question: the selection of paramilitary tactics raised doubts about the doctrine of minimum force, and the strict code of secrecy surrounding the decision drove a coach and horses through the concept of policing by public consent. ACPO, a body with no statutory basis, made up its own mind without informing, let alone consulting, the constitutional representatives of the public either in Parliament or in the local police authorities.

By the summer of 1983, the Community Disorder Tactical Options Inter-Force Working Group had done its work. Each police force was issued with a thick ring binder containing a detailed analysis of the stages of a riot and the police responses appropriate to them. A total of 238 tactics and manoeuvres are set out in its thirty sections, arranged in order of escalating force, from normal policing up to plastic bullets, CS gas and live firearms. ACPO had produced its national manual of *public order tactics for the eighties*.

An introduction signed by the President of ACPO, Kenneth Oxford, the Chief Constable of Merseyside, set the scene.

Since the street disorders of the summer of 1981, there has been intense activity within forces to ensure that their arrangements for the prevention of public disorder are adequate. Relatedly, above force level, the Association of Chief Police Officers has given full and urgent consideration to preparing guidance in relation to the perceived operational need taking account of related developments in training, equipment and organization. The objective is to provide for an integrated approach, under which common patterns and standards should enable forces to combine more effectively and enhance the success of mutual aid arrangements.

All Chief Officers of Police wish to preserve the philosophy of policing by consent, in the policing of public order as in that of other areas of activity, and wherever possible to respond to public disorder by the deployment of officers retaining the traditional image of the constable. There is equally no doubt of the need for the police service to have the capacity and professional skills required to maintain and, where necessary, to restore public order, making the most efficient use and deployment of the manpower and resources available.

To achieve these aims, all ranks should receive appropriate training both in the prevention of disorder and providing mutual understanding of the expectations and responses which may be made of them if violent disorder occurs. In turn, that requires full consideration to have been given to the use of particular tactics which are capable of dealing swiftly and effectively with large-scale street disorder, and which at the same time are clearly appropriate responses to the levels of violence experienced involving the use of no more than the necessary minimum force. And that can only be possible if all the officers deployed on a particular occasion are familiar with the execution of the 'tactics' chosen.

This manual defines and develops an extensive range of tactical options. The compilation of the manual is a further part of the Association's initial response to the recent experience of public disorder, and follows the publication of the Notes of Guidance booklet in January 1982. The final part of the Association's response is the development of comprehensive public order training packages, work on which is in hand.

This manual has been developed and produced by the Community Disorder Tactical Options Inter-Force Working Group. The Association is indebted to the group for the tremendous work which was done, and that within the short space of a few months.

K. Oxford, President.

The preface following these remarks emphasized that the manual had been produced with Home Office support and repeated the objective of obtaining common minimum standards of public order training for all forces. In plain English, it was announcing to its restricted readership that the *Public Order Manual* set out a detailed national response to riots, a response which carried the explicit approval of the Government.

It also apologized for the cumbersome presentation in a heavy binder, necessitated by the many amendments which would be made in the future. It was not, the preface whimsically observed, intended as a pocket edition. Nor was it intended for general publication, even within the police service. The restriction to officers of ACPO rank means that nobody below Assistant Chief Constable is authorized to read it.

3   Tooling Up

Once we start tooling up to declare war on society,
policemen become the unwitting victims of violence.
John Alderson, 2 September 1981

While work continued on a set of training materials for lower
ranks which would teach them the manoeuvres set out in the
Public Order Manual (which they, like the public, were not
permitted to see), an abbreviated version of the manual itself was
prepared for the eyes of middle-ranking officers, who would act
as commanders on the ground during disorders. It was distributed in April 1985 under the title *Public Order Guide to Tactical
Options and Related Matters*, under the imprimatur of the Chief
Constable of Cleveland, Christopher Payne, the Chairman of
ACPO Public Order Sub-committee. Chief Inspectors, Superintendents and Chief Superintendents were told that the *Guide* was
only the first step. Policing public disorder was 'an evolving
discipline' and new developments and emerging tactics would be
kept under review by a new body, the Public Order Forward
Planning Unit.

This planning unit was to become a permanent continuation of
the working group which had prepared the *Public Order Manual*.
Significantly, it reports to the ACPO sub-committee on public
order and is based in New Scotland Yard under the administrative umbrella of the Metropolitan Police. This effectively removes
the Forward Planning Unit, like the working group before it, from
even the semblance of control by local elected representatives on
police authorities. ACPO and its sub-committee are answerable
to nobody except their own members, and the Metropolitan
Police are (uniquely) answerable to the Home Secretary alone,
acting as the police authority for the metropolis.

An official document explaining this assumption of control at national level by ACPO and the Home Office presents the structure and purposes of the Forward Planning Unit. It says that Chief Constables should consult the unit when contemplating new proposals or equipment connected with the maintenance of public order. Officers throughout the country are asked to send new ideas, concepts and items of equipment up to the Forward Planning Unit so that they can be disseminated 'for the benefit of the police service as a whole'. (The document is reproduced in Appendix B.)

The official description of the Public Order Forward Planning Unit makes no mention of the Home Office. But in the course of explaining its operation, one senior officer with public order responsibilities made an important slip. He was discussing a particular tactic set out in the manual, which involves the use of a manoeuvre imported directly from Hong Kong. In Britain, the tactic had been found to contain a serious flaw, and a modification had been introduced to correct it. In line with the instruction that new ideas should be sent to the unit, this officer had not only changed the tactic within his own force, but had referred the change upwards. At first he said that the modification had been sent up to ACPO, but later he said it had gone to the Home Office. When pressed about this discrepancy he explained: 'ACPO or the Home Office? The two are sort of synonymous in this respect.'

Perhaps this interesting synonym lies behind another discrepancy. The author of the ACPO manual on public order is stated by the ACPO President in his foreword to be the Community Disorder Tactical Options Inter-Force Working Group, which was set up for the specific purpose of preparing such a manual and answered to the ACPO sub-committee on public order. But in a brief and apparently well-informed account of its preparation, the editor of *Police* (the magazine of the Police Federation) wrote in 1985 that 'it was prepared by the Home Office Public Order Liaison Group'. There can be only two explanations of this conflict of evidence: the first is that either the president of ACPO or the editor of *Police* is misinformed, which would be very surprising; the second is that the ACPO working group and the Home Office liaison group are, once again, 'sort of synonymous'.

Equipped with their new *Public Order Manual*, police forces up and down the country began training in its tactics late in 1983. They put a huge effort into it, to bring officers of all ranks in every force up to a common standard.

New recruits now find special training in public order tactics extended in their basic training. For the Metropolitan Police, this is conducted at Hounslow. Other forces use communal district training centres at Ashford in Kent, Bruche in Lancashire, Chantmarle in Dorset, Cwmbran in Gwent, Aykley Heads in Durham, Ryton-on-Dunsmore in Coventry and Kincardine in Alloa.

Male serving officers up to the rank of Inspector have been sent, in rotation, to learn the new tactics at training grounds within their own forces. Even those with long experience in crowd control have been dispatched to add the approved manoeuvres to their repertoire. Specialist squads of firearms officers have been taught to use new forms of weaponry which fire plastic bullets and canisters of CS gas. More senior men, up to Chief Superintendent, have been sent to classrooms in regional training centres, where they find themselves up against computers and facilitators in the hypothetical battleground of the Carruthers Estate.

The most senior officers, those of ACPO rank, have been sent back to the police staff college at Bramshill in Hampshire for between one and three weeks of intensive training in riots and the control of public disorder in general.

While all this training has been undertaken, orders for new equipment have become a matter of urgency. Protective clothing has been supplied, as have thousands of long riot shields. New short shields similar to those used by the Hong Kong riot squad have been stocked. Many forces store CS gas and plastic bullets in their armouries. Portable loudspeakers have been provided to issue warnings to disorderly crowds, and a few rudimentary banners have been made bearing legends such as DISPERSE OR SPECIAL WEAPONS WILL BE USED.

This transformation of the British police was completed, exactly as it started, in total secrecy. It is a mark of the tight discipline of the service that a fundamental shift in tactics of such enormous proportions was planned, and then codified in a manual, abbreviated in a guide, established in a Forward Planning Unit, translated into teaching packs, and then taught to tens of thousands of lower-ranking officers in the school of hard knocks, and to thousands of their superiors in Sandford, and to hundreds more of ACPO rank in the police equivalent of Sandhurst, without a word leaking out from anyone.

But while there was no published information, there were dire enough warnings of what would happen if the police departed from their traditional methods. Breaking ranks even before the crucial ACPO conference of September 1981, the influential voice of one insider was raised in public. John Alderson, the Chief Constable of Devon and Cornwall, had a reputation as a progressive thinker with liberal tendencies. He had increasingly set himself apart from more conservative Chief Constables and in particular from the Chief Constable of Greater Manchester, James Anderton. It is part of the voluminous police apocrypha that a weary Home Secretary once reacted to their bickering by announcing that he was sick and tired of the Andy and Aldy show.

By 1981, John Alderson had become convinced that his career would go no further. His outspoken advocacy of liberal (and later Liberal) policies, would deny him the job he most wanted, Commissioner of the Metropolitan Police. Having served in the metropolis as an Assistant Commissioner, and at the staff college at Bramshill as Commandant, he would collect his pension at the end of his days in Exeter. He had, therefore, little to lose by speaking his mind.

In an interview with the *Sunday Telegraph* in July 1981, he warned of the consequences of a hardline police response to disorder:

Alderson: There has to be a better way than blind repression. We must remember that this rioting is not a new phenomenon. Some 460 people died in the Gordon riots in the turmoil of the Industrial Revolution. Today, too, society has undergone a social revolution.

The violence stems from various disaffections – racial problems and other alienations – and this whole volatility has been detonated by the impact of the recession and the feeling of hopelessness. . . . The recourse to sheer force as a solution is very dangerous. We must tackle the underlying tensions and develop unorthodox, imaginative and radical solutions to keep pace with the free society and the cult of individuality. . . . The police and criminal justice alone can no longer be expected to control crime and violence. Police, probation officers and community workers must all come out of isolation and work together, sharing resources. If not, people will form vigilante groups.

Sunday Telegraph: While this may be a fine ideal, how do you reassure the public that the large-scale violence and destruction we have seen can be stamped out? Surely the police must urgently take a tough line with near anarchy?

Alderson: Of course. I'm explaining what's happened, not condoning it. Our men have to be equipped, trained and deployed to put down such excesses of violence. We must be seen to win and the rule of law vindicated . . . But having muscle is not enough; you have to use it wisely. A violent police reaction is not a panacea. It will not solve complex problems and will only make things worse.

Sunday Telegraph: We have already seen the use of CS gas in Liverpool. Would you approve of water cannon, rubber bullets?

Alderson: . . . and guns and machine guns? Where does the escalation stop? We are at a critical watershed and must not advance the police response too far ahead of the situation. It is even worth a few million pounds of destruction rather than get pushed too far down that road. That will only bring further violence . . . I repeat, force alone is not enough. Let us learn from Northern Ireland that you can't simply bring peace through great strength.

Sunday Telegraph: Without those constraints, should the police be doing anything more to curtail the violence?

Alderson: I think we are at the beginning of seeing a police response that none of us wanted. A repressive police force is inimical to our interests. . . . I don't think that even chief officers who may disagree with me on the extent of our reaction honestly want to see a paramilitary riot squad with all the paraphernalia on the streets of Britain.

I think we should rather learn from the United States, which had some appalling riots in the 1960s. They called in the National Guard and crack squads, but more and more people were killed. The presidential commission urged well-motivated social programmes to end alienation and they had some success, not least by employing more coloured and minority-group policemen.

John Alderson decided not to attend the ACPO annual conference at Preston in September 1981, due six weeks after his interview appeared in the *Sunday Telegraph*. According to one report, the mere mention of his name at a closing press conference produced an effect like shouting 'Paisley' in a Roman Catholic church. Instead, the Chief Constable of Devon and Cornwall presented his evidence to Lord Scarman's Inquiry into the Brixton riots, and instructed his public relations officer to put out a press release. It was dated 2 September 1981, just one day before the ACPO conference started. It expressed his resistance to paramilitary policing in even more stark terms.

Some people seem hell-bent on sacrificing a police style which is the envy of the world just because of a few hours madness on the streets. The official response in the aftermath of the rioting falls short of the stimulus needed to achieve a worthwhile solution. The Home Office has come up with de-humanizing equipment such as plastic bullets and CS gas, greater police powers and the prospect of a detention camp on Salisbury Plain. Meanwhile many police leaders seem unable to grasp the essential need for radical change. Once we start tooling up to declare war on the public, policemen become the unwitting victims of violence. They fill the hospital beds. If we are to save ourselves from incessant conflict, we must start talking hearts and minds, not CS gas and plastic bullets. We should be seeking to preserve our great tradition of policing with the people and declare our abhorrence of the alternative now on offer.

In the event, as we have seen, the policy ACPO adopted was precisely that which John Alderson so vividly warned them against. ACPO opted for the 'paramilitary riot squad with all the paraphernalia on the streets of Britain'.

At the press conference on 4 September 1981, which marked the only public session of their annual conference, the President of ACPO took the opportunity to distance himself from his dissenting colleague in the West Country. 'Mr Alderson polices a pleasant part of England,' said George Terry, the Chief Constable of Sussex. 'He can have a policeman to cover

hundreds of square miles with nothing but sheep. The philosophy in that environment is quite different from inner city areas.'
If these remarks seemed ungenerous in overlooking the years
John Alderson had served in Scotland Yard as Assistant Commissioner, during which he had trained the Metropolitan Police
for Grosvenor Square in 1968, they did at least end on an
incontrovertible note. 'I can only make clear,' concluded Mr
Terry, 'that the views Mr Alderson has expressed are not on
behalf of the Association of Chief Police Officers.' Six months
later, John Alderson took early retirement and left the police
service.

The word of the Lord

In November 1981, Lord Scarman presented his report on the
Brixton riots. Some Metropolitan officers found it a difficult
document to read because it was in places critical of the police,
pointing to acts of racial prejudice, harassment, lack of flexibility,
failure to consult, aggressive behaviour and excessive force. But
one paragraph was taken from it and remembered by those most
closely concerned with ACPO's decision to revise public order
policy. It was section 5, paragraph 72:

5.72. However good relations between the police and a local community
may be, disorder may still occur. The police must be equipped and
trained to deal with this effectively and firmly wherever it may break out.
In responding swiftly to disorder, the police deserve and must receive the
full support of the community. The analysis of the disorder in Brixton in
Parts III and IV of this Report, and the experience of the handling of
disorder elsewhere, underline in particular the need for:
  (i) means of ensuring that available police units are rapidly reinforced
      in the event of disorder by sufficient properly trained and equipped
      officers. Effective reinforcement arrangements both within and
      between police forces are particularly important, because the traditional British approach to handling disorder requires, if it is to be
      effective, the presence of large numbers of officers;
 (ii) increased training of officers, both at junior and command levels, in
      the handling of disorder. I have recommended earlier the adoption
      of common minimum standards and programmes for such training
      (paragraph 5.30 *supra*);

(iii) more effective protective equipment for officers – including better helmets, flame-proof clothing and, perhaps, lighter shields;
(iv) vehicles for transporting police officers which have some form of protection against missiles;
 (v) improved arrangements for communication between officers involved in handling disorder and their operational commanders;
(vi) a review of police tactics for the handling of disorders.

Part of this paragraph of Lord Scarman's report were committed to memory by some in ACPO rather as if it were a text of the scriptures to justify a policy they had already adopted. Indeed, one very senior ACPO member has the reference at his fingertips, 'Scarman page 97 paragraph 5.72', and has claimed that ACPO established its own review of public order policy as a direct response to this recommendation of Lord Scarman's. This seems to imply that members of ACPO possessed powers of foresight bordering on the clairvoyant, since they held their crucial session on public order two months before the Scarman Report was published.

Again resembling those armed with a convenient biblical text, some police officers have overlooked other parts of Lord Scarman's report which would not fit their case. The next page (page 98), for example, contains an unmistakable warning against ACPO's change of policy:

There should, I suggest, be no change in the basic approach of the British police to policing public disorder. It would be tragic if attempts, central to the thrust of my Report, to bring the police and the public closer together, were to be accompanied by changes in the manner of policing disorder which served only to distance the police further from the public.

Nor can Lord Scarman be quoted in support of ACPO's decision to proceed in total secrecy with its change of public order policy. Page 99 of his Report is categorical about the need for openness:

The need for an imaginative, dynamic attempt to tackle the tremendously difficult issues currently facing the police, an attempt which requires the co-operation of *Parliament, the Home Office, Chief Officers of*

Police, the police representative organizations, Police Authorities and local communities, is clear. I hope that the recommendations I have made will help to provide an agenda for a continuing dialogue between the police and the public about the nature of policing in today's society – a dialogue, which, if it be based on mutal understanding and respect, will serve to strengthen, without de-humanising, the forces of law and order. [my emphasis]

Of Lord Scarman's list of six major contributors to public discussion of policing issues, only two were actually included in the decision to opt for a paramilitary response to public disorder – the Home Office and Chief Officers of Police.

The battle of Orgreave

With an unblushing sense of timing, the last stages of training in the new public order tactics were completed in 1984. They were almost perfectly on cue for the first test of their effectiveness in Britain, which was not to suppress a riot but to defeat a mass picket of coal miners.

Early that year, the National Union of Mineworkers began picketing the coking depot at Orgreave in South Yorkshire as part of its dispute with the National Coal Board, and, indirectly, the Conservative government. It was in the course of this dispute that the Prime Minister, Margaret Thatcher, was reported to have made a comparison with the Falklands War two years earlier and to have told her party that, having defeated the enemy in the South Atlantic, it was time to defeat the Enemy Within. Day after day, as large numbers of pickets attempted to stop lorries from moving in and out of the plant, police officers from all over the country were seconded to keep the supply lines open. Some of them disliked their new role. One senior Metropolitan officer said that policemen were being asked to behave as soldiers. He gave a graphic description of coaches leaving Hendon every Sunday for the coalfields, saying that it was like watching an embarkation for a war. 'While the Army would call them platoons, ACPO calls them Police Support Units.'

A mass confrontation, sooner or later, seemed inevitable. It came on the morning of 18 June 1984. Thousands of miners converged on the road into the plant, arriving in large numbers from 6 a.m. They were met by thousands of police in riot gear, who confined them to the field adjoining the road. The following eight hours brought the most bitter and brutal clashes of the whole year-long coal dispute, and (perhaps inevitably) led to the most serious conflicts of evidence about what exactly had happened and in what order. Both sides suffered terrible injuries in the fighting, and television news sided with Fleet Street in blaming the miners for having started the violence. But a spate of radical books published eye-witness accounts to support the view that the police had provoked the worst of the conflict by attacking first.

The trial of Orgreave pickets charged with riot was remarkable in many different ways. In the first place, the charges against every one of the accused collapsed, suggesting that whatever may have happened on 18 June, there was no riot at Orgreave. Secondly, the defence team required the police to produce their own direct evidence of the day's events, in the form of a video recording of the main confrontation which had been made by a police cameraman from a nearby rooftop.

The existence of this official police video had not been mentioned by the police themselves, and it was not produced in court as evidence for the prosecution. A detailed account of its contents was presented in a *Guardian* article by Gareth Peirce, a solicitor acting for miners in the dock.

You see how men arrived at Orgreave on a beautiful summer's day from all corners of the country. You see them from 6 a.m. onwards being escorted by police towards an open field, being brought by police over open ground from the motorway, being steered by police from below the coking plant to the field above. For two hours, you see only men standing in the sun, talking and laughing. And when the coking lorries arrive, you see a brief, good humoured, and expected push against the police lines; it lasts for 38 seconds exactly. You also see – the film being shot from behind police lines – battalions of police in riot uniforms, phalanxes of mounted officers, squadrons of men with long shields, short shields and batons. You see in the distance, in a cornfield, police horses waiting, and down a slope, on the other side, more police with dogs.

Suddenly the ranks of the long-shield officers, 13 deep, open up and horses gallop through the densely packed crowd. This manoeuvre repeats itself. In one of those charges you see a man being trampled by a police horse and brought back through the lines as a captive, to be charged with riot. You see companies of 'infantry' dressed in strange medieval battle dress with helmets and visors, round shields and overalls, ensuring anonymity and invulnerability, run after the cavalry and begin truncheoning pickets who have been slow to escape.

You hear on the soundtrack 'bodies not heads' shouted by one senior officer, and then see junior officers rush out and hit heads as well as bodies. You see this over a period of three hours and you see men begin to react and throw occasional missiles. After 12 noon, they begin to construct defensive barricades against further police onslaught.

Ms Peirce's account concludes:

Orgreave was never to do with the niceties of police powers. It was to do with power, absolute power, exercised at will. Arbitrary arrests and brutality are hallmarks of any dictatorship – they were evident at Orgreave on 18 June and ignored. By our silence, we have endorsed the existence of a militia.

Ms Peirce compared the modern Chief Constable to a medieval warlord.

The account of the same events by the Chief Constable of South Yorkshire, Peter Wright, presents a quite different picture. Where Gareth Peirce emphasized the extent of police power and planning for the confrontation, Peter Wright stressed the preparations made by the miners and their supporters. His account makes no mention of some of the most serious incidents described in Ms Peirce's article, in particular the repeated use of mounted police charges into the crowd. Mr Wright tells a story of police responding in purely defensive ways to the increasing violence directed at them by the pickets. His account was published by his force in a detailed report called 'Policing the Coal Industry Dispute in South Yorkshire'.

Monday 18 June 1984 saw the worst and the last day of violence at Orgreave. Intelligence and information received indicated that many demonstrators would be arriving from Scotland, Kent, South Wales, the Midlands as well as South Yorkshire.

Pickets began arriving in Sheffield on the evening of Sunday 17 June 1984 and many more arrived in the early hours of Monday 18 June 1984.

The first incidents of note took place as early as 3.00 a.m. when 50 demonstrators began pulling stones from the walls of the Plant, and throwing them into the works.

A constant build-up of pickets continued through the early hours.

Some 700 left their coaches in Sheffield City Centre and commenced to walk in procession to the Plant causing traffic hold-ups on major roads. They were directed off the main roads with some difficulty. The build-up of pickets reached its peak about 9 a.m. when estimates of 10,000 were made.

In the meantime, because of this build-up of pickets, extra Police Support Units were requested and received through the National Reporting Centre.

The first convoy of 35 lorries to reach Orgreave had to be delayed on the M1 Motorway for 33 minutes whilst PSUs were deployed to prevent any likelihood of pickets blocking the approach road.

The convoy entered the Plant and loaded with coke. It was held for 28 minutes inside the Plant when fully loaded until it was considered safe for it to proceed. The convoy left without problem after which some pickets moved away, but most remained.

There had already been some scenes of violence and police officers in protective headgear and with shields had to be deployed to protect the police cordon from missiles being thrown by pickets.

. . . The second convoy of lorries arrived at 12.40 p.m. and went straight into the Plant without any hold up. The violence escalated; a barricade was erected using heavy boulders, a heavy steel girder, and angled steel spikes; also scrap vehicles were removed from a nearby dismantling yard, placed in the roadway and set on fire.

The second convoy left Orgreave at 1.10 p.m. without being interrupted. Usually after the second convoy had departed the pickets dispersed, but not on this occasion. They directed even greater violence towards the police, and this continued for about an hour.

. . . At the end of the day, 93 pickets had been arrested, 72 police officers and 51 pickets injured; 181 PSUs, 50 police horses, and 58 police dogs had been deployed (Sent our).

. . . Following 18 June 1984, Orgreave never again figured in the headlines.

In 1985, BBC Television's *Brass Tacks* obtained a copy of the official police video of the confrontation at Orgreave, which was by then being used at the police training college at Bramshill as part of the ACPO rank training in new public order tactics. It seemed to offer a unique opportunity to decide between competing descriptions of events. It could settle the question of who started the violence – the police, as claimed by the defence solicitor, or the pickets, as in the Chief Constable's version.

Brass Tacks invited John Alderson, by then into his fourth year of retirement in the West Country, to travel to Manchester and view the video. Having done so, his conclusion was clearcut: the pickets were not quite so peaceful and good-humoured as Ms Peirce had suggested, but there was no doubt that the police were responsible for the escalating violence:

Brass Tacks: You have looked at the police video of Orgreave. Judging from it, who attacked first?

Alderson: I think it is fair to say that although there was pushing and shoving by the miners and one or two throwing missiles of one kind or another, the general escalation, the first escalation it seems to me, came from the cantering of police horses into the crowd which merely heightened the tension and increased the violence. Which is contrary to what the police stand for. The police are there to diminish the violence, not to increase it.

John Alderson then viewed the video again up to the moment of the first police mounted charge into the crowd. He described the scene just before the order to advance was given:

Alderson: So far on this day, the majority of miners have been boisterous, there's been some pushing and shoving, but no greater violence than we saw in Grosvenor Square in 1968. I have seen one or two stones but that's about all.

Brass Tacks: If we stop the video at this point, imagine yourself as commander of the police on the ground. What would you be instructing your men to do?

Alderson: I would be certainly instructing my men to hold firm and try to retain their good humour.

Brass Tacks: Is there any sign that they could not hold firm?

Alderson: If I had seen a sign that they could not hold firm, I would have reinforced them, but I have not seen that.

The video was then played on, and John Alderson described the police tactics which had actually been used.

Alderson: Look what has happened. The commander on the spot has exercised one of his options, and that is his option to release the mounted police to charge in and to <u>intimidate the crowd</u>, in order to drive them back and relieve the pressure.

Brass Tacks: Would you have done that?

Alderson: I personally would not have done that at this stage because what is happening now is that this is causing the crowd, which is already tense and angry for reasons apart from on this particular day, now to become even more <u>angry and respond</u> you see. Now you find that after that mounted police charge, the throwing of stones at the police increases a little, though not, at this stage, on any great scale. So that has merely provoked anger and reaction and escalated the day's proceedings higher than I would have wanted to do at that stage.

Brass Tacks: How would you describe the decision to send in the police horses there?

Alderson: I would describe it as the sort of thing that you might read in a manual, but on the spot this is where judgment comes in. If you are trying to <u>police with minimum force</u> and get away from this field today <u>with few casualties</u>, then the police should not start the escalation on any scale.

There was a third remarkable outcome of the Orgreave 'riot' trial, which may prove even more significant than the collapse of all the riot charges and the revelation of the official police video. It was certainly the most unwelcome outcome so far as ACPO was concerned. It was the disclosure, for the first time, of the existence of their new *Public Order Manual*, and the training in its tactics. The point which brought it to light was not, in itself, central either to the prosecution case or to the defence. <u>It was alleged that some police officers at Orgreave had drummed on their shields with truncheons, and shouted battle-cries in unison.</u> When the commander of police forces on the ground appeared in court as a witness, the defence barrister, Michael Mansfield, decided to question him about these allegations.

The officer concerned, Tony Clement, Assistant Chief Constable of South Yorkshire, was himself a member of ACPO. He had spent 18 June at Orgreave directing his forces from just behind the front line of long shields. He said that <u>drumming on shields was legitimate in the circumstances</u> and was, indeed, authorized in the new manual.   *??? provokes ???*

What manual was this? asked the defence, and invited him to quote the relevant section. The Assistant Chief Constable referred to a section of the manual governing the 'tactical use of noise'. Later, other sections concerning long shields, short shields and horses were also read out in court and transcribed. ACPO's secret was out.

On 22 July 1985, a copy of what the Assistant Chief Constable had read in court was placed in the House of Commons Library, on the instruction of the Speaker following a request from Tony Benn MP. Journalists hurried to read it, and a number of indignant articles appeared drawing attention to its sometimes aggressive language. Three phrases caused particular comment:

manual language

* the instruction to short shield officers to 'disperse and/or incapacitate' demonstrators;
* the instruction that long shield officers should give a show of force by making 'a formidable appearance';
* the stated objective of using police horses 'to create fear' among a crowd.

It will become clear in later chapters that these are by no means the most contentious words in the manual. But their publication in the newspapers created enough antagonism for ACPO to insist that the rest of the document remain secret. If there were voices raised in favour of its publication, as some insiders suggest, then they were overruled by the majority which then, as now, maintained the manual's status as a restricted document, for ACPO rank only. Even the Shadow Home Secretary, himself a Privy Councillor, was told that he could not read it. What nobody outside ACPO and the Home Office could have known was that the sections on shields and horses which were read out in court had already been systematically edited to delete passages which might have provoked even greater comment (see Chapters 5 and 6).

In what is by now an extensive body of Orgreave literature, there is a consensus about the conflict's importance for the remainder of the coal dispute, which continued for eight further months without any further pitched battle on the same scale. Orgreave, 18 June 1984, has been presented as the place and time the police showed their power to defeat even the greatest and most dedicated forces of opposition. It has been mythologized as the day South Yorkshire regained what Birmingham lost in 1972 at Saltley gates. To one side in the argument, Orgreave represents a turning-point in the long struggle of the law against the dark might of trade union barons. To the other side, it symbolizes the victory of official violence in the form of Thatcher's army over the time-honoured civil liberties of workers. This conflict of inter-pretations has made Orgreave difficult to discuss without ran-cour, and has ensured its place in the dissenter's pageant of State repression alongside the General Strike and Tonypandy and Peterloo.

But in all that has been written about Orgreave, one key fact has been overlooked. From the standpoint of this narrative, it is the central point: Orgreave represented the unveiling of colonial policing tactics in mainland Britain. For the first time, manoeuvres learned from police forces abroad were put into practice not on a training-ground, but in a real dispute.

Immediately after cantering horses into the crowd, the police introduced their new cutting-edge: what ACPO calls short shield units, and Gareth Peirce calls 'companies of "infantry" dressed in strange medieval battledress'. It is the formation employed by the Hong Kong police in their riot squad. The police video shows clearly what happened. After the lines of long shields parted to let the horses through, paramilitary teams of police officers carrying truncheons in one hand and round shields in the other ran through behind the cavalry and set about members of the crowd, arresting and/or incapacitating them as laid down in the manual.

John Alderson watched this part of the police video with dismay. 'This is precisely how the Hong Kong riot squad would form up, with the same kind of equipment and the same tactics. In fact, this is a carbon copy of the Hong Kong riot squad.' He observed that some of the behaviour of officers of the short shield units was contrary to the doctrine of minimum force, and would legally constitute a crime. But his major concern was the general strategy.

The British people should never accept colonial-style policing. It is not democratic policing, it is forceful, repressive policing. Instead of export-ing the developed British traditions to the colonies, we are now import-ing colonial policing into Britain. The question that faces us all is this – if we have seen the Hong Kong police tradition used in Great Britain in 1984, what are we going to see in future on the streets of our big cities?

The fact that this fundamental change in police tactics was introduced without reference to Parliament or police authorities, and with public discussion muzzled by lack of information, raises another question: what is left of the constitutional tradition of policing by public consent? John Alderson says:

You need the consent of the people to police effectively. If you don't carry the people with you, your policemen will lose confidence in the public and begin to turn in on themselves. They will become alienated. They will, in fact, become a minority just like other minorities, and only by sticking together and using their force and power will they feel safe. If you can't walk about in police uniform in most communities by yourself and be reasonably well-received, there is something wrong in this country.

The secrecy surrounding the manual troubles many who wish the police well. In September 1985, the Police Federation magazine said that the manual 'has been the subject of a quite absurd degree of secrecy' and complained that neither the Police Superintendents' Association nor the Police Federation itself had been 'vouchsafed a sight of its contents'.

In 1986, one Chief Constable gave an interview saying much the same thing. Geoffrey Dear, by then Chief Constable of the West Midlands, told viewers of *Brass Tacks* that he did not know why his colleagues had decided to keep the manual secret.

I personally don't believe that there is anything in that manual that could not be made public. The tactics we have used and would seek to use in the future are pretty well known anyway. The only thing I think it is necessary to keep secret is the actual deployment on the day – the numbers of men you are going to use, where they are going to arrive and so on, which is a very different matter. I think the police service would be wise to allay suspicions about the manual and publish it.

The Commissioner of the Metropolitan Police, Peter Imbert, takes a more restrictive view, but is nonetheless in favour of public awareness of ACPO's new approach to public order policing: 'I do not believe that it is right that we should hide this training from the public. People should know what we are doing in their name, and either consent to it or not. I think that the more they know about it the better.' His approach to the manual is more limited in its candour, but he takes a dim view of ACPO's policy of secrecy: 'I do not think it would be helpful to publish the whole of the manual of tactical options, but we have been far too secretive with it.'

President Johnson's Commission on the United States riots of 1967, whose report became a nationwide bestseller in paperback, showed no inhibition about quoting from the FBI riot control manual. Indeed, the manual itself is a public document. It is also remarkably frank about the nature of police tactics in combating riots in American cities:

The organization adopted should be developed along military lines, ie., squads, platoons, companies and battalions. Military riot-control formations represent widely accepted uniform standards in general use by civilian law enforcement agencies.

Anybody who wants one can obtain a copy of this FBI manual simply by writing to the US Department of Justice.

But this spirit of candour has yet to permeate through the commanding ranks of ACPO. One of the Chief Constables most closely associated with the manual refuses even to discuss its existence, let alone its contents, in public. In an unattributable interview, he gave a vigorous defence of the policy of secrecy, and chose military language to make his point: 'No General would declare to the enemy his order of battle.'

1985 riots

In September 1985, rioting broke out again, this time in the Lozells and Handsworth areas of Birmingham. It was on a more serious scale than the West Midlands had suffered in 1981, and led to the deaths of two shopkeepers whose Post Office in Lozells Road was burned out. The men found themselves trapped inside the building and beyond the reach of rescue services, when fire engines were prevented from tackling the blaze by the crowd of rioters on the street.

Later the same month, there was a riot in Brixton. In October

1985, the most ferocious disturbances in post-war Britain took place on the Broadwater Farm estate in Tottenham. Many people were seriously injured, and a North London 'community bobby', Keith Blakelock, was hacked to death after he was caught on the wrong side of the police lines. Film and video of the night's events also showed clear evidence of a shot being fired from a block of flats on the estate. It seemed as if the ultimate 'scenario' of the Carruthers Estate war-game was moving from the table-tops of police training centres on to the streets of Britain.

The contention that riots almost always prove to have been triggered by police action was confirmed in each of these cases. In Handsworth, disorder began after police raided two premises, the Villa Cross pub and the Acapulco Café, looking for drugs. In Brixton, riots followed the shooting of Mrs Cherry Groce by the police. In Tottenham, Mrs Cynthia Jarrett died during a police raid on her home.

The response of police forces and the Home Office to these riots was in line with the policy that ACPO adopted in 1981. They continued to arm themselves against the possibility of further trouble, using weapons and tactics imported from Hong Kong and Northern Ireland. The Home Office urged the case for plastic bullets, which are a modern version of the wooden 'baton rounds' developed in Hong Kong twenty years ago. The Home Office also pressed for what the British colonial police had widely used as tear gas, now in its latest form known as CS gas.

The Chief Inspector of Constabulary, Sir Lawrence Byford, put the official view forward in his annual report for 1985:

The petrol bomb is now accepted by many disorderly elements as a legitimate weapon of first resort in confrontations with the police. With this in mind, and due to the stark escalation of violence in this country, the traditional equipment used for quelling public disorder may not be enough – as was evidenced at Tottenham. Reluctantly, therefore, the weapons of last resort, such as baton rounds and CS gas, need to be available to the police if their use may be the only means of dealing with major public disorder which seriously threatens life or property.

There were some Chief Constables who wanted these weapons but were denied permission to buy them by their police authorities. They were told by the Home Secretary, in a circular, that they could draw them from Home Office central stores in defiance of local wishes. The legal battle which ensued was to become a crucial test case for local accountability, as outlined in Chapter 9.

It was confirmed by the Commissioner of the Metropolitan Police, Sir Kenneth Newman, that police gunners with plastic bullets were brought on to the streets of Tottenham during the Broadwater Farm riot, though they were not ordered to open fire. This was the first reported occasion on which plastic bullets had been deployed in mainland Britain, and the Commissioner made it clear that it may not be the last. He told a news conference that he was prepared not only to deploy plastic bullets and CS gas, but to use them: 'I wish to put all people of London on notice that I will not shrink from such a decision should I believe it a practical option for restoring peace and preventing crime and injury.'

By the summer of 1986, every major police force in the country was 'tooled up', in John Alderson's terms, and ready to fight something very like a war on the home front. At the same time, they gave unprecedented emphasis to publicizing initiatives in community policing. It was as if they were working hard to present the reassuring face of the British bobby, dear old George Dixon, in order to soften the dramatic change which had taken place.

But within the police service itself, nobody was fooled by appearances. A number of startlingly frank statements illustrate the internal tension police officers feel, between their normal duties and the new paramilitary role they have been trained for. One senior officer argues against the creation of a separate paramilitary unit to complement the existing forces of police and the Army. It would be redundant, he claims, because Britain already has just such a 'third force': 'It exists in a hidden form, and goes back to wearing pointed helmets the next day'. The Chief Inspector of Constabulary made a related comment in an interview to mark his retirement in March 1987. Sir Lawrence Byford told *Police Review*: 'Now, even the rural policeman can be armed in riot gear one day and the next be required to return to his benevolent "Evening, all" attitude.'

Most candidly of all, an officer of the Metropolitan Police firearms squad told viewers of BBC Television's documentary *The Queen's Peace* in October 1986 that it had been hard to return to normal duties after Broadwater Farm because he was still on a high from the previous night. He said it was unfair to expect police to switch between these two roles. A fellow officer expressed the conflict precisely: 'We can't pat kids on the head one day and then shoot with plastic bullets the next.'

4   The Operational Knowledge

There was a need better to identify tactical options on an operational plane, to distil the knowledge and experience available within police forces which was largely unwritten and fragmented. That achieved, it was considered useful to convert the operational knowledge gleaned to this manual form.
        Preface to ACPO *Public Order Manual*

At first sight, the *Public Order Manual* looks like a maintenance handbook for use by car mechanics, or a thick file of lecture notes which a student might carry under the arm. It is an A4 size ring binder with a blue plastic cover bearing in gold letters its title, *Public Order Manual of Tactical Options and Related Matters*, a police shield, and the originator's imprint, *Association of Chief Police Officers*. At the top right-hand corner is its classification – *RESTRICTED For ACPO Rank Only*.

Its contents are arranged in five parts, with different coloured papers; each part is spaced into several sections, each of which, for ease of reference, is numbered on a card tab at the side.

Part One, in yellow, forms the introductory section. It begins by laying out the contents of each part, saying that Part One contains material which is either explanatory of the remainder, or is of a general nature. The Biblical status which police now accord to the manual appears to have been foreseen by its authors: 'It is intended that a reading of these pages will sufficiently enlighten recipients of the manual to enable it to be used primarily as a reference book. This is necessary, since the sheer volume of information prohibits that it be viewed as something to be read, learned and inwardly digested.' Part Two, it continues, will present the main body of the manual, the 'tactical options' likely to prove of operational relevance to chief officers. They will be presented, on white pages, in a hierarchy: 'reflecting an escalating application of force by police'. It says the options all relate to the way manpower can be deployed, with or without specialist equipment. Part Three, in blue, will cover evidence gathering, and deal with aspects of obtaining and presenting information and evidence in a pre-disorder, riot and post-riot situation. The role of CID will be included, though some aspects of their deployment could equally be viewed as tactical options. This seems to be a coded reference to the critical importance the manual places on good intelligence-gathering as a means of forestalling or containing outbreaks of public disorder.

Part Four, in pink, will give details of 'related matters' which have no common theme save that they are generally relevant to the subject of community disorder. Part Five, in green, will consist of appendices with lists of factual information about which police forces have certain equipment and specialist groups. The whole manual, it stresses, should be viewed as the latest state of the art at the time of printing, and there will be frequent or rapid developments in relation to some matters.

Then follows a list of the uses to which chief officers may wish to put the manual. It takes care to present its contents as no more than options, as the title claims, which chief officers may wish to consider when making their own decisions. 'Nothing in this manual', it emphasizes, 'indicates what must or should be done'. But there is a gentle reminder of the professional and political weight behind the 'options': 'The recommendations have the support of ACPO and the Home Office but in no way purport to supplant the authority of chief officers.' The point seems clear enough – any Chief Constable who chooses to ignore the collective view of his colleagues and the wishes of the Home Secretary and the Inspectorate of Constabulary, is perfectly free to do so.

The uses of the manual are listed as follows:

I. PLANNING
(a) To assist in perception of the relationship between escalation of community disorder towards rioting and the measured use of force by Police.

(b) To provide a reference point for chief officers who are deciding which tactical options they would wish to employ, (and therefore equip for if necessary), in the context of worsening community disorder.

(c) Against the background of centre core (national) training, to assist chief officers to assess their additional in-force training needs.

(d) To provide arguments in support of planned courses of action, in discussion with groups or authorities which may be involved in considering police deployments.

(e) To assist chief officers to consider additional resources, organization or deployments desirable in the event of serious disorder, which may require pre-planning.

(f) Generally, to assist chief officers in the formulation of Force Contingency Plans for serious public disorder, and/or directions to more junior officers.

2. OPERATIONS

(a) To assist in indicating the alternative police deployments possible when community disorder is on the increase; not least to show that the options are limited.

(b) To assist in advising divisional commanders on deployments when the social climate is such that the degree of tranquillity achievable has to be balanced against the risk of triggering a worsening situation.

(c) To provide a quick source to review the advantages and disadvantages of an operational option which is available by reason of equipment, training, etc.

(d) To enhance the appreciation of the consequences, for better or worse, which may be expected to flow from the employment of a particular tactical option.

(e) To enable chief officers to be fully aware of the manoeuvres through which tactical options are implemented, so that they can give effective directions in an operational situation.

(f) In an existing operational riot situation to provide something of a checklist of back-up arrangements that need to be brought into play.

Part One, section four presents the hierarchy of options which are now considered acceptable for police use in controlling disorder. It begins with the axiom that, as the degree of violence used by rioters increases, it will be necessary for police to increase the measured application of force. For that reason, the white pages of Part Two will appear in a hierarchical order, ranging from normal policing methods right through to the use of firearms. But placing tactical options in order is acknowledged to be 'a very inexact science' because it is impossible to decide the order either on the supposed acceptability to the public, or on the degree of risk of causing injury. Furthermore, some tactical options can be seen as approximately parallel alternatives which cannot be placed above or below each other. These problems are resolved by offering a ranking of the tactical options based on 'what might be thought to be degrees of acceptability' rather than levels of risk. The critical question is which tactical options are considered appropriate in different circumstances. If policing is supposed to be based on the minimum use of force, then matching police tactics to the threat of violence they face becomes an important art. The manual attempts some general guide-lines, by defining six stages of escalation of a riot and a further four stages of de-escalation, and then listing the tactical options which are considered 'appropriate' at each stage.

3. DEFINITIONS
(a) the following are the stages of a riot as defined below:

    1. NORMALITY
    2. HIGH TENSION
    3. SPORADIC DISORDER   } ESCALATION
    4. RIOTING
    5. SERIOUS RIOTING
    6. LETHAL RIOTING
    7. IMMEDIATE POST-RIOT
    8. SPORADIC DISORDER   } DE-ESCALATION
    9. COMMUNITY UNREST
    10. NORMALITY

(b) *Normality*
    The situation which requires no more than normal policing, which will itself vary from one area to another.
(c) *High Tension*
    The situation in the community when feelings are running high and the potential for disorder is perceived as considerably increased.
(d) *Sporadic Disorder*
    The situation in a community when there are frequent outbreaks of disorder, any of which might trigger a riot.
(e) *Rioting*
    This is taken to mean when an incident has in fact triggered serious public disorder in an area. This definition marks the shift in

emphasis from the general temper of the community to a specific incident. How widespread it may be is not relevant to the definition.

(f) *Serious Rioting*
Rioting which includes arson, use of petrol bombs, looting, occupation of premises, hostage taking, etc.

(g) *Lethal Rioting*
Rioting which includes the use of weapons designed to kill; in particular, firearms.

(h) *Immediate Post-Rioting*
This is the period of hours or days following rioting during which clearing up operations continue against a background of high risk of renewed rioting.

(i) *Community Unrest*
This is the much longer period during which a community settles down after a riot, against a background of media attention. The shift of emphasis is back to the temper of the community.

(j) *Normality*
This is when it is considered that 'normal policing' can be resumed.

The manual accepts that the stages of rioting as defined are not watertight compartments. For example, it says that high tension will certainly merge into sporadic disorder in a way which will defy identification of limits. None the less, police action must be tailored to the unrest they face, and the process of classification is therefore inevitable: 'The sole value in trying to identify the stages of a riot is the relevance to determining the weight or nature of the police response.' Two paragraphs later, the point is repeated with the specific advice that analysing a riot into stages affords assistance 'in deciding which, in the hierarchy of tactical options, is appropriate to the circumstances appertaining'.

It is easy to see how senior officers taking operational decisions during public disorder could come to read their *Public Order Manual* not merely as a list of options but as endorsement and approval from the highest level for action which falls within its guide-lines. The manual does not take from them the responsibility for making a judgment as to how police should act, but it does make crystal clear what is considered acceptable and 'appropriate' by those at the top of the political tree. An officer consulting it is likely to conclude that if he sticks to the manual his back is covered.

In the condition of *Normality*, the 'appropriate' tactical options are normal policing and the use of community intervenors.

In a state of *High Tension* the options are: normal policing, community intervenors, information management, intensive foot patrols and special patrol groups/task forces.

When *Sporadic Disorder* breaks out, the options extend to: normal policing, community intervenors, information management, intensive foot patrols, special patrol group task forces, protected officers, control of public/private transport, protected vehicles, Police Support Units, saturation policing, standoff/regroup, artificial lighting systems, cordons, check points, barriers, barricade removal, controlled sound levels, long shields, short shields, warning messages.

Once *Rioting* occurs, the appropriate tactical options are: community intervenors, information management, protected officers, protected vehicles, standoff/regroup, artificial lighting systems, cordons, check points, barriers, barricade removal, controlled sound levels, long shields, short shields, warning messages, mounted police, police dogs, arrest teams, baton charges (short baton), long batons.

When rioting gives way to *Serious Rioting*, four additional tactical options are considered appropriate: tactical use of vehicles, smoke, baton rounds, CS agents.

In the ultimate stage, *Lethal Rioting*, one further tactical option is added: firearms.

Once the worst is over, the four stages of de-escalation reduce the list of appropriate tactical options as follows:

Post-Rioting: options from community intervenors up to protected vehicles;

Sporadic Disorder: options from community intervenors up to special patrol group/task force;

Community Unrest: normal policing up to special patrol group/task force;

Normality: normal policing and community intervenors.

It seems likely that, at some stage, the working group compiling the manual considered one other option – water cannon. The option appears in this hierarchy, sandwiched between smoke and baton rounds, but there is no further reference to it and it does not appear among the tactical options listed in Part Two.

The manual then goes into some logistical considerations which will not be given in any detail here. They concern the timing of strategic decisions to make arrests, or disperse a crowd, to establish a police base-line while reinforcements are awaited, and in some circumstances to withdraw altogether. There is also an analysis of the chances of success of police operations under different numerical ratios of rioters to police officers. Again, nothing of this section will be reported here, for reasons outlined in Chapter 6 (see especially page 94).

There are then some general remarks about the approaches to crowd dispersal, beginning with an injunction to use only minimum force. The methods employed by the police, it warns, must be wholly appropriate to the temper of the crowd against the background of the local community situation.

An attempt should first be made to persuade crowds to disperse peacefully, without the need for direct or indirect physical contact with the police. This can be attempted on a voluntary basis, by using the least provocative method of achieving crowd dispersal, namely persuading a leader within the crowd to take the initiative and promote dispersal. If any community intervenors are available, they may be able to pull this off. If they fail, the next approach is by a display of force. 'This may be as ostentatious as possible, or more subtle.' The advantage of ostentatious display by the police is said to be that it may encourage curious spectators to disperse, separating them off from determined rioters. A more subtle display of force can then be made to those left behind, using officers with shields to suggest that the police strategy is to surround the rioters. Officers visibly displayed on rooftops, perhaps equipped with the paraphernalia of photography, will increase the apprehension of the rioters. 'Crowd dispersal, like crowd assembly, is infectious and once a crowd begins to disperse it should normally be allowed to melt away.'

If a display of force does not work, police can move on to verbal or visual persuasion, giving a warning message of the kind outlined in Section 20 of Part Two as a tactical option. The manual goes to some trouble to point out several pitfalls in this approach:

 (i) *Pleas* – requests based on moral grounds are more effective when made from a position of physical strength. Rioting crowds are well aware when police are numerically weak and public announcements from such a position may be counterproductive.

(ii) *Promises* – there is a risk that promises made in a confrontation situation may cause subsequent embarrassment. Officers in command must ensure that they do not exceed their authority to strike bargains, having regard to their duty to enforce the law.

(iii) *Warnings* – care must be taken to phrase warnings in such a way that they cannot subsequently be represented as threats. At the same time they should be credible to the crowd in that the police must clearly be seen to have both the capability and intention of giving effect to the course of action detailed in the warning.

At the same time, the manual says that it will probably still be desirable to reduce the size of the crowd by allowing some persons to disperse. If this is so, the crowd should be told that those wishing to depart peaceably may still do so, indicating a controlled exit point. At this stage, police may already have formed a baseline, which is a point beyond which the crowd will not be allowed to advance and behind which command and control systems for police officers on duty can be established.

Then dispersal can be attempted by physical means. The police may stick to their traditional way of policing crowds, namely close contact pressure. But this is said to be 'generally an inappropriate means of dealing with a rioting crowd'. Or they may decide to 'approach with impetus', in which case 'it is the menace or impetus of approach that proves the incentive for dispersal'. Several of the tactical options are based on this technique. Or the police may decide to use specialist weapons, about which no further explanation is offered in this section.

Then the manual explains the military origin and connotation of some of its new terminology, giving examples of military language it has adopted for use by the police. It leaves no room for fainthearts:

Such words constitute an important part of the vocabulary of strategic and tactical planning and for police officers, whose ordinary duties do not include such thought processes, it is necessary to make a conscious effort to tune in on this level. (This section is reproduced in full in Chapter 1, page 18.)

There is then another plug for the Public Order Forward Planning Unit based at New Scotland Yard, and Part One of the manual draws to its close.

The tactical options

Part Two opens with a sense of embarrassment. The first of the thirty tactical options it contains is none other than *Normal Policing*. Its inclusion in the hierarchy of options which culminates in plastic bullets, CS gas and firearms is said to be 'somewhat uncomfortable', and justified only by the need to preserve a progressive thread through the manual.

The exposition begins with a couple of truisms. In 'normal policing', it says, personnel are conventionally dressed and equipment and vehicles are traditional in appearance. It is only when normal policing has broken down that the other tactical options described in the manual become relevant: 'With the exception of community intervenors, normal policing methods are in direct contrast to every other section in this manual, particularly in relation to protected officers and vehicles, and the use of specialist weapons.' The significance of 'normal policing' for the rest of the manual is presented in terms of its potential for prevention of disorder. It can play a major part in ensuring that such incidents do not occur at all. The essential role of local beat officers is to counteract the escalation of minor incidents into fullscale unrest, and to serve as 'an invaluable dual channel of information between the community and police commanders'. The exact nature of this dual channel is left unexplained at this stage.

Local beat officers should be kept out of any police manoeuvre which could involve them in a violent confrontation within their own community. Their status and morale should be increased by recognizing their work in establishing local contacts, which can be a difficult and protracted task. They should be seen as specialists, not merely as a reserve of manpower. Four objectives for dealing with disorder by means of normal policing are laid down:

(a) To conform to an accepted and traditional image;
(b) To be seen to be policing with a minimum of force;
(c) To retain the greatest possible degree of public support and confidence;
(d) To avoid any action which may either provoke further disorder, or subsequently be used as an excuse for escalation.

These objectives represent the basis of traditional British policing. It is sobering to read them again with an imaginary NOT in front of each, bearing in mind the manual's comment that the rest of its tactical options stand in direct contrast to normal policing. As we shall see in later chapters, there are explicit warnings that other options can breach one or all of these four objectives.

The manual then sets out the reasons for abandoning normal policing methods in some circumstances. They appear formally as a list of disadvantages of normal policing. But they may be read as ACPO's private justification for the change of direction it introduced after 1981. They are as follows:

(i)   Is unable to contain other than minor incidents of disorder;
(ii)   Exposes officers to the risk of injury;
(iii) Officers may regard the risk of injury as unnecessary, and their apprehension will cause both their morale and effectiveness to diminish;
(iv)   If the Option (i.e. *normal policing*) is retained beyond the time it ceases to be appropriate, the range of Options and manoeuvres subsequently available can be considerably narrowed.

It then adds a 'special consideration' which goes to the heart of the matter: 'The police commander, using professional judgment, will decide when and where normal policing methods cease to be appropriate. It is a crucial decision, and forms the central dilemma of policing public disorder.' Then, just in case anybody has missed the point, the option of normal policing is formally recommended for use.

The next six options fall under Section 2 – *Community intervenors*. They expand the comments about local beat officers and the value of their work in forming local contacts. Four areas of contact are outlined in detail: liaison with elected representatives, community representatives, education services and centres of religion. They form options 1–4 of this section. Option 5 explains the tactical use of community intervenors before, during and after an outbreak of disorder, as exemplified by the uses made of Father Brown in tackling the problems of the Carruthers Estate. Option 6 covers the establishment of 'rumour centres' during periods of public disorder, in an attempt to counter any false or malicious stories which could inflame the situation.

The same point is covered more extensively in Section 3 – *Information management*, which presents eighteen recommended options for the management of rumours in times of tension. Police officers are recommended to set up rumour centres, to use their network of community links, and to open telephone information services. Their strategy should be to forestall rumours where possible, to refute them or minimize their content, or to create a diversion. They should keep a file of news clippings and use their own media information releases and filmstrips. They are told how to set up a briefing information service for journalists and how to approach television and radio news bulletins.

Two recommended options are particularly noteworthy. The first is the establishment of a 'media rumour clinic' within a local radio station or a local newspaper office, to which members of the public are encouraged to write or telephone stories circulating in their neighbourhood. The clinics should be operated with police assistance and should keep a finger on the pulse of local attitudes, anxieties and potential for community disorder. They can try to act as the link and mediator in any confrontation or misunderstanding, and publish or broadcast information accordingly. They can put an end to disruptive rumour by providing factual accounts. The disadvantages of such a rumour clinic are listed as its reliance on the integrity and objectivity of the media management, the inability of the police to control its running, and its potential for drawing police into a political arena 'with the real issues becoming overshadowed'. With these points in mind, a special consideration is recommended:

The motives and political leanings of media management require careful scrutiny before local police forces can contemplate participation in such a scheme since the ability for police to control information content is severely limited and the danger exists that certain disruptive elements could use the scheme as a political platform from which to attack the police. No such scheme is currently known to be in being in the UK, but the idea has worked successfully in certain US cities.

The second noteworthy option concerns 'restrictive measures'. The manual says that this tactic involves police forces taking the initiative in disrupting the information flow emanating from some person or organization intent on spreading anti-police or disruptive propaganda within a tense community. The essence of the tactic lies in making use of the type of information dissemination being used by hostile groups, and turning their own methods to the advantage of the police. Suggested measures are broadcast replies, open debate or the use of information leaflets: 'This Option does not involve the use of dishonest or unethical tricks, but places the emphasis on quick-witted response and an ability to turn methods of propaganda or rumour presentation to advantage.' Once again, it is stressed that the police should take care not to be drawn into political or stage-managed debate or confrontations.

The manual, in a departure from form, also takes the curious step of describing four further options which it insists are 'not recommended for use'. One is that no action be taken to combat rumours; another that rumour centres be established operated by a non-police agency; another concerns the appointment of rumour control monitors; and the fourth outlines tactics to discredit opponents.

Section 4 gives six options for *Intensive foot patrols*, which involve increasing the number of officers on each beat, or reducing the area to be covered, or both at once.

From Section 5 onwards, the tactical options move into a different style which abandons the 'traditional image' of British policing, in favour of the protective clothing, NATO helmets and riot shields which have come to symbolize the control of public order in the eighties. These new tactics and manoeuvres will be discussed in Chapters 5 and 6.

Before leaving traditional methods behind, it may help the clarity of this account to take one later portion of the manual out of order and consider it now. It appears after the full range of tactical options has been laid out, as the first section of Part Three. But it relates closely to the routine of normal policing, with an emphasis on foreseeing unrest before it breaks out, and taking steps to prevent it. It is the section concerning *Gathering and assessment of information/intelligence.*

Information / intelligence gathering by police forces

This discussion of information and intelligence gathering begins by distinguishing between the two. Information is defined as the hard facts coming to notice, while intelligence is the assessment and analysis of this information. Police operational intelligence before disorder, that is to say under conditions of normal policing, is presented as simply a designed system of gathering and processing information, which can and should do no more than provide the operational commander with a better understanding of the true picture facing him. 'The collation of information and intelligence should be the foundation upon which all plans for policing large scale public disorder are based.'

This emphasis on good intelligence echoes the view of Roy Henry, the Commissioner of the Royal Hong Kong Police when ACPO turned to them for guidance in 1981. He maintains that the first crucial area in controlling public order should be the intelligence network:

You have to have a special branch, an intelligence gathering machine which is charged with the function of warning and keeping the government alert to what the current situation is. If you know what is going to happen you can prepare for it. Even if there is no warning at all and a flash situation occurs, or a sudden mass reaction to something, then you still need an intelligence machine to follow it up and see how it develops. You have got to be well informed.

The *Public Order Manual* adopted for use in Britain divides information into three categories:

(i) Live intelligence, which is of immediate concern to effective planning of police operations;
(ii) Strategic intelligence, which is primarily long-range with little immediate operational value;
(iii) Counter intelligence, which aids the police to respond to or neutralize anti-police propaganda or rumours circulating within a community.

Sources of police information and intelligence are given as: informants; publications, including news clipping service and extremist literature; observation and surveillance procedures; comprehensive de-briefing of officers. Together, they form 'the total intelligence product'.

Collection of information is said to include 'development of sources of information in all levels of society within an affected community'. Processing this data is mainly carried out manually, but ACPO looks forward to an automated future:

With the advance of computerization of police records systems, many researchers see the time approaching when detailed decisions in the public order context will be possible using sophisticated equipment, allied to monitoring techniques and industrial methods.

Accompanying any such future system must be safeguards to ensure the accuracy of all data within the system, and the presence of all pertinent information. Controls must be designed to ensure accuracy and security of reports upon which management decisions are made. This section of the manual does not cover computerized data processing but mention is made at this stage to indicate the manner in which the system can be established and developed making use of modern equipment and techniques assuming that the political climate permits.

Some police forces, still working within the limitations of manual data-processing, have introduced a routine intelligence system known as 'tension indicators'. It is designed to offer local commanders and senior officers at force headquarters a regular assessment of the potential for disorder in different parts of their area. Each month, or each week in some cases, reports from police divisions are sent by telex to a central intelligence division, where they are compiled into a convenient digest of possible trouble. In some cases, a summary is prepared and added as a front-sheet, drawing attention to particular causes of concern. The whole document can be ready for the Chief Constable in the space of a morning.

The manual recommends this approach to every force and offers a check-list of indicators which lends formality to the traditional methods of predicting unrest; observation, experience and intuition. Police officers working in all parts of a force area are required to watch the approved indices of community tension, and report developments to their superiors. The official check-list is as follows:

(i) abuse and attacks on police officers and vehicles
(ii) increase in complaints against police
(iii) increase in disturbances between groups: such as school disturbances; volatile public area/park situations; racial, religious or nationalistic; serious conflicts between gangs; racial, religious or ethnic bomb/arson threats or incidents
(iv) racial attacks
(v) marches or demonstrations
(vi) all night parties/concerts by ethnic groups
(vii) anniversaries of significant events
(viii) attitude of the media or underground press.

This list is not considered exhaustive and local additions to it are encouraged. The manual points to a need for all operational police officers to be aware of tension indicators and to report their observations for collation and assessment. Recruits should learn the system in their training programme, and Special Constables volunteering for duty should be made aware of the 'unique opportunity' they enjoy to collect information. In turn, the staff at headquarters are required to report back to each division once information has been transformed into intelligence, and not merely to let it become the basis for statistics in a central department.

The manual recognizes that the tension indicators system carries a serious disadvantage in that police officers may perceive problems where in reality none exists and thereby distort the eventual assessment. It offers no way of avoiding this danger.

There is a detailed discussion of the use of *Informants*, which is said to be common in both overt and covert situations. CID, Special Branch and other departments are said to depend to a considerable extent on the cultivation and use of informants, and all branches of the police service are recommended to develop the practice with respect to public order. In particular, they should recognize the tactical significance of information direct from 'subversive groups'. Inside information is said to destroy the advantage such groups gain from their activities being clan-destine, and inside informants are described as being like an internal haemorrhage to the human body. There is a cautionary paragraph about the motivation of informants, which stresses that it would be naïve to suppose the majority of them to be prompted by public spiritedness rather than thoughts of gain, grudge against other individuals and in-fighting between criminal elements or militant groups:

The type of tense community prone to disorder tends to host a number of organizations purporting to represent the community and using the situation as a political platform. Invariably there is a degree of in-fighting between these groups with scope for the cultivation of informants.

There is then a long description of the legal limits governing the use of 'participating informants', that is, those who take part in the (sometimes criminal) activities about which they give information.

Other procedures are set out for establishing *Observation posts* within a tense community, like the spotter flat inside the fictitious Carruthers Estate, and for population surveillance in the form of observation of targeted individuals, vehicles, premises and locations to record activities. Reference is made to 'the already well-understood methods and range of technological aids' avail-able for this purpose:

Consideration should be given to the formation of composite undercover surveillance teams made up of experienced CID officers to identify organizers and perpetrators of offences, either from available staff or by mutual aid. A ready supply may be found in such areas as Special Branch and drugs squads.

It is recommended that all forces set up a central system of intelligence, linking divisions together through District Information Units. Among the advantages claimed for such a system, in terms of making best use of available information, is one which goes beyond the interests of the local force: it 'can provide a compatible system of information and intelligence for dealing with all types of disorder affecting the national scene and channelling of relevant information to a central point'. Those wondering what the authors of the manual might have in mind at this point, and what might be included under 'all types of disorder affecting the national scene', are not left to wonder for very long:

The need was recognized during the National Union of Mineworkers dispute to introduce a greater degree of co-ordination to improve national techniques between forces in receiving, assessing and disseminating information and intelligence relative to the dispute.

As a result, a Central Intelligence Unit was formed to co-ordinate and analyse selected information and intelligence, to identify trends and patterns affecting operational bearing on deployment and resources, and to identify individuals engaged in crime who cross force boundaries.

Appointing force Intelligence Officers selected for an ability in handling information and analytical skills, within those forces directly affected by the dispute, enabled the collation of relevant intelligence ensuring it was effectively processed and disseminated through to force command and control, interested forces and the Central Intelligence Unit.

The manual does not tell even its elite readership who it was who 'recognized' the need for this national centre of police intelligence, nor how it was controlled and to whom it answered. Nor does it say if the Central Intelligence Unit was disbanded at the end of the dispute which gave it birth.

5   Tactical Options I

*Police officers deployed against hostile crowds during
public disorder are likely to experience emotions ranging
from anxiety and fear to outright anger.*
ACPO *Public Order Manual*

The manual sets out thirty categories of police response to unrest. They form a hierarchy of applied force designed to meet the various stages of disorder defined in its Introduction. As we have seen already, the first four categories involve the use of police officers in traditional uniforms.

From Section 5 onwards, most of the recommended options require the new look of British policing introduced in the past decade – what is officially known as 'protective clothing' and routinely referred to as 'riot gear'. Sections 5 to 18 present tactics which are generally defensive in nature, designed to protect officers against attack while giving minimum cause for escalation of violence. It may, of course, be argued that the mere sight of well-defended police officers in 'battle-dress' is itself potentially provocative (see the remark of the Special Patrol Group officer quoted in Chapter 2, that people who would not normally throw anything at an unprotected officer have been known to have a go at those with riot shields). Indeed, the manual itself draws attention to the danger that ostensibly defensive or protective measures may be counterproductive if they are taken as a declaration of combat and thereby precipitate increased hostility against the police. But a clear distinction remains between manoeuvres which are intended to provide defence or protection, and those which are deliberately, in the military sense of the word, offensive. These latter options will be the subject of Chapter 6.

Section 5 covers the uses of *Special Patrol Groups* both alongside home beat officers in traditional uniform and in protective clothing after other officers have been withdrawn from a scene of disorder. SPG officers may be on foot or in mobile patrols in their transit vans. The significance of SPG policing has been recognized since its introduction by the Metropolitan Police in 1965, and it may well be a mark of the controversies it has raised that different forces have adopted their own names for the same type of unit. The manual lumps them all together under the heading 'tactical group':

Tactical group – an established group of police officers trained and equipped for specialist duties, including containment of public disorder, known variously as 'support group', 'special patrol group', 'tactical aid group', 'task force', 'operational support unit', 'immediate response unit', 'special operations service', etc.

In January 1987, the Metropolitan Police renamed their SPG units 'Territorial Support Groups'.

Section 6 presents the long list of special clothing which is supplied to *Protected officers* and the balance of advantages and disadvantages set out in Chapter 1. Only one detail need be added here, concerning the sensitive subject of police officers' numbers which are supposed to be displayed at all times on their shoulders:

Overalls – when overalls are worn there is a problem identifying officers, and this may be the subject of adverse comment from civil liberty groups and cause police investigating officers a good deal of work in any subsequent complaint investigation. Consideration should therefore be given to forces issuing personalised identification badges that can be readily attached to the overalls.

It would presumably aid identification if the badges could not equally readily be detached from the overalls.

Section 7 sets out various options for the diversion or control of *Public/private transport* near the area of a disturbance. It recommends the establishment of routine links between police and transport operators and the identification of diversionary routes prior to disorder. With the approval of an officer of ACPO rank, there is also the option of routing public and private transport through an area of disorder as a means of preventing assemblies.

Section 8 covers *Protected vehicles* and the procedures for taking officers into and out of a scene of unrest. It also sets out arrangements for transporting casualties and prisoners away from the area, and moving stores and equipment.

Section 9 details the basic unit of all later paramilitary operations – the *Police Support Unit*. It is remarkably similar to the riot-control unit used for public order control throughout the British colonies, and to the basic unit of domestic civil defence planning. In colonial police forces, it has had a variety of names including: Riot Control Unit, Police Mobile Unit, Police Motorized Company, Police Field Force and General Service Force. But they all shared a distinctive structure, consisting of one Inspector, one NCO and eight men. Acting together as a highly trained fighting unit, they could fit into a police Land Rover.

This colonial system for transforming ordinary police officers into a paramilitary company, and the implications of its adoption in Britain, are discussed further in Chapter 8. When ACPO developed its own units for use in a domestic crisis, it had to ensure that they would fit into the current British command structure and means of transport. A transit van is slightly more spacious than a Land Rover, and for domestic policing an Inspector can manage more than twice as many men. The *Public Order Manual* gives its own definition: '*Police Support Unit* – a contingent of male police officers trained together for the containment of public disorder, comprising one Inspector, two Sergeants, twenty constables'. Together they fit into two transit vans.

The manual, echoing the procedures used in Hong Kong, makes possible the mobilization of every policeman in Britain into one of these units. It represents the culmination of a gradual process of mobilization which began with the appointment of the first Special Patrol Groups.

Others were included when an almost identical formation was taken as the basic unit for emergency planning of police action in the event of a nuclear war. The term 'Police Support Unit' was given to this grouping in another restricted manual, prepared in 1974, which sets out the emergency plan for police contributions to civil defence. Its title is *Police Manual of Home Defence*, and its stated purpose is to prepare police forces for nuclear war by informing them about the effects of nuclear weapons, the organization of emergency services, the scheme of wartime regional government and the responsibilities of the police in such an emergency.

The concept of the Police Support Unit as the basis for these contingency plans is introduced as a means of providing the flexibility which will be needed 'before and after an attack'. Each PSU is to form a mobile contingency unit whose duties include the guarding of key points, reinforcement of public warnings, control of essential service routes and freezing of petrol stations. At the head of this list of police tasks is the enforcement of 'Special measures to maintain internal security, with particular reference to the detention or restriction of movement of subversive or potentially subversive people'. The mobilization of police officers into Police Support Units in a national emergency would begin, according to the *Police Manual of Home Defence*, with a message from the Home Office to Chief Constables to form PSUs in accordance with agreed plans. No specialist training was envisaged for these units in 1974, but the Home Office did suggest that 'Chief Constables will have opportunities to practise the units in peacetime when suitable policing tasks arise.'

Lord Knights recalls that ACPO seized this opportunity when preparing its own plans for control of public order in peacetime, following the confrontation at Saltley Gates. The PSU formation was adopted for general use: 'We decided to borrow this wartime conception from civil defence and use it to organize police officers in peacetime as well'.

When ACPO prepared its own *Public Order Manual* in 1983 the process of mobilization was extended to all policemen in the country. Its tactical options for switching into Police Support

Units are now taught to officers as part of basic training. On a word of command, twenty-three policemen can be taken from their normal duties and transformed into the 1:2:20 structure. If necessary, an entire police force can be mobilized into PSUs on an order from HQ. In Hong Kong, where they have been practising this transformation for several decades, the police pride themselves on being able to complete it in a matter of a few hours.

Section 10 involves officers in traditional uniform as well as those in protective clothing. It outlines five techniques of *Saturation policing*. The introductory comments stress that saturation policing requires a level of police activity 'substantially above that of intensive foot patrols' and says that the concept must be seriously considered in the immediate pre-disorder stage and in the period of de-escalation once disorder has subsided. It offers no definition of saturation policing, but does include one memorable suggestion to help visualize it: 'The phrase "army of occupation", although it has been used only in condemnation of the police, is a useful one to reflect the top end of the scale of this Tactical Option.' The objectives of saturation policing are then listed as: to deploy a large number of uniformed officers for the purpose of preventing potentially serious disorder from developing into a major problem; to discourage local bands of unruly persons from associating together in large groups which cause concern to law-abiding citizens; to allow a quick response to incidents; to allow early detection of trouble; to improve communication between police and the public and thereby increase the flow of intelligence regarding possible disorder. It depends on 'a background of unarguable numerical and physical supremacy'. The five techniques cover:

* reinforcement of beats by traditional or heavy foot patrols, initially wearing conventional uniforms;
* reinforcement by mobile patrols in protected personnel carriers;
* maintenance of patrols with reserves;
* sectorization of the area in the post-riot period;
* deployment of special teams to stop and search suspect vehicles and persons in an effort to detect weapons and obtain intelligence.

The advantages are set out, including: potential for defusing a serious situation, provision of a pool of officers available for action, no requirement for special equipment, and increased police confidence and morale from knowing that adequate resources are in the area. Then, with equal frankness, come the disadvantages, including:

* Removes resources from unaffected areas thereby increasing the possibility of crime being committed there;
* Officers drafted in may be insensitive to the needs of the area and unaware of local conditions;
* Individual officers, detached from their normal duties, may not have worked as a unit on previous occasions with consequent reduction in effective communications;
* May be regarded as 'provocative' in some quarters and serve to heighten tension within the community;
* Sometimes places police officers in an exposed position physically;
* Occasionally places individual police officers in an invidious position legally, particularly when provoked by radical or hostile elements.

It is recommended that the minimum ratio of supervisory officers to constables is as laid down for Police Support Units, that is one Inspector: two Sergeants: twenty Constables.

Section 11 presents three manoeuvres for *Standoff/regroup*, which are intended to strengthen police lines when they are over-whelmed or unprotected, and even when under fire from lethal weapons. In this extreme case, unarmed officers may be removed from the line of fire 'until after tactical firearms units, deployed independently from the public disorder operation, have located and eliminated sniper fire'. There is also an outline procedure for reducing police strength in structured stages once the worst violence is over.

Section 12 covers *Artificial lighting*, with seventeen options for different types of lights – floodlights, spotlights, overhead lights, vehicle-mounted lights, helicopters with lights – and the tactical uses of created pools of darkness to conceal police operations.

Section 13 sets out the traditional techniques of crowd control using officers with linked arms to form *cordons*. Often known as 'trudging and wedging', these tactics once characterized the police response to large-scale outbreaks of unrest. They provided the unarmed thick blue line which was familiar to CND demonstrators in the fifties and student protestors in the sixties. They are as remote from the policing style which has dominated the eighties as Aldermaston is from Stonehenge, and Grosvenor Square is from Wapping.

They involve large numbers of police officers shoving themselves right up to a crowd in order to contain or move it, or forming running human wedges to break it up. The potential of these tactics for causing injuries on both sides of the line should not be underestimated. Those inclined to romanticize past confrontations as if they were no more than boisterous and gentlemanly line-outs, should remind themselves of the numbers of policemen who were taken to hospital afterwards, and the catalogue of allegations that protestors in the front of the scrum were kicked, punched and secretly truncheoned by over-heated officers.

Section 14 is about *Checkpoints/interceptor tactics and motorway disruption*. It shows how to establish a checkpoint for vehicles and/or pedestrians, as happened most controversially during the coal dispute in 1984–5. Indeed, the manual anticipates the resistance this option may meet: 'Police check/Interceptor points can be detrimental to community relations in sensitive areas. It can also generate antipathy towards police, being viewed as a gross infringement to civil liberties.' With this in mind, the manual warns that friction must be minimized by using only experienced, tactful and well-briefed officers for this purpose. The duration of any particular checkpoint must also be carefully judged: 'Check/Interceptor points retained for protracted periods have a very detrimental effect on police and public relations and will inevitably be viewed as a rather draconian and politically sensitive measure.'

Section 15 gives seven manoeuvres for containment of crowds using *Barriers*. Most of them involve the use of tape to define a psychological limit, or tubular hurdles to lend it some physical substance. Two are more drastic, and can only be used on the order of an officer of ACPO rank: one option explains the use of police vehicles to form a barrier and says that, in the absence of police vehicles, 'private vehicles may be commandeered for barrier purposes'; the other suggests using 'unorthodox vehicles/ material to form barriers to protect police lines'.

Section 16 goes into the technique of *Barricade Removal*, some of which is recommended only if authorized by an ACPO rank officer.

Section 17 is mysteriously entitled *Controlled sound levels*, and recommends one of the most controversial techniques of recent policing – the use of battle cries and rhythmic drumming. It was the controversy surrounding these tactics which first brought to light the existence of the manual, when the Orgreave trials heard the Assistant Chief Constable of South Yorkshire refer to this section of the tactical options as justification for his men's behaviour (see chapter 3). The practice is explained under the heading of *Unifying sound*:

Use of a battle cry or other sound to unify police personnel deployed at scene of disorder – despite training, confidence and levels of suitable equipment, police officers deployed against hostile crowds during public disorder are likely to experience emotions ranging from anxiety and fear to outright anger. The use of chanting, shouting or the rhythmic beating on protective shields can act as a morale booster prior to deployment and also serve to release stress in police officers.

Advantages
  (i) the training requirement is minimal
 (ii) police morale may be increased
(iii) a sense of unity will be instilled into police officers
(iv) police officers' anxieties about impending deployment will be lost in the sense of group confidence engendered
 (v) noise levels draw attention to a police show of strength
(vi) tension in police officers may be released by chanting and beating on shields.

Disadvantages
(i) such action may be interpreted as a lack of police discipline with
    resultant complaints or critical comment.

Special considerations
Officers embarking on an active manoeuvre spontaneously produce a
cry. Even in defensive positions they may resort to shield tapping or
chanting which is very difficult to stop.

Recommendation
Option recommended for use only when necessary to lift morale of a
beleaguered police unit to enable it to break through to safety.

Lord Scarman's report on the Brixton disorders of 1981 records
that this tactic was used by police at the time. He compares their
shouting to that of ancient warriors going into battle and says it
was unfortunate and unworthy of a disciplined force. In spite of
the need to keep morale high while under ferocious attack, the
report finds that the behaviour of the police was calculated to
arouse fear and apprehension in those citizens who heard it, some
of whom were no doubt perfectly peaceful. Lord Scarman's
conclusion is terse: 'Such behaviour, despite extenuating circumstances, must be stopped.' The authors of the manual, and those
who approved its contents, clearly thought otherwise.

    There is also a description of two options which involve police
using no sound at all – silently approaching a scene on foot or in
vehicles.

    One other tactic in this section involves the use of sound to
soothe a crowd. It is as close as the manual's authors come to
surreal, if unintended, humour. They begin with the observation
that practical use is already made of the well-recognized effect of
music on human and animal behaviour. The tunes piped into
dentists' waiting rooms are given as an example, and a suggestion
of similar tactics is made for the police: 'Recorded sound or
music, preferably of a soothing nature or consisting of popular
songs to induce members of a crowd to begin singing, can be
delivered using conventional loudspeaker systems, either hand-
held or vehicle.' Among the advantages listed is that police
officers present will also experience the calming effect, though

the manual does not specify whether they too should begin singing.

But there are, of course, disadvantages as well. These include a warning that the sound levels produced may offend local authority noise officers under the provisions of the Control of Pollution Act 1974. There is also the risk that singing could impair police communications. Finally, timing is said to be important, and ACPO does stress that this tactic is 'of little value once actual fighting, arson and looting has begun'. In all, it might be simpler to take the advice of one user of the manual, who suggests that this tactic should be turned into a threat: 'Why don't we just hold up a large banner saying – DISPERSE OR WE PLAY BARRY MANILOW?'

Section 18 concludes the catalogue of defensive options with eighteen manoeuvres for officers equipped with *Long shields*. Parts of this section were placed in the House of Commons library after appearing as evidence during the Orgreave 'riot' trials, but some key elements were omitted from the version read out in court. The full text of the House of Commons document is reproduced in Appendix C; in addition to long shields, it also covers some manoeuvres involving short shields and mounted police which are discussed in Chapter 6.

The long shield manoeuvres can be used either as a display of strength, or for 'general crowd confrontation', or approaching and entering buildings, or recovering police trapped on the wrong side of the front line. There are also instructions on the use of portable fire extinguishers, designed to prevent any repetition of the scenes in Brixton in 1981 when some officers were appalled to find that petrol bombs could send flames round or underneath their shields. Some even found that the foam padding on their 'protective' shields caught fire itself.

Only the first seven manoeuvres in this section have been made public. Manoeuvres 8 to 18, though little different in principle, were not introduced as evidence during the Orgreave trials and have not made their way to the House of Commons library. A sample of 'brief descriptions' will indicate their nature: wheeling at junction, starburst, three man overhead, recovering injured officer – the pick-up, rescue/ambulance teams. More significantly, the court heard nothing of the lists of advantages and disadvantages which follow each manoeuvre. For example, the 'show of force' described in manoeuvre one is qualified by the following observations:

Advantages
  i) may intimidate some elements of the crowd and discourage riotous behaviour
 (ii) may bolster the morale of foot officers in close contact with the crowd
(iii) easily executed and withdrawn as situation changes.

Disadvantages
  (i) may trigger a worsening in behaviour of the crowd
 (ii) may be seen by some elements of the crowd as an invitation to discharge missiles towards police lines.

The disadvantages of manoeuvre two, the unit shield cordon, include one which is a common complaint among front-line officers: 'May be regarded by the officers as an "Aunt Sally" position without seeing the reason for it.'

Other listed advantages and disadvantages of manoeuvres in this section are mainly practical considerations concerning speed of movement, the dangers of opening gaps in the police line, and particular points of vulnerability to attack.

One final remark about defensive shields may be relevant, before moving on to the short shields police use when they go on the attack. Lord Knights, formerly Chief Constable of the West Midlands, recalls the fear his officers felt when they came under attack in the mid-seventies and had nothing but milk crates and dustbin lids for protection. The police began looking for better defences. 'We had seen shields in use in Northern Ireland both by the military and by the RUC, and it was that image we cottoned on to', he told *Brass Tacks* in 1985. He remembered that similar shields had been ordered up for police use, the appropriate supplies coming 'from military sources', because nobody else was making them at the time.

6   Tactical Options II

> *Use of baton rounds establishes a dependency on the weapons and creates both a reluctance on the part of the user to revert to normal methods and a tendency to use increasing levels of weaponry.*
> ACPO *Public Order Manual*

When Chief Constables decided to keep secret their new *Public Order Manual* for fear of 'declaring to the enemy the order of battle', the final twelve categories of tactical options must have been foremost in their minds. These closely typed pages give the initial appearance of a 'how-to' handbook, setting out in laborious detail a sequence of technical procedures which might fascinate the specialist reader but offer apparently little to interest the uncommitted. Some of the pages also read like the ballroom dance-step guides which were popular thirty years ago. In this case, though, the formation team-work is designed not for *Come Dancing* but for the streets of Britain, and its purpose is to suppress public unrest and rioting. Here are set out in neutral terms the control techniques of the modern police force. They cover the operations of colonial-style riot squads, the use of dogs and police horses, the most effective ways of mounting a baton charge, and the technology of putting up a smokescreen. At the top of their hierarchy of police offensives are the three ultimate weapons: plastic bullets, CS gas and live firearms. Together, these twelve sections form a book of instruction in a radically new approach to British policing. The technical word for it is 'para-military': '*Paramilitary*: on military lines and intended to supplement the strictly military; organised as a military force.' (*Chambers 20th Century Dictionary*)

The decision to publish here extracts from these most forceful *Tactical Options* is not taken lightly. No journalist ought to overlook the possibility that disclosure may be against the wider public interest, and there are senior members of ACPO who maintain that public awareness of their tactics may obstruct the conduct of future police operations.

This anxiety is not shared by all serving police officers, nor even by all members of ACPO. We have already noted, in Chapter 3, the opinion of the West Midlands Chief Constable that the *Public Order Manual* should be published in full in order to allay suspicion about its contents, and the Metropolitan Commissioner's view that police have been far too secretive. The official spokesman for the Police Federation, representing the lower ranks, is also on record opposing the 'quite absurd degree of secrecy' which has surrounded the document. It is even suggested by some in a position to know that the Home Office would favour publication of the manual, and may take the view that ACPO has aimed a shot at its own foot by insisting on secrecy.

There is a practical consideration, too; that police tactics are designed for use in public. If they were truly to depend on secrecy to be effective, they could only be used once each. But the manual contains nothing to suggest that this is so. Indeed, it is presented to its readers as a broadly definitive guide for the foreseeable future.

There is also a powerful constitutional argument in favour of publication. One pillar of the British tradition, the principle of policing by public consent, has clearly been by-passed by ACPO. Any move towards militarization of the police service raises serious issues of public policy, and it is sophistry to suggest that the public can consent to developments which are kept secret from it. It is also possible that some of the approaches enshrined in the new *Public Order Manual* challenge the other pillar of our police tradition – the principle of minimum use of force. Nothing short of a detailed public debate can settle this second question, and such debate must surely depend on public access to information. It does not, however, require that precise details be given of individual manoeuvres. These will, therefore, not be included in the following pages.

Section 19 of the manual introduces what John Alderson describes as 'a carbon-copy of the Hong Kong riot squad'. The official title is less dramatic and makes no allusion to colonial styles of policing – it is simply *Short shields*.

The short shield unit is defined as a specially equipped grouping of one Inspector, two Sergeants and twenty Constables – the standard formation of a Police Support Unit. What marks them out from their colleagues is that they carry light circular (sometimes rectangular) shields on their left arms, and a striking baton in their right hands. One senior officer responsible for public order training fancifully compares their appearance to that of Roman gladiators. It is undeniable, though, that the colonial policing model has been influential in the use of tactics and equipment. If a British short shield unit were dressed in khaki shorts instead of blue overalls, they would indeed be the Hong Kong riot squad as it appeared in the late sixties.

The manual lays down some guide-lines for the selection of short shield men. They should be young, fit and properly trained, with a quality of maturity and strong self-discipline. They will be required to operate at speed and will need very strict supervision. Their shields will not afford them the same protection as long shields, and they should never be left alone under bombardment with missiles and petrol bombs. But they gain extra protection from the nature of their tactics: 'Because the manoeuvres are offensive, the shields do provide sufficient protection to the fast-moving, advancing units, especially if the officers have the added advantage of protective clothing.' The shields themselves are described:

Equipment
The majority of forces possess short shields made from polycarbonate (trade name MAKROLON) measuring 762 x 578 mm. These shields have the same qualities as long shields. Additionally, a number of forces use round black shields made from polycarbonate (514 mm. diameter). Apart from not being transparent, these shields have the same qualities as the standard short shield. It is considered an advantage, however, to have the word 'POLICE' on each shield as this may have an inhibiting effect on rioters.

The first of the seven manoeuvres in this section was left out of the version which was read in court at the Orgreave trials, though it is not especially controversial. Manoeuvre one is designed to protect Inspectors or other officers in charge of a long shield unit, while giving them the advantage of a lighter and more manageable short shield.

Each of the remaining six manoeuvres is as set out in the trial transcript which is reproduced in Appendix C, but there are significant omissions. Just as with long shields, the lists of advantages and disadvantages have been edited out, so that the court never heard, for instance, the list of advantages and disadvantages attached to manoeuvres five and six, which send short shield units into action with their batons drawn:

Advantages
  (i) provides a fast aggressive action
 (ii) allows a good degree of manoeuvrability
(iii) psychological effect on the crowd will probably cause them to disperse
(iv) provides a good distraction for arrest teams to move in.

Disadvantages
   (i) affords less protection than the long shields
  (ii) in advanced position the shield carrier may become more concerned with his own safety than what is going on around him
 (iii) over a sustained period the shield will place a strain on the officer's arm
 (iv) it is possible for rioters to grapple with the short shield, and there is a risk of the shield arm being twisted and injured
  (v) fitness of individual officers is essential
 (vi) speed of advance will be dictated by that of the slowest team member
(vii) unless objectives are firmly set, control of the teams may be lost
(viii) there is a possibility of teams being overwhelmed by crowd
 (ix) in certain circumstances the use of short shields by arrest/dispersal squads may be regarded as over-reactive and aggressive. This factor may be used as anti-police propaganda
  (x) possibility of serious injury to crowd if they have insufficient room to disperse in safety.

For manoeuvre six, a further disadvantage is also listed:

(xi) officers require training in use of batons to incapacitate instead of causing serious injury.

We may only guess at why this interesting list was not presented to the court. But it does contain a revealing illustration of police double-think. The manoeuvres are commended in Advantage (i) for providing an 'aggressive action', while at the same time Disadvantage (ix) warns that they may be regarded as exactly that and contribute to anti-police propaganda.

The manual recommends all seven of the short shield options, but stresses that manoeuvres five, six and seven may only be used on the authority of an officer of ACPO rank.

Section 20 sets out the rules for giving *Warning messages* before certain options are used against a crowd. Some warnings are couched in general terms, such as:

THIS IS A POLICE WARNING. YOU ARE CAUSING AN OBSTRUCTION AND YOU MUST LEAVE THIS STREET.

or:

THIS IS A POLICE WARNING. VIOLENCE HAS BROKEN OUT. PLEASE LEAVE THIS AREA.

These might be used in the early stages of disorder, and given out over hand-held amplifiers, backed up by the local media and even police helicopters. At the same time, large printed banners may also be held up bearing the same message. Police officers are told to make a written note of the time and date of each message, its contents and method/s of delivery, the name of the officer issuing the warning, and the 'crowd situation' before and after it. 'It is recommended that if force is to be used to clear the area then if practicable and time permits, three warnings should be given to the crowd prior to tactical deployment of force.'

Once disorder has turned into rioting, serious rioting or lethal rioting, other warnings should be used to announce that the police are about to launch an offensive:

THIS IS A POLICE WARNING. UNLESS THE DISORDER STOPS,
POLICE HORSES WILL BE USED TO CLEAR THE AREA WITH-
OUT FURTHER WARNING.

THIS IS A POLICE WARNING. DISPERSE OR BATON ROUNDS
WILL BE USED.

THIS IS A POLICE WARNING. UNLESS THE RIOTING STOPS,
TEAR GAS WILL BE USED WITHOUT FURTHER WARNING.

Once again, officers are told to give such warnings three times 'if
practicable and time permits'.

The specimen warnings given in this section do not include
those relating to the last resort of police planning – the use of live
firearms against members of a crowd during lethal rioting. They
do, though, include a warning that water cannon will be used,
which may be taken as another indication that water cannon were
considered as a tactical option at one time, and omitted from the
manual only during the latter stages of preparation.

Section 21 deals with *Mounted police*. Seventeen manoeuvres
cover the use of police horses to provide a display of strength, to
make cordons, to open gaps by making wedges in a crowd, to clear
a street and to sectorize an area. Edited versions of the most
controversial of its manoeuvres, numbers ten and eleven, were
read in court during the Orgreave trials, and are transcribed in
Appendix C. The manual says that they may be authorized only by
an officer of ACPO rank. Manoeuvre eleven involves cantering
horses into a crowd in a manner indicating that they do not intend
to stop. The version read out to the court omits, once again, the
customary list of advantages and disadvantages of the option, and
also omits the 'Special Considerations' which are given for the
benefit of officers contemplating the tactic. The court was not
informed of these omissions, and no explanation has been offered
for them. The deleted parts could hardly be more strongly-
worded:

Advantages
(i) extremely effective for crowd dispersal in an 'in extremis' situation.

Disadvantages
 (i) advance at such speed is very difficult to control. The rioters and horses, the foot police and the public are all at risk of very serious injury or death.
(ii) carried out at faster speed the publicity aspect might well be angled against police, especially in built-up areas.

Enhancement
If the circumstances justify adoption of this extreme tactic, there is little doubt that the mounted officers will be wielding their batons.

Special considerations
THIS MANOEUVRE MUST ONLY BE USED IF THE CIRCUMSTANCES ARE SUCH THAT IT COULD BE TIGHTLY CONTROLLED AND IN PARTICULAR THE CHIEF OFFICER MUST BE CERTAIN THERE IS AMPLE SPACE INTO WHICH THE CROWD MAY DISPERSE.

The risk of injury to everyone concerned increases proportionally to the rate of advance.

A warning to the crowd should always be given before adopting mounted dispersal tactics. A fast rate of advance may subsequently need justification. Manoeuvre Eleven is capable of physically sweeping away all opposition by weight and force – but the risk to life is very considerable. The laws regarding manslaughter and cruelty to animals may both be brought into play if a crowd fails to disperse in sufficient time, resulting in serious injuries.

Recommendation
The manoeuvre is recommended for use on authority of ACPO rank only. (The risk is thought to exceed that arising from use of baton rounds.)

We may only guess how the court (and the public) might have reacted to the disclosure that one of the police tactics at Orgreave is officially considered to carry the risk of 'very serious injury or death' for all parties concerned, and to be more hazardous than the use of plastic bullets. It is also worth noting that the FBI equivalent of the ACPO manual, which is called *Prevention and control of riots and mobs*, specifically rules out this tactic in its own instructions on the use of horses: 'Under no circumstances should horses be used to charge the mob.'

Section 22 is about *Police dogs*. Their use by the police to deal with disorder is said to be a sensitive and emotive subject with the potential for public and political reaction against the police service. The manual does not make clear whether such reaction is more likely to come from civil liberties groups or from animal-lovers. It stresses, however, that the limitations of police dogs in dealing with disorder should be understood and that police commanders must consult with their dog section officers to seek specialist advice.

The manoeuvres with dogs include the guarding of vulnerable property, isolating particular areas during serious disorder, supporting a police cordon, dispersing small hostile groups, and running towards a hostile crowd ahead of an advancing shield line. This last manoeuvre is recommended only if authorized by an officer of ACPO rank. The manual expresses 'serious reservations' about it and says it should only be considered 'as a desperate measure where other means of dispersal (e.g. CS agents or baton rounds) are not available'. Some idea of the implications of using dogs against a crowd can be gained from the discussion of this 'desperate measure':

Advantages
(i) the use of dogs conserves manpower, which may then be deployed elsewhere.

Disadvantages
 (i) the use of dogs may appear provocative and invite hostility.
(ii) the use of dogs may attract adverse publicity.
(iii) the use of dogs in immigrant communities could draw undesirable parallels with some foreign police forces.
(iv) handlers and dogs could be vulnerable to attack from petrol bombs or other missiles.
 (v) the advance of dogs and handlers may panic a crowd, and cause injuries.
(vi) danger of indiscriminate biting to public and police alike.

Commanders are told to think about withdrawing handlers and dogs as soon as there is a heavy missile attack or where petrol bombs are thrown.

Section 23 sets out a 'new concept' for British police – the *Arrest team*. The purpose is to target ringleaders and agitators involved in disorder in much the same way as active criminals may be targeted at present. The arrest teams identify their targets and attempt to prevent disorder by arresting them promptly for any offences committed prior to the outbreak of disorder. They may also catch up with them during and after disorder. Once arrested, the ringleaders and agitators find the same team collecting evidence against them, interviewing witnesses and in other ways supporting the prosecution of cases.

This tactic appears to have been learned directly from the Royal Hong Kong Police, where the teams are commonly called 'snatch squads'. Their former Commissioner, Roy Henry, cites it as one of the clear influences of colonial policing methods on the new direction adopted by ACPO.

Section 24, by contrast, presents what it says is one of Britain's oldest tried tactics, the *Baton charge*. It is commended as a fast and effective way of dispersing and arresting rioters, with one considerable advantage: 'What is perhaps more important is that the public accept it as a legitimate tactic, provided that it is controlled, and within the bounds of reasonable force according to the scale of disorder.'

The batons involved in these eight tactical options are the ordinary police truncheons known as short batons. They may be used to present a display of strength, to assist in making arrests or to disperse a crowd. The police unit concerned is instructed to form up out of sight of the crowd and then march smartly into view, making sure that the crowd is shown 'a well-organized, highly-disciplined unit of baton-armed officers'. Then they form a line facing the crowd with their batons drawn. For arrest manoeuvres, they next go forward in pairs to protect and assist each other. In some circumstances, they may also carry short shields, and it may be decided that they should go in groups of four. For dispersal manoeuvres, they may all charge towards the crowd at once, or go in smaller groups. Their primary purpose is to cause a riotous crowd to scatter; they must therefore not use this tactic against a densely-packed crowd where there is no avenue of escape.

The manual is quite explicit about the dangers of these options. It says that any commander is bound to be reluctant to order a baton charge since it 'will probably result in injuries'. In spite of the long tradition of using truncheons, it gives a clear warning about their potential for injury: 'There is surprisingly little training given in baton techniques. It can be a lethal weapon, particularly if used as a club directed at the head, but it can also be used as an invaluable aid for restraining prisoners.'

This section also contains some general points about the use of force by police officers, which could apply to many tactical options throughout the manual. It is the closest ACPO comes in the whole document to defining the traditional principle of minimum force. Its appearance among the techniques of the longest-established police weapon may be intended to remind officers that even a familiar weapon may be 'lethal', and that even policemen are subject to the law on assault and may be called upon to account for their conduct:

Legal Constraints
  (i) There is a clear and absolute duty on the police to enforce the law and maintain the Queen's peace. There may therefore be occasions when the application of lawful force will be necessary.
 (ii) During serious public disorder, it is the duty of the police to protect life, prevent injury to any person acting lawfully, and prevent damage to property. In performing these duties, the police may use such force as may be reasonable in the circumstances.
(iii) The degree of force to be used in order to maintain or restore order must always be the *minimum* necessary in the particular circumstances applying at the time. And force should be used only with the objectives of restoring order, preventing crime or arresting offenders.
 (iv) The principles governing the use of force are: No more force should be used than is necessary; Force must not be used as a punitive measure; Force must cease immediately the objective has been achieved.
  (v) Nothing in these guide-lines will affect the principle, to which section 3 of the Criminal Law Act 1967 gives effect, that only the

minimum force necessary in the circumstances must be used. The degree of force justified will vary according to the circumstances of each case.

The baton charge is recommended for use only on the authority of an officer of ACPO rank and with the condition that it should be used only 'where other methods of control have failed or are unlikely to succeed'.

Section 25 covers much the same ground, but with ordinary truncheons replaced by *Long batons*. The recommendations for use are similar, but most of these options are restricted to conditions of 'extreme disorder'. Confusingly, this is a term which does not appear in the 'Stages of a riot' set out in the introduction of the manual.

Section 26 concerns the *Tactical use of vehicles*, which it says is an emotive subject. The vehicles involved are those designated 'protected vehicles', that is to say, specially reinforced police vans. They may be lined up in a display of strength or, to give a greater sense of display, shown off amid great noise from their engines, klaxons and the like. They can also be used to aid intelligence-gathering, by monitoring the periphery of disorder. They may be used to divide a crowd, to tow other vehicles out of the way of an advancing police line, or to deal with vehicles being driven at a police line. As in other sections of the manual, it is the techniques for crowd dispersal which receive the greatest attention and carry the clearest warnings to police officers. This, for example, is the comment on breaking up a crowd by driving into it:

Advantages
 (i) A method of dispersal which does not require a substantial commitment of manpower.
 (ii) Can be used to relieve pressure on foot officers, and will boost their morale.

Disadvantages
 (i) this is a dangerous manoeuvre which may result in serious or fatal injuries.

(ii) adverse criticism is inevitable.

(iii) there will be civil liability for any injury caused.

(iv) drivers may be affected by concern over their criminal liability for any injury caused.

(v) vehicles may be encircled and attacked.

(vi) unless the manoeuvre is supported by foot officers, the crowd may only move aside rather than disperse ahead of the vehicles.

This is one of the most potentially dangerous manoeuvres considered in this section.

IT CANNOT BE EMPHASISED TOO STRONGLY THAT THE MANOEUVRES CONTAINED IN THIS SECTION ARE ONLY TO BE CARRIED OUT BY TRAINED OFFICERS, USING ALL THE SAFE-GUARDS DESCRIBED.

As an enhancement, it is suggested that the use of a sufficient number of vehicles to confront the whole width of the crowd will increase the effectiveness of the manoeuvre. The general tactic is recommended only where other methods of control have failed or are unlikely to succeed, in conditions of 'extreme disorder', which remain undefined.

Section 27 marks a transition. None of the tactical options set out in the final four sections of the police hierarchy has yet been used in mainland Britain, though they are all now available in almost every city and in many rural forces. The first of these untried manoeuvres concern the use of *Smoke*.

Smoke is not the same thing as tear gas, which is covered in a later section. The smoke dealt with here is intended for use as a smoke-screen, which can act to conceal movements of the police or to confuse a crowd by isolating some parts within it. It can also be used to encourage a crowd to disperse.

These two tactical options involving smoke are said to depend on suitable weather conditions. Once the smoke grenades have been fired, there is no available method of controlling the direction or speed of the drifting clouds. As the manual expresses it: 'The random effect of the spread of smoke, coupled with the safety factor, makes these less than simple options'.

The description of the manoeuvres makes it clear that the cloud would have to be dense enough to block out all visibility in the target area. The smoke grenades land well short of the crowd, leaving the wind to take the smoke on towards its target, to avoid the chance for rioters simply to pick up the smoking grenades and hurl them back at the police. These tactics may also be used to smoke out a crowd, and arrest selected individuals as they run out of the cloud.

Being an untested option, the advantages and disadvantages must be considered theoretical, and they are presented in some detail:

Advantages
   (i) Individual crowd members are visually and psychologically isolated from each other, thus breaking down the group unity so that leaders no longer effectively exercise control.
  (ii) Psychologically, most rioters will associate obscuring smoke, harmless though it may be, with the fear of fire, tear smoke, or an increase in police offensive measures.
 (iii) Smoke may decrease the amount of physical contact within the crowd, which will limit violence to persons and property.
 (iv) Smoke can obscure police manpower and resources from the crowd and gain a short term advantage.
  (v) Results in minimum of contamination and annoyance to residents and to areas with schools, hospitals, etc.
 (vi) Smoke dissipates rapidly, whereas chemical agents such as CS linger and contaminate the area.
(vii) Smoke can be useful in determining wind direction and area coverage as a prelude to the use of CS.
(viii) Respirators are not required by police.
 (ix) Relatively inexpensive, non toxic.
  (x) Obscuring smoke, combined with good tactical evaluation and application, could provide a 'soft' but powerful weapon in controlling disorder with the minimum of force, expense and casualties.

Disadvantages
  (i) No police operational experience in the United Kingdom in the use of smoke in an urban environment.
 (ii) Dependent on type and height of surrounding buildings, control of smoke could be very difficult if not impossible. Once smoke is generated, there is no method of dispersing it or controlling its direction.
 (iii) To maintain a screen of smoke, constant supply must be available.
 (iv) The effect of smoke on rioters in this country is unknown:

    (a) They may panic, causing injury;
    (b) Advantage may be taken of screen to cover increased looting or
        damage;
    (c) They may imitate police and create their own smoke by offenses
        of arson.
  (v) Police will be prevented from observing rioters' behaviour unless
     officers were using expensive thermal imaging systems.
 (vi) Benefits provided to police by using a smoke screen would also
     afford equal benefits to rioters.
(vii) Successful use of smoke is entirely dependent on favourable
     prevailing wind.

One particular use of a smoke-screen is mentioned, namely to obscure the movement of police officers when a 'strategic withdrawal' is a necessity. The two tactics using smoke may only be employed if authorized by an officer of ACPO rank.

Section 28 outlines the uses and dangers of one of the newest 'specialist weapons' in the police armoury. In plain English they are universally called plastic bullets, but ACPO follows colonial practice by referring to *Baton Rounds*. The original baton rounds were developed in Hong Kong during the mid-sixties to deal with widespread political and industrial unrest. They were made of wood, like a policeman's truncheon, and fired from a wide-barrelled discharger. The name 'baton round' was chosen to convey the sense of a little truncheon being loaded up as a form of ammunition.

    In 1970, the practice was introduced in Northern Ireland, using rubber instead of wood. Experience in Hong Kong had shown up a serious danger of splintering in the original design, and a more predictable round was wanted for use in the United Kingdom. In 1974, rubber gave way to plastic bullets. One of the principal suppliers is Brock's, the firework company. Each round consists of a fat black metal cartridge just over 4″ long, which houses a small explosive charge and the bullet itself. This is a flat-nosed cylinder of solid plastic weighing only slightly less than a cricket ball. It is fired at a speed of 160 m.p.h.

The decision to include seven manoeuvres using plastic bullets in the ACPO manual has effectively sanctioned their use in any part of the British mainland. That which was controversial in Northern Ireland and politically unthinkable for the rest of the United Kingdom in the seventies, has now become a fact of life for the whole country.

The manual's introductory remarks about baton rounds make no attempt to play down the risks they carry:

Baton rounds can cause serious and even fatal injuries. They are to be used only as a last resort when conventional methods of policing have been tried and failed, or must from the nature of the circumstances obtaining be unlikely to succeed if tried, and where the Chief Officer judges such action to be necessary because of the risk of loss of life or serious injury or widespread destruction of property.

The danger of severe or fatal injury is said to be greatest if the weapon is used at short range:

Baton rounds are not to be fired at a range of less than twenty metres, unless there is a serious and immediate risk to life which cannot otherwise be countered. Rounds should be fired at selected individuals and not indiscriminately at the crowd. They are to be aimed directly at the lower part of the body, and never at the head or neck.

Police forces are told to take urgent steps to ensure that early medical attention is provided for any casualties. They are also reminded of the legal considerations outlined earlier (in Section 24) on the lawful use of extreme force. Every police officer called upon to use baton rounds must be instructed that although they may not be intended to cause death, they are capable of doing so if they hit a vulnerable part of the body. The principles governing the reasonable use of force are repeated, and a new point is added: 'Every officer using force must be able to justify the legality of his conduct which cannot be done merely on the basis that he is acting under the orders of a senior officer.'

This is a summary of the Nuremberg principle. Its potential for conflict with the demand for obedience and discipline in a paramilitary unit is left unexplored. The manual says that it is essential that all officers are fully informed by their seniors as to what is happening, if this principle is to be honoured. But it leaves open a possible loophole: 'The law however recognises that it is not always easy to apply careful consideration of legal niceties in stressful situations.' The comment of the Lord Chief Justice in 1972 is quoted with approval: 'In the circumstances, one did not use jeweller's scales to measure reasonable force.'

The seven manoeuvres follow. The first is designed to create a show of strength, without actually firing the weapons. It carries a clear warning that the sight of baton gunners may precipitate the crowd to increased disorder and escalate rioting.

Manoeuvre two is the real thing. Baton gunners are brought up to the front line of long shields, where they go down on one knee, load their weapons and then bring them up to eye-level for the firing position. They take aim, and on the order to fire, they shoot plastic bullets at the crowd. After the order to stop, they retreat into the main body of police, regroup well away from the front line and await further instructions.

To date, this manoeuvre has been used only on training grounds in Britain. If it were ordered against a real crowd, the manual's customary list of disadvantages would represent immediate dangers. They make sombre reading. Members of the crowd could be seriously injured or even killed; the police themselves could become dependent on their new weaponry and reluctant to settle for anything less; and the crowd might respond to the use of police weapons with firearms of their own. In blunt terms, plastic bullets could set off a shooting war on the streets of Britain. The prospect of this manoeuvre must be considered imminent, as almost all major police forces have already trained and equipped themselves for it. Its consequences could scarcely be more grave. Yet public debate has been denied information about how the police themselves view these preparations.

Here is how the Association of Chief Police Officers, with the approval of the Home Office, consider this crucial tactical option:

Advantages
 (i) Can be used with discrimination.
(ii) Will distance crowd from police preventing or reducing further injuries.

(iii) Will lead to dispersal of some rioters.
(iv) Ringleaders within front ranks of a crowd can be incapacitated.
 (v) Confirms police determination to take offensive action by use of baton rounds.
(vi) Maintains confidence of police cordons of the intention to use necessary force.

Disadvantages
 (i) If a baton round strikes a vulnerable part of the body serious or fatal injuries may result.
(ii) Innocent parties may be injured.
(iii) Cannot be safely used at short range.
(iv) Use of baton rounds establishes a dependency on the weapons and creates, both a reluctance on the part of the user to revert to normal methods and a tendency to use increasing levels of weaponry.
 (v) Baton round dischargers are single shot weapons, with a necessity to stop and reload after each shot with inherent difficulties involved.
(vi) Crowd experience may bring about armed response to use of this weapon with associated cycle of escalation.

The remaining five manoeuvres in this section amount to variations on a theme. Each of these tactics carries the explicit instruction that it must only be used on the order of a Chief Constable or his deputy. The line of command is set out as follows: the Divisional Commander (or deputy) makes a request to the Assistant Chief Constable in charge of operations as soon as he considers the use of plastic bullets to be necessary. The ACC evaluates the request in the light of all the information available to him and then, if he wishes to proceed, seeks approval from the Chief Constable (or deputy). If this is granted, the ACC mobilizes the gunners and orders the release of the appropriate weapons and ammunition to the Divisional Commander. The Commander then directs and controls the actual operation. Exactly the same hierarchy applies to the use of weapons in the next set of options.

Section 29 is about *CS agents*. The use of noxious chemical clouds can serve two distinct purposes for the police. On a small scale in a confined space, they can be directed against individuals or groups under siege in a building or in an incident involving hostages. The purpose is to clear a specific area, such as a room, using the technological development of the old art of smoking-out familiar from tales of the Wild West. The appropriate gas cartridges and their dischargers have been held in British police armouries for at least twenty years. A quite different approach, using different weapons, is now recommended for a second purpose – the control and dispersal of large crowds gathered in the open air.

The confusion between these two uses of chemical weapons is not always appreciated even by the police themselves. When the Merseyside force used CS gas against a crowd for the first time in mainland Britain during the Toxteth riots of July 1981, they made the serious mistake of firing the wrong kind of cartridges. As the *New Statesman* reported the following week, some of those actually fired had been intended for shooting through doors when storming a besieged building, and were clearly marked 'Specifically designed for barricade penetration only. Do not fire at any person or crowd. Projectile may inflict serious injury should it strike anyone within a range of approximately 300 yards.' The reporter was Rob Rohrer. In evidence to Lord Scarman's inquiry, the Chief Constable of Merseyside, Kenneth Oxford, said he was 'fully aware that some of the equipment should not be used again to deal with public disorder', but defended his decision to use CS gas as the correct use of minimum force which was necessary and available.

There are also different types of chemical which can be used for both police purposes. The original tear gas, developed in 1871, is a synthetic compound customarily abbreviated to CN. A more potent type was produced in 1928 in the form of a white powder known as CS. It is roughly five times as irritating as its predecessor. A third type was synthesized in 1962 of even greater potency – thirty times the original – which is called CR.

The type approved for use in the ACPO *Public Order Manual* in 1983 is CS. It is the same as that used throughout the colonies and sometimes known as tear gas. More usually, to avoid any link with gases used in the trenches during World War I, the colonial police forces referred to it as 'tear smoke'. This was supposed to sound more calming not only to the public but also to serving police officers, who were apparently untroubled by the order to put on a 'smoke mask', but could have been alarmed by the dangers still resonating in the words 'gas mask'.

To colonial police, CS gas offered a cheap alternative to the crowd control techniques which had been developed for mainland Britain. According to Michael Macoun who was a British police officer in the colonies for twenty years, and then Inspector General of Police (Dependent Territories) under the Foreign and Commonwealth Office, the traditional British domestic tactics were far too wasteful of manpower: 'I know it's a dirty word – "tear smoke" or "tear gas", but a few well-directed rounds of tear smoke can save an awful lot of sweating and heaving and punching and thumping and so on.'

In the colonies, the preferred method of using CS gas was by firing small cartridges from dischargers known as pistols. Police were taught to fire over the heads of a crowd, and in general, according to Michael Macoun, a couple of rounds would be enough to make a crowd run away. For him, this represented the 'disciplined' use of tear smoke. His anxiety is aroused by the decision to bring this tactic to Britain, particularly if large amounts of CS gas were to be used:

Let's face it, we have seen enough tear smoke being used recently in South Africa. I mean indiscriminate discharge of tear smoke; and if it is not very strictly controlled it can be counterproductive. It merely antagonizes the whole population.

Michael Macoun retired in 1979 and has not seen the ACPO *Public Order Manual*. If he were permitted to read it, he would find some of his own apprehension reflected in it. But he would also find that his favoured technique of firing small CS rounds from a special pistol is only one of the tactical options it recommends.

Section 29 begins with warnings which are very similar to those given for plastic bullets. The use of CS gas carries risks for both the public and police and is to be authorized 'as a last resort', only when conventional methods of policing have failed or must from the nature of the circumstances be likely to fail. There must also be a risk of loss of life or serious injury or widespread destruction of property. Authority for use can be given only by a Chief Constable or, in his absence, his deputy. An oral warning should be given beforehand that unless the crowd stops rioting or disperses, CS will be used without further notice, though such a warning need not be given if the officer in charge considers it 'impracticable'. Then the 'Conditions Of Use' are laid out:

CONDITIONS OF USE
(a) Only approved CS equipment authorized by the Home Office for dealing with a riot or serious public disorder in the open air is to be used: that is to say
    (i) Grenade, anti-riot irritant L11A1 (this is the preferred weapon as it cannot be thrown back by rioters);
    (ii) Cartridge, anti-riot irritant L3A1;
    (iii) Grenade, hand, anti-riot irritant L1A2.
    A description of the characteristics of the approved equipment is given below.
(b) Wherever CS is used, attention should be paid to the direction in which the wind is likely to carry the smoke cloud. Police officers downwind without respirators are likely to experience severe discomfort. Respirators should therefore be worn by police wherever possible.

Once again it is stressed that records must be kept of the use of CS gas with full details of the background of the incident, the reasons for using the weapon and information about the outcome. Any injuries should also be noted, and early medical attention must be provided for casualties as a matter of urgency. Then the principle of minimum force is restated and attention is drawn to Section 3 of the Criminal Law Act of 1967 which gives it effect. The degree of force justified is said to vary according to the circumstances of each case.

The effects of CS gas are listed as follows:

CS smoke is a powerful lachrymator and sneezing agent. It produces a stinging in the eyes, a painful burning sensation of the nasal passages causing severe coughing, pains in the chest and irritation of moist skin areas. These effects are immediate and last for two to five minutes after removal to an uncontaminated area. The smoke is visible and has the appearance of a dust cloud.

The objectives for its use are given under six categories:

(i) To warn a disorderly crowd by the open display of protected officers equipped with respirators and CS launchers.
(ii) To subdue a disorderly crowd by a small discharge. This could be followed by a further and larger use of CS or the employment of an entirely different tactical option.
(iii) To lay down a barrier along a prescribed area to control the movement of a disorderly crowd.
(iv) To select and disperse a small section of a disorderly crowd, by the use of a minor discharge.
(v) To achieve complete crowd dispersal, if the level of disorder has reached such proportions that this becomes necessary.
(vi) To protect both the individual and small groups of officers.

Then come the tactical options in the form of eight recommended manoeuvres. They provide instructions for CS gunners firing singly or in formation, and give detailed orders for different patterns of firing. Some of them carry the important warning that 'it is inevitable that some innocent persons will be affected'. As in other parts of the manual, the most sensitive comments come in the discussion of pros and cons of each tactic. Manoeuvre two, for example, stimulates the following catalogue:

Advantages
(i) A small and controlled escalation from the display stage, which gives both time and opportunity for dispersal with only minimal offensive action having been taken.
(ii) Confirms the determination to take further offensive action if necessary.
(iii) The discharge over the crowd breaks its cohesion and causes maximum disruption for minimum use of force.
(iv) Maintains the confidence of police cordons of the intention to use necessary force.
(v) Air-burst grenades disperse the CS preventing the crowd throwing back the grenades.

Disadvantages
(i) A favourable wind direction, or the absence of wind, is an essential element in the discharge of CS. Unfavourable wind direction limits this option if personnel without respirators are in the vicinity.
(ii) Will affect innocent persons as well as rioters.
(iii) Heavy use of CS can contaminate an urban area for periods between minutes and months.
(iv) Police officers and members of the emergency services who become seriously contaminated will require medication.

  (v) Imposes on officer in command an increasing level of responsi-
      bility and accountability.
 (vi) Requires rigid control of gunners and must be applied exactly, to
      limit the effect of the tactic.
(vii) Use can increase anti-police propaganda.
(viii) Use of CS establishes a dependency on this option with resultant
      reluctance to revert to lesser options for riot control.
 (ix) Crowd experience increases to meet new options and causes
      natural cycle of escalation.

A vivid illustration of the effects of CS gas on a crowd came
during a boxing match in February 1988, when a canister was set
off near the ringside at Bingley Hall in Stafford. A member of
Margaret Thatcher's government, the Sports Minister, Colin
Moynihan, was present as a member of the audience, and spoke of
'the appalling nausea that results from CS gas being thrown'
which had been produced throughout the whole stadium: 'It was
sickening in every sense of the word.' The Minister also criticized
the 'disgraceful scenes' that followed, in which brawling was
reported as hundreds of people were overcome by fumes, and
'panic-stricken spectators – many with handkerchiefs over their
faces – scattered in all directions' (the *Sun*). It was also reported
that a policeman was taken to hospital after a canister blew up in
his face.

   The phrase 'as a last resort' is routinely introduced into
discussions of police use of plastic bullets and CS gas. It is written
into both the relevant sections of the *Public Order Manual*. HM
Inspector of Constabulary wrote in his report for 1985 that these
measures are 'weapons of last resort' for the police. They do not
mean what they say. Plastic bullets and CS gas are to be reserved
for extreme conditions of disorder, where life is at risk or the
widespread destruction of property is threatened. They may only
be drawn from the armoury once other policing methods have
been tried and failed, or where they would have no hope of
succeeding. But they are not the last resort.

   The *Public Order Manual* completes its catalogue of tactical
options with no more than a heading for the options to come, a
blank space waiting for details of the real last resort.

Section 30 is to present the approved tactics for use of *Firearms*.
At the time the manual was prepared, it could say little:

FIREARMS
The question of the use of firearms by police in public order situations is
currently under review by the ACPO Joint Standing Committee on the
police use of firearms.

When their findings are known, an entry on this subject will be
prepared.

In February 1986, the Home Secretary, Douglas Hurd, set up a
formal working party on police use of firearms under the chairmanship of a Home Office official. Two of its leading members
were Kenneth Oxford and James Anderton, the Chief Constables
of Merseyside and Greater Manchester. Other members represented the Metropolitan Police, Devon and Cornwall Constabulary, HM Inspectorate of Constabulary, the Police Complaints
Authority and two trades unions, the Police Superintendents'
Association and the Police Federation.

A year later, in February 1987, they produced new guide-lines
for all forces in the use of firearms, and a summary of important
points to be issued to every firearms officer (see Appendix D).
Some of their phraseology is identical to sections of the ACPO
Public Order Manual sections on plastic bullets and CS gas.
Firearms are, for example, to be fired 'only as a last resort when
conventional methods have been tried and failed, or must, from
the nature of the circumstances obtaining, be unlikely to succeed
if tried'. The statement of the principle of minimum force, too, is
strikingly similar to that given by ACPO in its section on CS gas.

The working party recommends that further work on the
implementation of its guide-lines should be left in the hands of
the ACPO Joint Standing Committee on police use of firearms.
Section 30 of the tactical options is in preparation.

One subject the manual passes over in silence is the use of water
cannon. Opinion polls have recorded a marked reluctance among
the public to accept some of the tactics recommended in the
tactical options, such as plastic bullets, CS gas and firearms. But

water cannon have consistently scored high in popularity, and their omission from the approved list may strike some people as curious. No explanation is given, though, as was noted earlier, the authors of the manual seem to have contemplated their inclusion at one stage, and the Metropolitan Police still have two of them sitting almost literally like white elephants in the car-park at Hendon. The official reasons for rejecting their use were given on 18 March 1987 in a written answer to the House of Commons by a junior Home Office Minister:

Any benefits in the deployment of water cannon would be outweighed by their operational and tactical disadvantages, including lack of manoeuvrability, quick exhaustion of water supply, and vulnerability to attack. It is not therefore proposed to add water cannon to the range of equipment now available to the police to deal with serious disorder.

In private, Metropolitan officers have concluded from their experimental testing of the two models of water cannon they bought that there is a real danger of killing innocent people with the force of water produced in their jets. It also became obvious during the operational tests that weapons of crowd control which work well in vast open spaces, like the Place de la Concorde in Paris, can be less useful in pursuing rioters through the back alleys of Brixton. Half a million pounds were spent on official evaluations of water cannon, only to conclude (in the words of *Police Review*) that they got 'the thumbs down'.

7 Related Matters

Women are capable of doing anything to discredit the police, including striking their own children and making accusations agains the police.
ACPO *Public Order Manual*

Part Four of the manual is printed on pastel pink pages and covers the 'Related Matters' referred to in the title of the whole publication. The reader is offered no guidance on what exactly its strange assortment of matters might relate to. They certainly bear little relation to one another, and the pages could aptly have been labelled 'Odds and Ends'.

The section on *Hand signals/whistles and flags* need not detain us, nor the systems for deployment of *Traffic department, Police observers, Casualty bureaux* and the *Special constabulary* during public disorders.

The much-discussed topic of *Operational stress* affecting police officers during and after riots is raised in one section, but nothing of substance is said about it except that ACPO is commissioning workshops on a national basis to look into it.

The section on police *Staff associations* recommends the 'tactic' of consulting with representatives of the lower and middle ranks in the formulation of policy on public disorder. But this apparent rush of democracy into the police service goes no further than to note the importance of striking 'the correct balance' with union officials, and ACPO's notion of balance is robustly uneven. The Chief Constables have ensured, for instance, that even the manual in which these benign generalities on consultation are written has been kept secret from both the major staff associations – the Police Federation and the Superintendents' Association.

Amongst this mass of clay, there are a few hidden gems. Three sections in particular reveal a great deal about current police

attitudes to themselves and their place in the social order. They
set out the ground rules for contact with other centres of localized
influence and power: schools, town halls and the media. Another
section gives a sketch of official masculinism in the form of notes
on the perils of *Women and children* in public protests. Lastly, a
description of *Inter-force liaison* which is buried away alphabeti-
cally between helicopters and Interpol, gives the clearest available
statement of ACPO's drive towards a national police blueprint for
containing public disorder. (Details of this section are given in
Chapter 9 which examines the emergence of national control of
the police.)

Taking the town halls first, the manual confirms what has often
been claimed by radical local authorities: that co-operation
between municipal services and the police in quite uncontentious
matters can suddenly be hi-jacked by a Chief Constable and
turned against pickets and protestors. A hostile line of argument
has been put forward by some councils that joint planning for an
emergency, including civil defence planning, is a trap designed to
win their complicity in police operations against subversion or
unrest. The manual connects the two spheres of operation in
explicit terms:

EMERGENCY SERVICES AND LOCAL GOVERNMENT LIAISON
Liaison between the police and other emergency services is essential in
respect of contingency planning for major incidents such as flooding,
rail, train or plane crashes. Many aspects of that planning can be applied
to police arrangements with regard to situations of potential or actual
widespread large-scale public disorder.

Police forces are then told that the precise form of liaison will vary
between different areas, but that it will involve their well-
established formal and informal links with the ambulance and fire
services and extend to the local government utilities.

There has been a similar reluctance by some education authorities to develop projects with the police in their area, because of
their suspicion of police motives. Some schools have cancelled
previous arrangements for police officers to give lessons in crime
prevention, on the ground that visits of this kind can be exploited
by the police for partisan purposes and may also be used for

gathering low-level intelligence about pupils and their neighbourhoods. Once again, the manual explicitly confirms the
motives suspected behind police liaison with schools. Two of the
advantages listed for this kind of approach are that it can
'engender pro-police attitudes conducive to good citizenship' and
that 'useful intelligence can be obtained once dialogue is established'.

The manual also notes that political opinion within the education system in certain areas limits police involvement, and warns
forces to be aware of the political implications of using this tactic,
though it stops short of telling them what those implications are.

This is the *Education* section in full:

Description of tactic
Involvement of police officers in the education system to deter young
people from participating in public disorder.
Relation to state of disorder
 (i) during normal policing conditions;
 (ii) during escalation towards disorder;
(iii) following public disorder.

Existing expertise
(a) Most forces have regular input to schools by accident prevention,
    schools careers department, schools liaison officer, community
    contact officers and periodically by local operational police officers.
(b) Many forces operate community contact projects involving young
    people, e.g. establishment of sports clubs, camping holidays, visits to
    police stations.
(c) Forces foster good relations by encouraging school visits to police
    premises.
(d) With police assistance young people are encouraged to undertake
    educational and community ventures.

Alternative developments
(a) Some United States police forces recruit young people as a volun-
    tary peace corps or anti-vandal patrol;
(b) Some United States police forces permit young people to patrol in
    company with operational police officers.

Advantages
(a) Police contributions can engender pro-police attitudes conducive to
    good citizenship;
(b) Young people can be persuaded against public disorder;

(c) Regular contact with schools and youth clubs will identify causes of tension;
(d) Useful intelligence can be obtained once dialogue is established;
(e) It helps police officers involved to keep in touch with the needs and aspirations of this section of the community;
(f) Radical groups seeking to influence young people lack unity and have conflicting aims. The police service can take advantage of this situation, to counter subversive information;
(g) Police usually identify well with young people in a non-conflict situation, thus countering the image that they are hard on the activities of youth.

Disadvantages
(a) Political opinion within the education system in certain areas limits police involvement;
(b) Police projects are costly and involve a non-operational manpower commitment;
(c) Police projects can involve entering the political arena;
(d) Involvement of young people as a peace corps is not yet acceptable in the United Kingdom.

Training
Already undertaken:
(a) Forces train officers for community contact duties;
(b) Community contact is taught to officers at all levels during periodic courses.

Considerations for use
None, but forces must be aware of political implications.

Conclusion
Most forces have facilities for formal liaison with schools through the education system. This is an area which falls within the sphere of community relations and one which is vital to the continuation of good police/public relations. It is therefore necessary to continually monitor and review this type of contact in order that new initiatives may be fully exploited.

The decision to include two 'alternative developments' in this section is unusual in the manual. ACPO does not often mention possibilities from police forces in other countries without actually endorsing them. It may well be, as Disadvantage (d) states, that the recruitment of young people as a police peace corps is 'not yet acceptable' in the United Kingdom (though there is nothing in the manual to indicate who has declared it so.) But the fact that it is raised at all suggests the ACPO would like it to become acceptable (to the Home Office?) in the future. The same may be true about the suggestion of young people patrolling with operational police officers. The links between police and schools in some parts of the country, and also these 'alternative developments', may find a readier political climate as control of school curricula shifts from local to central government. A sympathetic Cabinet could find scope for further educational developments to support the ACPO curriculum of engendering 'pro-police attitudes conducive to good citizenship'.

Relations between some police forces and the media, particularly television and radio, have been notably antagonistic in recent years. A conference held in 1986 brought fifty representatives of the two sides together in Cumberland Lodge, next to the Queen Mother's home in Windsor Great Park. They met in almost total incomprehension, as if divided by a mental barricade. Some senior police officers have become convinced that journalists are seeking to get at them by publishing accounts of police corruption or allegations of brutality with a close attention to detail while leaving no space for the hard daily graft of honest coppering. On the other side, a number of experienced and respected journalists now regard the police as potential obstacles to their daily task of honest reporting. Even some who are far from the political left have made formal complaints of systematic harassment by police officers in uniform apparently trying to prevent them reporting or filming scenes of police action against public disorder. One distinguished BBC news reporter maintains that, on occasions, squads of policemen have broken cameras and other equipment, blocked direct views of a scene and even attacked journalists with physical violence in order to stop them going about their lawful business. After a violent night at Wapping in January 1987, BBC TV News lodged a formal complaint against the Metropolitan Police over the treatment of Kate Adie, a reporter, who claimed that she had been hit on the head with a truncheon.

A photographer for the *Independent* newspaper, Jeremy Nicholl, was quoted as follows:

The police have come to regard the press as a legitimate target. Now when I am sent to cover a public disturbance, I always take an extra flash equipment, knowing that police usually aim to rip that from the camera.

He too claimed to have been hit by a truncheon at Wapping. There are mainstream journalists who are convinced that their phones are tapped by the Special Branch or others, and some of them say they have evidence in the form of tape-recordings or tip-offs from inside sources. It is a remarkable aspect of London life in the late eighties that guests at a media cocktail party can stand in small groups holding glasses of champagne, while swapping stories of their harassment by the police. Some of the police reaction to these complaints has been combative. The editor of *Police*, the magazine of the Police Federation, wrote after Wapping:

Incidents between police on duty at Wapping and the press led to official action last year, when the police were told not to treat the media as the enemy. The message was received with a certain amount of resentment by the 'troops', who felt that if anyone was doing the harassing, it was the lads with the lenses.

An editorial in the same edition expressed mocking bitterness at the complaints made by journalists against their treatment by police officers:

The media, counting its casualties and licking its wounded ego, joins the chorus of disapproval of police 'over-reaction', and the Commissioner sets up an investigation, accompanied by announcements from the Police Complaints Authority . . . Once the rule of law has been defended, and public tranquillity restored, we put the police in the dock. Not for nothing was Lewis Carroll British.

The manual's section on the media was written before these attitudes had hardened, but reflects some of the same suspicion of journalists. It contains nothing at all to suggest that police forces, as public services, owe a duty of openness to the public. Not one of the listed advantages of liaison with news media even hints at the concept of the public's right-to-know through newspapers and broadcasting networks. Press relations are presented as another 'tactic' to be used for specific police purposes, and to be handled with care or, more usually, with suspicion.

The warnings are clear: 'The media is controlled by financial interest. Concern to produce a story can override the requirement to be accurate'; and: 'Close liaison with politically motivated factions of the media requires careful control.'

Scenes of disorder are treated as if they are police property, rather than public events with a presumption of free access to reporters. Police commanders are told that 'the media are *allowed* access to events and scenes of disorder' [my emphasis].

The reasons given in favour of good press relations tend to concentrate, perhaps inevitably, on the advantages for the police: 'All police forces are aware of the need to liaise with the media and the value of fostering the police image through media releases'; and: 'Public confidence, approval and sympathy can be gained from media interviews with police officers, for example officers in hospital following injuries sustained during public disorder.'

There is also the potential for issuing mass orders: 'Police forces can make use of the media to publicize instructions to the general public'; and the suggestion that something like a propaganda battle is under way: 'Representatives of extremist groups make full use of media coverage. The police service can take similar advantage of the media facilities to influence public opinion.'

Any underlying resentment of the independence of journalists, is tempered by one conciliatory observation: 'In general, media reporters will try to give a balanced story if there is a flow of information from the police.' The actual point of balance which police officers have come to rely on from Fleet Street was identified by the editor of *Police Review* in one of the more entertaining of his consistently candid leaders, which was published in December 1986:

There's a general (and only sometimes justified) police complaint that the media deals in bad news about the police but ignores the acts of quiet heroism, the commitment beyond the call of duty, the boring daily dedication. So how would you bet on the space allocated, to the following stories? A chief inspector caught in compromising circumstances in a public lavatory; a WPC who saves a baby from a fire; a sergeant suspected of cheating in his promotion examination; a dog handler coming to terms with life after losing his legs to a terrorist's bomb.

If you bet on the lavatory and the cheat coming top, you would have lost your money. The four stories appeared in most papers last week. The chief inspector made no more than two inches in two papers; the exam cheat possibly rated twelve inches; the fire heroine made almost every daily paper; and the disabled dog handler was the subject of a two-page feature. And if you're still convinced that the media are biased against the police, think of the coverage given to the death of PC Olds, the memorial to PC Blakelock, and the struggle to live by PC George Hammond.

While we're about it, might we not admit, too, that we read the bad news much more thoroughly than the good? Those of us who had nothing to do but browse through the papers last weekend probably remember the full details of the episode involving the chief inspector, including the bizarre titbit that one of the other men arrested wore suspenders and stockings. We may also recall that the promotion exam story involved Freemasons and the Royal and Diplomatic Protection group. But can we remember just how the WPC came to rescue the baby, or what the incident was in which the dog handler lost his legs?

We don't remember good news.

The section dealing with *Women and children* seems out of place even by the loose criteria governing the manual's 'Related Matters'. Much of its content deals with circumstances of public order rather than disorder, in which women and children are behaving in apparently law-abiding and peaceful ways. A possible explanation of their inclusion is suggested early on: their non-violent actions are said to be 'calculated not necessarily to breach the existing law but to cause frustration to police officers or police arrangements'.

It is noticeable that many of the most serious recent disturbances have been almost exclusively male events, both on the side of the public and among the ranks of police. As John Alderson remarked after watching the police video of Orgreave, the young men of each tribe are sent forward for the fray. But ACPO (which is a male forum) includes a warning on the guile which can be shown by the second sex:

Experience in Northern Ireland has shown that women . . . are capable of doing anything to discredit the police, including striking their own children and making accusations against the police. There is no reason to believe that such a ploy could not be used in mainland Britain.

The main concern about policing women and children is their considerable potential for arousing public sympathy if the police use violence against them. The manual presents this in fighting terms – as part of the continuing propaganda war between the police and unspecified forces of darkness:

Mishandling of the situation could provide adverse publicity for the police which subsequently can be used as grounds for criticism and propaganda . . . It is often possible to capitalize upon emotional factors; physical lack of endurance and the dislike of discomfort of women and children. Should force become necessary, the less its degree, the less will be the adverse propaganda value . . . The deployment of specialist equipment such as baton rounds against women and children, has heightened public/media negative emotive response potential.

This last point almost certainly refers to experience of the Royal Ulster Constabulary in Northern Ireland, where outrage has followed incidents in which young children have been killed or maimed by plastic bullets fired by security forces in the course of disturbances. The campaigns such incidents have generated have attracted considerable support, which seems to translate through ACPO's word-processor into 'heightened public/media negative emotive response potential'.

The manual concludes this section with the observation that a variety of tactical options has been considered for use against women and children, including the deployment of mixed sex or all female Police Support Units.

Methods of effecting removal of demonstrators presenting passive to aggressive resistance (short of open violence) have been examined, and specific information can be obtained through direct liaison with the Public Order Forward Planning Unit, A8, New Scotland Yard.

8   The Colony Within

I sometimes think that if I'd done something terribly wrong the rubber-stamp would have endorsed it. That's its danger. It's a controlling force without the ability to judge.

District Superintendent Ronald Merrick on the Indian Police in *The Raj Quartet* by Paul Scott

The history of Britain's colonial police force is sometimes told with a tinge of romance. Nowadays, if it is told at all, it tends to be in the fond drone of reminiscence by men who are comfortably returned to the safety of the home counties, mixing the first gins of the evening as their retirement clocks chime six. The tales take a familiar range of topics – excitable natives forever plotting against the Crown; mass rallies whipped up by fiery demagogues; sanity restored only by the relentless cool of men in khaki shorts cracking a few well-chosen heads; ringleaders thrown into gaol; new waves of plotters going underground to prepare the next show. The best of these stories could happily serve in the long-running radio series *A Book at Bedtime*, and have, indeed, been both edited and rehearsed with considerable care over the many years of their re-telling. Outside this small and diminishing world, the importance of the real legacy of colonial policing is only now becoming apparent. It is, in an unforeseen way, the key to British mainland policing in these latter years of the century.

The two British police traditions of the past century and a half were never intended to be mixed together. One was for use at home, the other for export. They embodied different styles, different technologies and, most important of all, different attitudes toward the populations they policed. Policing at home in mainland Britain was to be as gentle as possible among citizens who were (at least) the political equals of their constables. The consent of the people was the very foundation of the constabulary. Overseas, on the other hand, none of these considerations applied. The populations concerned were not British citizens but 'natives' who could be treated with whatever degree of force was required to do the job. The job itself was control and, where necessary, repression. The idea of seeking the consent of the local people simply never arose.

These two traditions are separate no longer. They have been brought together in an extraordinary historical circle which stretches over a hundred and fifty years. It began with the creation of a police force for London in 1830, and continued through the establishment of a unified paramilitary constabulary to police Ireland in 1836. Then on through the policing expansion of the nineteenth century, as force after force was set up to take care of different parts of the empire, all of them based on the Irish model and trained in Dublin. For a century they carried on their business of policing the colonies, while other forces modelled on the Metropolitan Police proliferated throughout mainland Britain. Then, after the Second World War, these two traditions slowly started to mingle. In 1981, they began a formal relationship involving regular meetings, the institutional equivalent of going steady. In 1983, ACPO arranged a marriage and in 1984 it bore fruit when the first colonial police tactics were ordered for use against the citizens of mainland Britain. The long courtship was complete.

Those involved in the early stages of policy-making had no idea that the story would end as it has. They intended no such marriage. When Whitehall established two major police forces in the 1830s, they were meant for quite separate purposes. The Metropolitan Police were created under the Home Office to replace the militias as law-enforcers and keepers of the peace in the nation's capital, and what became the Royal Irish Constabulary was set up as a merger of four provincial military commands in Dublin to put down rebellions by Irish republicans. One force, the Peelers, was for domestic use among a population whose consent to their authority could be won. The other was tailored for action across the water, among a divided population which was in armed conflict over the very issue of Whitehall's authority to govern it. The tactics of the two forces were quite different from the start – the unarmed citizen constables of Georgian London would have been fatally vulnerable in Dublin, while the armed patrols of the RIC would have represented a mere continuation of the military if they had been seen in mainland Britain. There was a clear difference of outlook which stemmed from their different purposes. An officer in the Metropolitan force might face real danger in the backstreets of his beat and earn the undying resentment of those he arrested and gave evidence against, but he could rest his general approach to the public on the understanding that most of London was behind him. Even some of the felons who were busy breaking the rules would accept the legitimacy of the whole game. Not so, of course, in Ireland. An officer of the RIC, in contrast, could face outright enmity from local residents who not only resented his intrusion into their affairs but also denied the very authority of his uniform.

By the middle of the nineteenth century, Whitehall needed officers for the new police forces which were set up to keep order in the empire. It also needed a style and structure for these colonial police forces, and found that it had a ready-made model in Ireland. After all, the gentleman officers of the streets of London, the imperial capital, could hardly be thought suitable for the distant lands still waiting for civilization. So for a hundred years, Ireland became the base for an enormous training operation controlled from London. Officers of the RIC were sent abroad to recruit and give basic training to police forces all over the world, and on the return trips officers who needed advanced training for promotion returned to Dublin. A few 'native' senior officers were signed up in the colonies, and they too made the long journey to Phoenix Park for training. When self-government finally established an Irish administration in Dublin, the RIC tradition continued in the six counties of Northern Ireland. After partition, the force, renamed the Royal Ulster Constabulary, simply carried on the same business of training colonial police officers from its new address in Belfast. Training on a large scale was transferred to mainland Britain only after the Second World War.

The rugged nature of colonial policing is not in doubt. The model developed in Ireland and then copied in British colonies around the globe was deliberately far removed from the civilian police forces which reproduced the Metropolitan Police throughout Britain.

For a concise description of its nature, the colonial police force can speak for itself in the person of Michael Macoun, who (until his retirement in 1979) was its most senior officer. After Stowe and Oxford, he joined the Tanganyika police in 1939 and then became Commissioner of the colonial force in Uganda. For the last thirteen years of his working life he was at the very top – Inspector General of Police for all the Dependent Territories and Overseas Police Adviser to the Foreign Office. Michael Macoun is an engaging and hospitable man who tends to express his views as he chain-smokes his cigarettes – both are unfiltered. His family background in Ireland ('I am a de-tribalized Ulster Scot') and his long experience in the colonies give him a unique qualification to define the nature of the British colonial police tradition. He calls it an armed constabulary with a limited civil police capability:

Right up to the end of the last war, training in the colonial police locally was almost entirely what one might call 'paramilitary' – military exercises, weapon training and drill. There was just a basis of law and police procedures, but the great emphasis was on the paramilitary side.

This concentration on paramilitary training was almost inevitable given the nature of the Royal Irish Constabulary which had trained the colonial police forces:

The composition of the Royal Irish Constabulary was largely ex-military officers in the senior ranks. The rank and file lived in barracks and the training was confined to quasi-military exercises.

My own personal experience was to arrive in East Africa having spent a year being trained by the Metropolitan Police, to find that there was barely a senior officer who'd ever had any police training at all. They'd been soldiers.

But colonial police forces were more than mere extensions of the British Army. They maintained their own proud traditions of independence from the military. An occasional Army officer might be seconded across to help with weapons training, but the police controlled their own affairs and organized their own command structure. They existed alongside the Army and were, as the dictionary says (see Chapter 6), intended to supplement the strictly military, while being organized along military lines. They were, and are still, paramilitary police forces.

The tactics they used, in their most sophisticated form, were developed to deal with a wave of uprisings and urban riots which swept through the colonies after the Second World War. Riot Control Units were established in many countries based on a common pattern of organization. One Inspector, one NCO and eight men formed a single unit and could be neatly transported in a single Land Rover. Riot Control Units were strategically positioned at various parts of a colony so that they could quickly be sent to put down any local disturbances. In later manifestations, these units took on a galaxy of new names: Police Field Forces, Police Motorized Companies, Police Mobile Units. But their basic organization remained the same, and their tasks were clear: to control riots in the towns and fight insurgents in the country-side.

In quieter times they were used for ceremonial and guard duties. Michael Macoun saw a dual purpose in giving them these other tasks: they were useful duties in their own right, and they also kept the troops occupied: 'It was particularly important that they should be employed on other duties. Otherwise they would get stale and discontented and possibly mutinous.'

The weapons of the Riot Control Units were initially firearms and truncheons, with little in between. They carried riot shields and developed a series of manoeuvres which could be carried out by ten men acting together to attack or arrest members of a crowd. They called these new formations riot squads and snatch squads. Later, in the fifties, they got hold of tear gas and began to use it widely. Before long, their crowd control techniques came to depend on tear gas not as a last resort, but as one of their first resorts, using it even before there had been a serious outbreak of violence from the crowd. Michael Macoun set the policy:

We worked under the concept of early intervention before disturbances snowballed. The use of tear smoke was justifiable if it meant you dispersed the crowd quickly and could contain the situation. You might lose a number of arrests in the process, but it was worth dispersing them so that you could regroup and decide what to do next.

In the sixties, one colonial police force, the Royal Hong Kong Police, developed (as was noted in Chapter 6) a new type of intermediate weapon. Wooden sticks, like little police batons, were loaded up and fired from guns in place of live ammunition. Word of this development spread rapidly. The official report of the Commission established by President Johnson to investigate the 1967 riots in American cities recommended that the Pentagon begin research immediately into new, non-lethal, types of ammunition for use in civil disorders. It said: 'British units in Hong Kong, for example, fire a wooden peg that . . . is reportedly highly effective'.

These 'non-lethal' weapons did not cause colonial police forces to put away their live firearms, though Michael Macoun claims that they continued to use them against crowds less frequently than is sometimes supposed. If they were thought necessary, they were still used:

If it were a very large crowd and the police could not persuade them to disperse with the use of tear smoke, they would be given a formal warning. A banner would be held up saying: DISPERSE OR I OPEN FIRE.

It is worth noting how closely this procedure, even down to the wording of the banner, corresponds with that adopted by ACPO in 1983 and incorporated in Section 20 of the tactical options (see Chapter 6).

Once a warning had been given, the colonial instructions were to open fire on the crowd aiming at knee-height. The idea of firing over their heads was rejected because it would give the impression that the firearms were ineffectual if, as one officer put it, there were no bodies squirming on the ground after the shots.

The most significant aspect of colonial policing is not its technology or its paramilitary structure. It is the habit of mind which determined the whole process of the empire. Colonial police forces were set up to keep order on behalf of the Government in Whitehall. Their relationship to the populations they police is that of master to servant, characterized by instruction on one side and obedience (coerced if necessary) on the other. Michael Macoun makes this key point rhetorically, saying that colonial policing has a different philosophical basis from British domestic policing, and was drawn from the imperial precepts of Rome:

The British domestic tradition grew from the Anglo-Saxon philosophy that the law reflected the will of the people and that every free man had an obligation to uphold it.

The function of the British police overseas was closer to the Roman tradition. It had an organized force at the disposal of the administering power to maintain public order by pragmatic action rather than worrying about accountability to the community as a whole. The authority of government could be deployed by all means at its disposal without reference to public opinion.

We had the force to maintain order, simple and straight, and if people didn't like it that was too bad.

With the benefit of hindsight, Michael Macoun now thinks that blurring of the distinction between domestic policing and its colonial counterpart started in the late forties. A formal programme of visits was set up by the Foreign Office, which involved senior British policemen touring the colonies to learn how their opposite numbers operated. For an officer sitting at his desk in Manchester or Newcastle, it must have seemed a most attractive offer. A few weeks in the sunshine without an in-tray, and with little to do except soak up the distilled operational experience of officers from another world. There was no shortage of takers.

James Anderton, then the Assistant to the Chief Inspector of Constabulary at the Home Office, was sent on a six-week fact-finding and lecture tour of Asia which included visits to Ceylon, India, the Philippines and Hong Kong. John Alderson was sent to West Africa on a shorter trip, during which he had all his belongings stolen from a beach in Sierra Leone, including his passport and money, while taking a swim. Other senior officers found themselves seconded to colonial forces for active service.

Sir Derek Capper, Chief Constable of the West Midlands, was
sent to the Gold Coast. Assistant Commissioner Peter Brodie
went to Ceylon. Two successive Commissioners of Police in Fiji
were British police officers, one from Cumbria and the other from
the East Midlands. Throughout the seventies, Michael Macoun
supervised a rota which kept more than forty British policemen on
a variety of secondments throughout the remaining colonies,
including Hong Kong.

Those fortunate enough to be offered an expenses-paid short
tour were expected to look and learn as they went and to report
what they found. The Foreign Office title for these exercises was
'familiarization instructional tour'. They were also supposed to
give the benefit of their experience to the colonial officers whose
hospitality they enjoyed. Michael Macoun was eager to make the
exchange as engrossing as possible: 'We made them sing for their
dinner. All these high-powered police officers had to give
lectures. We had a fairly tight programme for them so they
wouldn't spend all their time on the beaches or in the knocking-
shops in Bangkok.' Along their route, the seeds were sown of a
lasting and influential relationship. It was still below the surface
when Michael Macoun retired in 1979. He left office convinced
that the practices of colonial police forces had no effect whatever
on British domestic policing: 'It would have been out of the
question because of the different circumstances and the fact that
we only had a limited accountability.'

Looking back from the vantage-point of his retirement home in
Surrey, he now sees those early contacts he fostered between
British officers and their counterparts abroad in a different light.
Inadvertently, he thinks, they began the process of bringing
colonial policing to mainland Britain:

That must be a key to it. So many UK officers over the last decade and a
half have served overseas that some of them must have learned something about public order tactics which presumably they brought back
with them. I should have realized that.

It was a reversal of the customary colonial process. As John
Alderson tartly remarks, the usual practice was for developed

British traditions to be exported to the colonies. In police circles, the first time this import came to light was at the ACPO conference of September 1981 (see Chapter 2) when Richard Quine, Director of Operations of the Royal Hong Kong Police was invited to attend and outline the colonial police systems for dealing with public disorder. Outside police circles, this visit was kept secret, of course. ACPO and the Royal Hong Kong Police hit it off well enough for their link to be made formal and permanent. Richard Quine's superior, the Commissioner of Police, was invited to attend all future meetings of ACPO and to bring other senior colonial officers with him. In 1982, the Commissioner, Roy Henry, began coming to Britain for ACPO meetings on the whole range of policing matters, with special emphasis on public order. His status at ACPO conferences was that of participating observer.

Immediately after the visit by Richard Quine, ACPO asked if their specialists in public order could visit Hong Kong to see the colonial techniques in practice. Roy Henry was more than happy to accommodate them, and the group studied the Hong Kong force during their exploratory tour of foreign police tactics in many countries. In 1983, a formal agreement was concluded between ACPO and Hong Kong to permit regular exchanges of operational officers. Three Superintendents from British forces were sent to Hong Kong for extended periods of secondment, in exchange for three colonial Superintendents who visited Britain. Roy Henry says he was flattered by the interest which was suddenly shown in his Hong Kong tactics, and was keen to help introduce them to Britain: 'We had several requests for police officers of middle strata level who were experts in the field of public order to visit us and see what they could lift from Hong Kong which would be useful to them.'

The exchange arrangement has continued, with the purpose of tightening the police liaison between Hong Kong and Britain. The transfers are managed through the office of the Chief Inspector of Constabulary at the Home Office. The visiting British officers have been receptive to the tactics of their colonial partners. According to Roy Henry's account, they have raised no objection to adopting what they have seen in operation: 'Oh no, the very opposite. There has been great understanding. There is no doubt that when they looked at our systems, our methods and our tactics they said "We like that, yes".'

In November 1987, the Royal Hong Kong Police advertised in *Police Review* for British police officers to go out and join them. Their slogan ran: 'Royal Hong Kong Police – the proving ground for natural leaders'.

The significance of Hong Kong is that it embodies the British colonial police tradition in the most important colony left and the most difficult to police. Its public order tactics are a compendium of methods which have been tried and tested for forty years in all the former colonies. They have repressed dissent and put down uprisings in the Caribbean, up and down Africa, in the Middle East, the Indian sub-continent and in the Far East.

Roy Henry has now retired (since 1985) and is living comfortably in Surrey surrounded by his collection of presentation police shields from visiting forces. He is an ebullient raconteur who takes great pride in the contribution his men have made to shaping British domestic police tactics. His background, like that of many colonial police officers, is military, and he has the bearing for which tweed jackets and cavalry twill trousers were invented. He sports a pipe with an enormous bowl, and punctuates his anecdotes by frequent and near-lethal use of a Zippo lighter.

Where Michael Macoun's practical experience was in colonial Africa, Roy Henry's was in the Far East. He was sent to Malaya first, worked his way up to Commissioner in Sarawak and then Fiji before his career reached its peak for six and a half years as Commissioner in Hong Kong:

Hong Kong had the advantage of being one of the last of the Crown Colonies and was therefore able to look back at history in other territories. We studied the internal security mechanisms of past colonies such as Malaya, Borneo, Kenya and Cyprus. They had a public order problem in each of those territories. So we were able to pick and choose the best from all of them and adapt it into the Hong Kong machine.

Attendance at ACPO conferences between 1982 and 1985 gave Roy Henry a privileged view of the system and tactics adopted for use in Britain and enshrined in the *Public Order Manual* produced in 1983. He has not yet acquired ACPO's habit of silence, and shows no hesitation in confirming the extent to which the tactical options adopted for Britain are those of his Hong Kong machine:

They reflect it in several fundamental ways. There are many things which are now being taught and practised in United Kingdom forces which were in existence in Hong Kong. There is a definite reflection of similar methods.

The details are even more significant. ACPO has imported manoeuvres and tactics from a wide variety of sources. But close examination reveals that its main escalations of offensive police action are those developed in Hong Kong. The formation of riot squads armed with truncheons and short shields; their training in specialist techniques for dispersing a crowd or making selective arrests from it; the use of sophisticated intelligence-gathering to target individuals; the development of CS gas and plastic bullets as weapons of penultimate resort. All reflect the tactics of colonial police forces.

The language used to describe the new police approach is striking. Roy Henry talks about 'the projection of police units in an efficient, effective and *formidable* manner which creates an atmosphere in the riotous mobs of apprehension and awe which could be close to *fear*?' [my emphasis]. ACPO talks, as we have seen earlier, about the need to present a *formidable* appearance and the purpose of creating *fear* in a disorderly crowd. Both present the ultimate aim of police attacks in the same term: 'dispersal'. Roy Henry says that if the police get it right, a crowd will scatter: 'They run like the dickens!'

ACPO also draws heavily on colonial experience in its blueprint for a control structure which enables a Chief Constable to transform his force on command into a paramilitary fighting unit. This is the chassis of Roy Henry's Hong Kong machine, and ACPO has imported it direct. Normal policing involves officers scattered throughout the force area going about their normal range of duties and this is called the 'watch and ward structure'; in an emergency, orders are radioed to all officers to get into paramilitary gear and await instructions on a force-wide basis, and this is called the 'public order structure'. The Hong Kong police force has been training so long that it can now switch from one structure to the other in a matter of hours. This is precisely the skill which ACPO has brought to Britain and which hundreds of thousands of man-hours have been spent practising since 1983.

By the time of the Broadwater Farm riot in October 1985, the Metropolitan Police were so skilful at this transformation that they could carry it out even on a Sunday evening. The officer in charge at the Wood Green control room, Commander David Polkinghorne, gave an authoritative account of the operation to an international police conference in London in September 1987. He accepted that the battle had gone badly for the police for several hours, and said that at 9.45 p.m., almost three hours after the first disturbances, his men were losing so heavily that he requested the Commissioner at New Scotland Yard to approve the use of baton rounds, a request which was immediately granted. In the event, the riot receded and no plastic bullets were actually fired. Commander Polkinghorne was frank in his speech about police shortcomings on the night. But he spoke with pride of their success in getting more than a thousand men into riot gear and out on the estate in disciplined units:

Our Force Mobilization Plan worked exceedingly well: 400 police were deployed within the estate in the first hour; 500 within an hour and a half; 750 in three hours and more than a thousand by 11.30 p.m. [four and a half hours]. Control was able to despatch and account for all those serials on the ground.

He then outlined the new public order structure which the Metropolitan Police have introduced to ensure that this feat can be repeated whenever it may be ordered:

The District Support Units have merged with the Special Patrol Group to form the Territorial Support Group. We have now got eight such units throughout London of 100 men each, under their own command structure. Normally, they are under the divisional Chief Superintendent, but when they are employed on public order events they will be under the cadres of senior officers or under their own command. So that is 800 fully trained shield men with equipped vehicles that we have got throughout London to deal with probable problems.

This arrangement is the British equivalent of colonial riot control units stationed at strategic points and occupied with other duties until the call comes for them to drop everything and deal with a local disturbance.

Roy Henry defines it as the switch into a paramilitary role and argues that its implications for the police could hardly be more profound:

Public order structure is almost the very opposite of the normal watch and ward structure. In normal policing, the constable is on his own, he is told to think for himself and act on his initiative, to be an individual. In the public order structure it is the very opposite. He is part and parcel of a group, a platoon or a company. He is told *not* to act on his own but to wait for orders, *not* to use his initiative. So it is a complete volte-face.

As we shall see in Chapter 10, this view is repeated almost exactly in the study notes given to Metropolitan Police recruits during their training at Hendon and Hounslow. The required 'volte-face' involves a complete change of principles. For while the watch and ward structure needs officers to act as policemen, the public order structure demands that they behave like soldiers. It does not, of course, actually turn them into soldiers, but it does depend on their ability to accept military discipline and conduct manoeuvres with military precision. Most significantly of all, it requires them to think of themselves as members of an army rather than a constabulary. This aspect of the transformation is explicitly recognized in the *Public Order Manual* under the section on military concepts entitled 'Borrowed terminology' (see Chapter 1).

The relationship between British police forces and their mentors in Hong Kong continues today as warmly as ever. It has become such a strong habit that Roy Henry regards it as part of the routine to keep Britain up to date with the colonial state of the art:

If something new should evolve in Hong Kong I am sure that it would flow to the United Kingdom – and vice versa. If there should be new equipment, new thoughts, new tactics, then both sides will gain on a mutual exchange of information.

To its supporters and practitioners, there is cause neither for surprise nor for alarm in ACPO's policy of importing colonial police practices into Britain. To them, the worsening situation confronting the police justifies the measures adopted. They point to picket-lines at Grunwick, Warrington, Orgreave and Wapping and to riots in Brixton, Handsworth, Toxteth and Tottenham as evidence of increasing violence in public places. They also assume a general level of public consent on the ground that the police are acting to hold the line for the rest of society. This view leaves one fact unexplained. ACPO has taken great care to shroud its new policy in secrecy. It is difficult to see this as a sign of faith in public support. It suggests, to the contrary, that a profound shift in thinking has taken place among some senior police officers which leads them to treat parts of Britain like colonies. Tactics which were previously reserved for use against subject peoples overseas, are now considered appropriate for the control of British citizens at home. Whether or not it was ever morally right to employ them for foreign suppression, the decision to import these tactics into domestic policing is of the greatest political significance. ACPO has decided in secret that parts of Britain's population should be treated, on occasion, like hostile aliens. Can they avoid the conclusion that, for some purposes, it is no longer their intention to police by consent?

The policy adopted in 1981 represents the most radical break with police tradition since 1830. It is hard to imagine that it was undertaken without the support of ACPO's political masters. Such support would be unlikely under the decentralized structure of political control which theoretically governs British police forces. Nobody could seriously expect the wide variety of local government police authorities to welcome a policing revolution with such dramatic implications. But a way was found to by-pass the disobedient processes of democracy. The matter was decided by the Home Office and the police themselves.

9   The Golden Concept

*We are accountable, I suppose, essentially to ourselves as a
responsible body.*
James Anderton, ACPO President, May 1987

The question of police accountability is usually considered a dull
corner of the forest. Any journalist who suggests it to the editor is
likely to see a tell-tale glazing of the eyes in response, followed by
the unanswerable judgement that it is hard to find a new angle.

In a country with no written constitution, it is perhaps not
surprising to find national policy for police forces made by an
informal grouping of unelected Chief Constables meeting as an
association which has no basis in statute. Nor, apparently, is it
remarkable that the leader of this association should declare in a
television interview (in the *Secret Society* series on BBC2) that they
are accountable only to themselves for their actions. Imagine the
uproar which would greet a similar declaration by the FBI or, for
that matter, the KGB.

The theory of British policing is quite different from this
reality. Peter Imbert, the Commissioner of the Metropolitan
Police, speaks of 'the golden concept of policing by consent'
which governs each force. In theory, each police headquarters
answers to a democratic authority which ensures its compliance
with the wishes of the public. In London, this authority is
embodied in the elected Member of Parliament serving as Home
Secretary. Everywhere else, it takes the form of a watchdog
committee composed mainly of elected local representatives.
Control of the coercive power of the state as exercised by a police
force, is theoretically held between the Chief Constable, who
decides day-to-day operational policy, the local police authority
which oversees general policy and decides the budget, and the
Home Office which inspects standards and gives specialist advice.

This arrangement is sometimes compared to the balance of forces which makes for stability in a tripod.

In practice, the control of public order policy in the eighties has come more to resemble a shooting-stick. Almost all important decisions have been made by just one leg of the tripod, the Chief Constables. Their association has organized the crucial meetings, established the framework of committees, drawn up and agreed the central document, and arranged relevant training materials. The only known intervention by an elected authority has been the approval given by a Home Secretary, William Whitelaw, to the draft of ACPO's *Public Order Manual*. Local authorities have simply been ignored throughout the process, neither informed of ACPO's intention to prepare a manual nor consulted about its contents.

This is a break with historical precedent. The origins of the British police force are commonly traced back to the Saxon office of tythingman, elected by the common people in his own locality to perform a variety of functions including the maintenance of the peace. The authority of his office derived from those who had appointed him, the members of his own community. His style of policing was, correspondingly, by consent rather than brute force. The Royal Commission on the police in 1929 referred to the tradition that held police officers to be ordinary citizens who were paid to do their job in uniform:

The police of this country have never been recognized, either in law or by tradition, as a force distinct from the general body of citizens. Despite the imposition of many extraneous duties on the police by legislation or administrative action, the principle remains that a policeman, in the view of the common law, is only 'a person paid to perform, as a matter of duty, acts which if he were so minded he might have done voluntarily'.

. . . This attitude is due, we believe, not to any distrust of the police as a body, but to an instinctive feeling that, as a matter of principle, they should have as few powers as possible which are not possessed by the ordinary citizen, and that their authority should rest on the broad basis of the consent and active co-operation of all law-abiding people.

The report went on to stress the 'peculiar degree' to which the police in Britain are dependent on the goodwill of the general public. 'The utmost discretion must be exercised by them in overstepping the limited powers they possess.' If these sentiments seem outmoded, even slightly pious, today, then it is worth recalling that they survived for more than a thousand years as the definitive marks of what we now call the British police tradition. The extent to which events seem to have overtaken them, is a measure of how far recent changes in policing have strayed from these origins.

This process of change did not begin with the election of Margaret Thatcher as Prime Minister, though it has certainly been accelerated throughout the eighties. It was already under way by the time of the Royal Commission of 1962, which examined the complex structure of accountability of police forces. The report of that Royal Commission set out what seemed merely common sense at the time, namely a spirited defence of the balance of power between central and local government. It is, again, a mark of how far the political fulcrum has been shifted that these simple nostrums should now seem so dated:

In our opinion, the present police system is sound because it is based upon, and reflects, a political idea of immense practical value which has gained wide acceptance in this country, namely the idea of partnership between central and local government in the administration of public services. This idea, working itself out in a variety of ways in our education, health, housing and other services, admirably suits the British temperament. It gives free rein to discussion and ample scope for compromise, thus promoting the growth of an enlightened and mature public opinion. It provides for the central pooling of knowledge and experience gathered from the whole country, but for the local application of this knowledge and experience to suit the needs of each particular community. By bringing into the administration of public services large numbers of men and women of goodwill it encourages the development throughout our society of a sense of civic responsibility. These are imponderable but very real gains. They ought not to be lightly surrendered.

At the time, the Conservative Party welcomed this approach. The Home Secretary in 1963, Henry Brooke, commended the maintenance of local police forces to Parliament and spoke of the 'immense value' of local interest and local initiative in the working of the system.

Yet even in 1962 it was evident to the Royal Commission that the balance between local and central government was tilting:

A realistic appraisal of the present arrangements for control must consequently recognize that for many years there has been, under the guidance of the Home Departments, a centralizing process which has steadily gained momentum. As a result the police service cannot with any precision be described simply as a local service.
. . . Much of the evidence we heard indicated that the influence of the central Government is now dominant.

The freedom of Chief Constables from democratic control in large areas of decision making, was also clear to the Royal Commission. It concluded that they enjoy a position of 'exceptional independence':

They are subject to little legal control in carrying out their duties. Like everyone else they are subordinate to the law; but the effect of this is rather to restrain them from unlawful activities, than to order the manner in which they carry out those that are lawful.

The Royal Commission concluded that the problem of controlling the police could be restated as the problem of controlling Chief Constables. It spoke of the unfettered discretion a Chief Constable could exercise:

He is accountable to no one, and subject to no one's orders, for the way in which, for example, he settles his general policies in regard to law enforcement over the area covered by his force, the disposition of his force, the concentration of his resources on any particular type of crime or area, the manner in which he handles political demonstrations or processions and allocates and instructs his men when preventing breaches of the peace arising from industrial disputes, the methods he employs in dealing with an outbreak of violence or of passive resistance to authority . . . and so on.

This is a *carte blanche* which Lord Denning, in a celebrated judgment of 1968, put like this: 'The responsibility for law enforcement lies on him; he is answerable to the law and to the law alone'.

At the heart of the 1962 Royal Commission report, and the 1964 Police Act which followed it, lies an unresolved conflict between the desire to maintain local public control of police forces and the requirement to keep Chief Constables free of any semblance of operational accountability. It is the conflict between the demands of democracy and those of independence. The evidence of the 1980s suggests that police independence has won the contest. It would certainly be difficult to square the recent behaviour of ACPO with any customary concepts of democratic accountability.

As ACPO's president said later in the *Secret Society* interview, the guide-lines ACPO issues are matters for Chief Constables, not for public discussion. 'Why should we consult people outside the police service when we are determining operational policies and tactics?' ACPO may be, as Mr Anderton maintains, a responsible body in the sense that its decisions are taken with care, but it is not, it seems, responsible in the more literal sense of having to answer to anyone at all.

Yet ACPO as a body is not mentioned in any Act of Parliament and has no more standing in law than a village gardening society. So how has it managed to exert such influence over the direction of police strategic planning? The explanation lies in its success in undermining resistance to the paramilitary drift of its policies among all three legs of the constitutional tripod – the Chief Constables, the Home Office and the local police authorities. There are serving police officers who complain privately that ACPO is run by a self-perpetuating group among its membership. A small number of forceful Chief Constables are said to control the committee which makes all important decisions, including the appointment of association officers. Those outside this circle wield relatively little power within the association. It is not only John Alderson who has felt the chill of repeatedly being excluded.

The breadth of ACPO's influence over individual Chief Constables is considerable. When *Brass Tacks* invited police contributions to a documentary about the *Public Order Manual* in October 1985, a formal approach to ACPO got nowhere. Individual ACPO members indicated that they might be willing to appear in the programme but, because of their position as office-holders within the association, felt obliged to seek the advice of their colleagues first. In the event, they said no. So *Brass Tacks* wrote separately to each Chief Constable in Britain asking him to take part. They all refused. Significantly most of them refused in exactly the same terms, saying: 'I regret I am unable to assist . . .', as if some unseen central spirit had guided their hands. Then one Chief Constable wrote: 'The question of police participation in such a programme was raised at the autumn conference of ACPO. I do not intend to depart from the decision of my association.' So ACPO apparently decides even the relatively minor matter of which television invitations to accept.

ACPO has the ear of the Home Office. There are regular meetings between its senior office-holders and high-level civil servants to discuss policy matters. The Home Secretary attends the annual meeting of ACPO which is held each autumn over a period of three days. The importance of these links is that the Home Office exercises statutory powers in the appointment and dismissal of chief officers. The career path of an ambitious Chief Constable can depend to a great extent on the goodwill of successive Home Secretaries, which would be difficult to secure without the co-operation of senior civil servants. The Home Secretary is also responsible for the Inspectorate of Constabulary, which reports annually on each force, and which can, in theory, trigger a cut-off of government funds amounting to half the force budget if it does not like what it finds.

It would be possible for a Chief Constable to defy ACPO and the Home Office if he disagreed with a particular policy. But he would be a brave man to try it in view of the constitutional power held over him in Queen Anne's Gate. One former Chief Constable tells the story of Home Office pressure on him to accept water cannon after the riots of 1981. He resisted all the way, until at last the Home Secretary himself became insistent. The point was silenced only after the Chief Constable banged his fist on the table and shouted 'I'm not bloody having them, Willie!' He carried the day, just as Lord Denning said he should under pressure from the executive, but it is significant that the Chief Constable concerned had already built an unchallengeable reputation within the service, and was within a few years of retirement when he made the stand.

But while ACPO has avoided the emergence of dissent within its own ranks, and formed a close working relationship with the Home Office, it has run into far greater opposition among some individual police authorities. Discussion with dissenters has been avoided by declaring the tactical options of public order policing to be operational matters, which are therefore outside the remit of the police authority. This is entirely in line with the constitutional position set out by the 1962 Royal Commission. Chief Constables have upheld their lack of accountability for the way they handle political demonstrations and industrial disputes and for the methods they employ in dealing with outbreaks of violence. But the Royal Commission, while presenting its account of the facts of the case, argued for greater accountability in some areas of policing. Chief Constables, it urged, should be controlled and supervised more closely. The Home Secretary, Henry Brooke, said in Parliament during the debates leading up to the 1964 Police Act, that new measures were needed to provide arrangements by which Chief Constables could be called to account, both centrally and locally: 'Even as we accept that the Chief Constable is not subject in these matters to orders or directions, we must make sure that he is fully accountable for what he does.' When a Liverpool MP, Sir Kenneth Thompson, asked about the accountability of a Chief Constable who ordered the use of mounted police to restore order in the event of trouble, the Home Secretary gave a clear answer in favour of public debate of the issue:

Mr Brooke: Unquestionably, the police authority could ask for a report from the Chief Constable on that and could discuss the report with him.
Sir K. Thompson: But he could refuse to give it.
Mr Brooke: If he did, the matter could be settled in the end by the Home Secretary. But in a case like that I can see no reason why the Chief Constable should not supply a report on request.

This democratic impulse, however, was notably absent from discussion of police tactics in public order control among some police authorities in the eighties. Indeed, matters became so serious in Greater Manchester in March 1982 that the police authority called its Chief Constable to account for a speech he had made supporting the abolition of police committees and saying that the link with local government was no longer needed. Mr Anderton had spoken in terms which, with hindsight, seem to foreshadow the Prime Minister's 1984 speech about the Enemy Within:

I see in our midst an enemy more dangerous, insidious and ruthless than any faced since the Second World War . . . I recommend that police committees should be totally abolished and replaced by non-political police boards.

Mr Anderton's reply to his police authority's questioning on this speech was forthright. He said that it was not incumbent on him to report back in any shape or form on what he had said. The meeting grew increasingly acrimonious. At one point, Mr Anderton refused to answer questions about the speech, saying that he felt like Christ must have felt before his crucifixion. Three years later, the police authority was abolished by the Government in a local government reorganization.

Not all police authorities, by any means, have been so robust in their approach to the job of calling the police to account. Research conducted by the University of Bath was made public in August 1987, showing a wide variation in attitudes among members of authorities throughout the country. An unnamed Conservative chairman of a police authority describes the change which has been brought by the arrival of a number of Labour members determined to challenge the Chief Constable:

The police authority has changed. Meetings never used to last beyond 12.30 p.m. and we all used to go into another room and have a glass of white wine or sherry and go home. Within that meeting there was always a chance for us to enjoy a presentation from the Chief. He would explain something, show some slides or whatever. It's different now. Meetings go on until 2 or 3 p.m.

The most significant of these anonymous remarks from the point of view of police accountability echoes this tone. It is attributed to the leader of the Conservative group on an unnamed authority:

After all the police do control the country. If they are to be effective they must be above politics, under the control and answerable to the Home Office. The police authority is like a sub-committee of the Home Office, a sort of local tier of management.

Where these views have prevailed, there can have been little, if any, resistance to the change in public order policing decided by ACPO and approved by the Home Office. There is, however, no record of any Chief Constable presenting an explanation or a slide show of ACPO's plan for the mobilization of police units. In other police authorities where members have decided to test the limits of their powers, as before they have been over-ruled in favour of central decisions. A case in point arose over the decision of Douglas Hurd as Home Secretary to make two of the most forceful tactical options available to forces whose authority members opposed their acquisition. In a Home Office circular issued in May 1986, Chief Constables were told that they could draw stocks of CS gas and plastic bullets from central stores under Home Office control if their police authorities refused to authorize their purchase. It was the clearest possible instance of central government offering to help Chief Constables to override the wishes of local government representatives.

The Northumbria Police Authority decided to test the matter at law by taking the Home Secretary to court for exceeding his powers and infringing their own influence on policy. In the High Court in London the case was given its first hearing in December 1986. The Northumbrians claimed that the Home Secretary's circular went beyond his powers as set out in the Police Act of 1964 and that his circular should be set aside by the Court. They lost the case. The Court decided in favour of the Home Secretary but on significantly restricted grounds. It agreed that the Police Act gave him no power to overrule a police authority in a matter of this kind, but declared that he had a general prerogative power invested in him as an office holder under the Crown. This prerogative power was considered by the Court to be sufficient to justify the circular.

The Northumbrians decided to appeal against the decision. In

July 1987, at the Court of Appeal in The Strand, they argued against the lower court on two grounds: firstly that the right of prerogative had never, as a matter of precedent, been interpreted so widely as to give a Secretary of State the power to supply arms to a police force under local democratic control; and secondly that the Home Secretary's powers under prerogative had been superseded by the elaborate statement of his position in the 1964 Police Act.

Those closely involved in the case from the Northumbrian side felt that the judges in both courts were eager to side with the Chief Constable, and by implication with all Chief Constables, in making available to him whatever he requested to maintain public order. The Northumbria Police Authority is Labour controlled and not particularly left-wing. As in much of North-East England, the Labour tradition leans towards the right of the party. The chairman of the police authority, Councillor George Gill, decided to press the case in Court on constitutional grounds. Little more than a year earlier, he had been appointed to chair the new police authority after the abolition of its predecessor under the Tyne and Wear County Council. He remembered the briefing papers he had been given, setting out the tripartite balance of power which, in theory, governed his force, and was horrified to find the Home Secretary apparently undermining it by his circular. The offence was compounded, in Councillor Gill's eyes, by the failure to discuss this disagreement openly. He expected the Home Office to call a meeting of Chief Constables, local authority representatives and civil servants to settle their differences. But there was no such meeting. The Home Secretary, he decided, was going beyond his remit and attempting to establish a national police policy without the involvement of his proper partners in power, the local authority. For Councillor Gill, the question went to the heart of policing in a democratic society:

You can only ever police by consent because there are not enough policemen to do the job in any other manner. We could not afford to employ enough officers to take on the status of an army.

There has never, in the history of the police, been a greater need to have the support of the people. The country is at a crossroads and the police require our support. But if it is seen that the representatives of local people are not even taken account of when decisions are made, then it will do the police no good.

His authority's decision to refuse expenditure on plastic bullets was made on practical grounds as well. Their force was seriously undermanned, down by 550 men, one sixth of its total establishment. If there was money to spend, Councillor Gill wanted it spent on recruiting more officers to fill some of these gaps on the beat.

Relations between the police authority and the Chief Constable of Northumbria remained good in spite of their disagreement. The force had taken pride in avoiding most of the tactical options in the ACPO manual even during the conflicts of the eighties. For the whole of the 1984–5 coal dispute, they kept their riot gear in lockers and never once put it on. Visiting police units from other forces were told to put theirs away too because Northumbria didn't do things that way. But the Chief Constable wanted plastic bullets as a precautionary measure. He was worried that trouble might blow into the Tyneside area from outside. More importantly, the force was concerned that officers from other police forces might be brought on to their territory to restore order if they failed to do so themselves. The Deputy Chief Constable expressed their fears vividly:

If the unthinkable did happen, in other words if RentaMob decided to come here from Manchester or Liverpool, then we would have to make sure that we could manage them. The only way we can do that is by training. We need plastic baton rounds to make sure that our officers are properly trained to use them. The last thing we want is officers from another force coming into this area and having to discharge those weapons.

The case was decided several months later, on 18 November 1987. The Appeal Court accepted the general scheme of the 1964 Police Act as a deliberate separation of powers: the police authority to maintain, provide and equip a force; the Chief Constable to control and operate it; and the Home Secretary to supervise and regulate. But the Court decided that these functions were not as closely limited as the Northumbrians believed.

The Home Secretary, for instance, had a power to provide central services for the police. The Court ruled that the supply of equipment constituted a service. So the Home Secretary was entitled, after all, to issue plastic bullets and CS gas from a central store, under the terms of the 1964 Act. There was thus no conflict between statute and the Royal Prerogative, and the Northumbrian case was decisively rejected. They were denied leave to appeal to the House of Lords.

The outcome of this seminal case has weakened, perhaps even demolished, the tripartite arrangement of control over police forces. It sets a clear precedent for any future dispute between a Chief Constable and his Police Authority. If the Home Office backs the Chief Constable, then the third part of the traditional tripod, the police authority, could find that it has no leg left to stand on. In the specific instance of riot equipment, the Home Secretary's Circular 40/1986 has been upheld:

Where a chief officer decides that he needs plastic baton rounds or CS equipment, and anticipates that he will have difficulty in obtaining the approval of the police authority, he should consult HM Inspector of Constabulary . . . If the HMI endorses the officer's assessment of need, but none the less the police authority withholds approval for such equipment, the HMI will make arrangements with the Home Office for equipment to be supplied from a central store.

Just as the Northumbria case was going to Appeal, the 1987 Birthday Honours list caused a stir among police forces by elevating a former Chief Constable to the peerage. Sir Philip Knights, after long years of service in the West Midlands force, was to become Lord Knights of Edgbaston. No previous Chief Constable had ever been honoured in this way. The new peer was, of course, delighted. The honour had been awarded to the whole police service, he said, and he intended to act as the voice of the police in the House of Lords. Then came the barb. Lord Knights said he would continue to press as a peer those issues which had most concerned him as a Chief Constable. He mentioned only one, in his interview with *Police Review*:

I am disturbed by the increasing influence of central government on the police. The proper level for police control and accountability is in local government, whose members should have a say in deciding police priorities . . . Effective policing requires marked local affinity, which can be much better achieved with local forces.

Lord Knights knows from the inside how far ACPO wishes to move in the direction of national co-ordination of the police. The *Public Order Manual's* section on *Inter-force liaison* summarizes the current attempts at standardization, and looks forward to further joint developments. The political debate over control of the police is not mentioned in this section. Instead, moves towards a common policy are presented in terms of professionalism. The present arrangement is set out under the heading *Existing expertise*. Two 'alternative developments' are noted with approval:

(a) Consideration of the regular deployment of officers to neighbouring forces for familiarization in preparation for any mutual aid commitment;
(b) Interchange of senior officers between forces on temporary attachments for familiarization.

Nowhere does the manual give any indication that ACPO wishes to see its members combined into a national police force. But it clearly does encourage the establishment of still greater uniformity throughout the country in terms of operational policy. That indeed, was its justification for producing a manual in the first place:

Conclusion
There is at present a high degree of co-operation and liaison between forces and departments.

  This will be further enhanced by the establishment of A8 (Public Order) Forward Planning Unit, which will be staffed by officers from a variety of forces. Whilst already reality on a limited basis, it is recommended that all forces consider mutual aid interchange of PSUs, and senior officers on temporary attachments, particularly to be deployed during public disorder. This will afford valuable training and familiarization and give officers from both the receiving and sending forces the opportunity to gain expertise that otherwise would not necessarily be possible. These are valued options worthy of consideration by all forces.

There is a further aspect of police accountability which has become increasingly important with the preparation of the *Public*

Order Manual. It is the thorny question of how to adjudicate complaints against individual police officers after a serious public disturbance. The theory, as we saw earlier in this chapter, is that constables enjoy no special protection from the law against the consequences of their own actions. A police officer who hits an innocent person with his truncheon, for example, is supposed to be as liable for this assault as anybody else who did the same thing.

The extension of this principle to cover the tactical options is of the greatest importance. If police officers firing CS gas canisters or plastic bullets are to be held individually responsible for their actions, then some could find themselves, in theory, facing murder charges if they kill people. With intentionally lethal weapons, such as live firearms, the legal jeopardy of officers carrying out their duty under orders is even greater. As the *Public Order Manual* itself repeatedly emphasizes, every officer using force must be able to justify the legality of his conduct, which cannot be done merely on the basis that he is acting under orders (see Chapter 6).

Once again, though, this theoretical accountability in law bears little relation to the practice applied in real policing. Consider three instances of public order policing in the mid-eighties. First the twelve-month coal dispute, during which the riot squad tactics imported from Hong Kong were first used in the British mainland. Those who watched television news reports of the major confrontations during the strike saw line after line of police in riot gear taking the strain of protesting miners and their supporters. They also saw a number of spectacular scenes of brutality by individual policemen either on foot or on horseback. Within police ranks today it is commonly accepted that some officers 'went over the top' in their zeal to beat the demonstrators. Yet the law has apparently overlooked them. Not one police officer has been charged with an offence as a result of the year-long public order operation, though more than ten thousand charges were brought against individual miners and demonstrators.

Two other events share a similar pattern of failure to bring guilty police officers to book. Some assaults on students demonstrating against the visit of the then Home Secretary, Leon

Brittan, at Manchester University on Friday 1 March 1985 and on members of the 'peace convoy' at Stonehenge on Saturday and Sunday 1 and 2 June 1985, have not been cleared up because the police officers who carried them out have never been identified. In both cases, elaborate inquiries were made by officers of other forces on behalf of the Police Complaints Authority, and established unlawful behaviour by some constables present. But a wall of silence has prevented these constables being brought to account for their actions in court. In the case of the Manchester students, the Police Complaints Authority concluded that: 'In eight cases where evidence clearly showed that police had assaulted students it had not been possible to identify the individual officer responsible, the Authority made this quite clear to the complainant.' For the Stonehenge hippies, the conclusion was similar: 'In the act of making arrests some officers clearly used excessive force, but it has not been possible to identify them amongst the 1363 officers involved and therefore disciplinary proceedings, which demand a clear identification of officers, are impossible.'

In both cases, the complainants and the general public are left with the result that established breaches of the law by some police officers go unpunished because those responsible cannot be identified. The presence in Manchester of more than sixty trained police officers, and at Stonehenge of more than a thousand, is apparently no help when it comes to identifying the perpetrators of these crimes.

It may also be relevant that inquiries by outside forces have depended upon the co-operation of the very police force under investigation. In Manchester, for example, as an edition of the BBC2 *Out of Court* series showed, the investigating team of officers from Avon and Somerset police were billetted in Greater Manchester police accommodation, used GMP offices, were driven about by GMP drivers, and even socialized in the Greater Manchester police bars. When press releases covering Manchester University and Stonehenge were issued by the Police Complaints Authority, the word 'Independent' had been inserted into the Authority's title.

Perhaps the most telling comment on the current system of investigating complaints against individual policemen comes from a man who, as a Deputy Chief Constable, had been responsible for discipline within a police force. It was John Stalker, as DCC of Greater Manchester Police, who supervised the response to allegations of ill-treatment which were made by four dozen students and lecturers after the police cleared the steps of the Students' Union during the demonstration against Leon Brittan. In May 1986, Mr Stalker was removed from duty over allegations of misconduct in his relationship with a Manchester businessman. He was subjected to detailed investigation himself amid suspicion that he had been 'nobbled' to get him off his own inquiry into the conduct of Royal Ulster Constabulary Officers in Northern Ireland. Eventually, he resigned in frustration, telling reporters that he now held opinions which he had rejected during his thirty-year career as a policeman:

I am less than sure now that the present system of investigating the police is the best. Having read the report of the investigation into me, I now recognize something that people outside the force have long recognized about policemen investigating policemen.

10   Shooting in the Dark

Eventually, all the top people who have held back the tide of paramilitarism for the last ten to fifteen years will have gone. The whole nature of policing will have changed by the beginning of the next century if the trend continues.
John Alderson, BBC *File On 4*, September 1987

With the objections of police authorities swept aside, the most forceful of ACPO's tactical options, including plastic bullets and CS gas, have secured their place in the armoury of every major police force in the country. Tens of thousands of constables have been trained in the techniques of front-line riot control. Thousands more belong to elite squads whose job will be to conceal and protect specialist gunners as they are brought forward to fire one of the new weapons into a crowd. The prospect of paramilitary policing is no longer confined to futuristic fantasies in the anti-establishment press. It has become a present reality of British life, stamped day after day into the tarmac of our police training grounds. It can be a matter only of time before some Chief Constable gives the order to open fire in the streets.

In doing so, he will take an enormous gamble. For not even the ACPO hierarchy can be sure what would happen next. They hope that the police would gain ground, quell the disturbance, make arrests and go home victorious to public approval. But this result is not guaranteed. ACPO itself explicitly acknowledges in its *Public Order Manual* that the consequence could be disastrous – an escalation of violence and an armed response from the crowd precipitating gun warfare in the High Street and the back alleys. How long it would last is anybody's guess. The days and weeks that follow could be marked by futher disorder, or by intermittent sniper fire, which would make it impossible to resume normal policing by unarmed foot patrols. The effect on other cities would be incalculable.

These fears are shared, and discussed with candour, by many senior police officers. They point to an inescapable conclusion: every plastic bullet or CS gas canister fired in a British city will be a shot in the dark. It could prove fatal not only for those at the scene, but ultimately for the police tradition which Britain has pioneered.

It might be comforting to dismiss these speculations as alarmist. But the comfort would hardly survive a visit to one of the inner-city areas already scarred by rioting, the very areas which are most likely to see the use of ACPO's toughest tactical options. In July 1986, *Brass Tacks* reported from Handsworth in Birmingham, where rioting had been so destructive only nine months earlier that the Chief Constable had abandoned his earlier opposition to plastic bullets. As the West Midlands force began to lay in stocks of this new weapon and train gunners to shoot them, the crucial question became what would happen if they were used against a crowd. The answers were startlingly consistent. As we spoke to leader after leader of the black communities, they all expressed their grave fears for the future. It proved impossible to find a youth worker or project co-ordinator who did not foresee armed retaliation against the police if they were to fire plastic bullets. These are not, by any means, people who relish the prospect of street warfare (though there are others who clearly do). They are the patient men and women who help everybody carry on life in poor black neighbourhoods and keep the lid on most of the resentment around them. They run scruffy advice centres in church basements, organize literacy projects for the Manpower Services Commission and help ex-offenders. One of them is a former officer of the British Army, who has spent many years suppressing uprisings in the colonies and has himself fired plastic bullets into crowds on many occasions. They all draw compari-sons between Britain and South Africa. They watch events in Crossroads and Soweto and apply their conclusions to Lozells and Handsworth: if the police are tough, a crowd grows tougher;

if shots are fired, they are answered in kind. They have weighed their warnings carefully, and issue them with little hope:

1. Part of my job is to reduce the level of violence on the street and prevent serious injury to people living in the community.

We don't want plastic bullets used in Handsworth. There were meetings throughout the area and the audiences voted overwhelmingly against plastic bullets. So I am disappointed that the Chief Constable is planning to increase the level of violence. There is an old saying that you fight fire with fire. I am worried that if the police use plastic bullets, people who have got guns within the community will start using them.

Year after year, people have watched the use of plastic bullets against brothers and sisters in Africa, and they know exactly the type of damage they can do. What I fear is that the introduction of these weapons into Handsworth will inflame the situation.

2. If the Chief Constable decides to use plastic bullets, there will be total panic, chaos and then a form of retaliation. People are not going to stand by and be shot at, they will actually fight back. The moment you bring in plastic bullets or any other sort of heavy weaponry, they will see it declared as a war zone. The police will be declaring war against the community. I don't see that as deterring riots, it will increase them alarmingly. If somebody shoots at you, you are going to shoot back.

3. If they resort to plastic bullets, the next step will be hit squads that will hit out at the police. The police are put there as a front for the government. But people can't go and stone Margaret Thatcher's house. The police are going to be there in front of it, so they become the obvious target. The fight is not really with the police, it is with the government. But the police become the jam in the sandwich.

4. Bullet will be met with bullet.

5. I spent nine years in the British Army, and had specialist training up to a high level using firearms and plastic bullets. I was trained to oppress people but in the long run they did not sit down and take it, they fought back. People would regroup, learn new strategies and come back the following day. I think people in this community will do that too.

Those uttering these warnings believe that they would be powerless, in a real confrontation, to stop them becoming reality. The tide of anger and frustration would run so strongly against the police that not even the most respected community leaders could turn it.

From the police side, the dangers look surprisingly similar. Those responsible for policing inner city areas sometimes privately express their nightmares in terms which are hardly distinguishable from those above. They know only too well the potency of the apartheid image of white police officers facing a mainly black crowd. They fear that it could become even more potent if they were to adopt a repressive, technological approach to unrest in Handsworth, Brixton, Tottenham or Toxteth.

The officer who developed Handsworth's show-piece community policing scheme in the seventies, Superintendent David Webb, has now left the force after a series of internal disputes, and runs a sportswear business in the same area. His differences with former colleagues reached a peak with the decision to buy plastic bullets for riot control. He knew from intelligence sources when he ran the divisional police station that there were many licensed gun holders in Handsworth and a large number of unlicensed weapons as well. He also knew of the existence of stocks of hand grenades:

We know that all those weapons are down there. The moment the police start using plastic bullets, it is my fear that those weapons will come out onto the streets. The police will find themselves in very serious trouble and people will be killed.

Ex-Superintendent Webb's fear is compounded by his informed guess as to what would happen next. He believes that a combination of guns and hand grenades could force the police into a tactical withdrawal, but only for a short time. They would come back with live firearms of their own, to reply to the shooting from the crowd.

The Chief Constable of the West Midlands agrees with him. He calls the possibility of armed retaliation from rioters 'a very serious risk that has to be taken into account'. He knows that there are people in Handsworth who already compare their lot with that of blacks living under apartheid, and though he might disagree with their analysis, he accepts their conviction:

They will no doubt go on to argue that they should respond in the same way as blacks in South Africa, and that is obviously one of the risks that I

have to take into the equation when deciding whether to use plastic
bullets on the night.

What concerns him most is the unpredictability of the next few
days. He has little doubt that the police would be able to win the
immediate battle, by virtue of superior weaponry and training. 'I
don't think there is a great army waiting to come into action if we
use plastic bullets.' But he is less confident about the following
days. He can make no useful estimate of the strength of response
the police would encounter once their opponents had regrouped
and drawn on their own reserves of firepower. There would be a
real possibility that the police could be outclassed within a day of
their initial shot: 'We could win the first round in a pyrrhic victory,
and the next night be losing.'

Another risk is that retaliation could take a less organized form,
with sporadic sniper attacks on police officers returning to the
beat after the disorder. It is a common concern among police
officers of all ranks that they should not be expected to perform
riot duty in their normal beat area, partly for fear of personal
retaliation. But there is a more general danger that uniformed
officers could be attacked just for being policemen if local feeling
ran high after a pitched battle. The Chief Constable has little
reassurance to offer them:

What happens when they go back the next day is debatable. A lot of
people would probably welcome them with open arms for restoring
order. But there would equally be a number, one hopes a minority, who
would be deeply displeased that they had lost and the police had won.
The response from them could be anything. It could be glowering
hostility, passive acceptance or active physical opposition of all sorts.

The significance of this last sentence lies in its acknowledgement
that police officers returning to normal duties after a battle could
find themselves targets for lethal attack. If this were to come about
in fact, the potential would exist for indefinite periods of militarization in certain places. For which Chief Constable would dare to
send his men and women out undefended against the threat of
sniper fire?

It is a relatively simple matter to train police officers to act like soldiers, as ACPO has demonstrated in the eighties. It takes considerable reserves of public expenditure and the support of the Home Office, but given these political clearances the process has proved straightforward. It is also comparatively easy to escalate police response to disorder into the paramilitary realm. But how easy will it be to go back again? Once the battle-lines have been drawn and the first shots fired, how will the mechanism of de-escalation operate? The *Public Order Manual* gives clear instructions on each shift up the gears of increasing force, but then offers only an outline of how to put the machinery into reverse. ACPO has thus provided a detailed blueprint for turning policemen into soldiers, with relatively little guidance on how to turn them back into policemen.

The effect on public opinion is equally unpredictable. If the battle goes well for the police, with victory on the night and little violence afterwards, then senior officers may well prove right in their assumption that the public will applaud their success. It is, though, worth recalling the consistent finding of opinion surveys over many years, that people in Britain like their police officers unarmed and in ordinary uniform and that they oppose the use of plastic bullets and CS gas in cities on the mainland. The only additional weapon the public says it wants deployed against rioters is the very one the police force rejects – the water cannon. Lord Knights, the former West Midlands Chief Constable Sir Philip Knights, argued for restraint shortly after his retirement in 1985:

I never felt during my period as Chief Constable that there was any necessity to stockpile weapons of that kind. We have had CS gas to deal with armed, besieged criminals but not for use on the streets, and neither have I ever felt that plastic bullets were necessary. If we ever reach that stage then we have got to recognize that we have lost the support of the community in maintaining the law. If I said I needed plastic bullets as a last line of defence, it would have been as good as saying that I did not trust the public.

What the public would make of a police attack which went wrong, leading to increased levels of violence and the possibility of armed hostilities, is quite another matter. Some ACPO members believe that public confidence in the police could be damaged almost beyond repair by such a misjudgement. The stakes have been raised very high for a Chief Constable contemplating the use of these weapons.

Former Superintendent David Webb of Handsworth spent years building a relationship with leaders of each ethnic group in his division, in an early experiment with community policing which attracted national attention during the seventies. He found it an uphill struggle against deep-seated suspicion of police, often bordering on outright opposition. In spite of these odds, the scheme could boast some success. David Webb today maintains that the contacts he built would stand little, if any, chance of surviving a street battle in which police fired plastic bullets – whatever its immediate outcome:

The worst casualty is going to be the relationship between the police and the public as a result of firing these plastic rounds. There will be a very serious breakdown and long-term the traditional relationship would be finished. It is already seriously harmed in the inner city and if the police start firing plastic bullets, it will be gone forever.

You cannot go down into an area to do community police work, trying to solve the local problems, if the day before you and your colleagues have been firing plastic baton rounds at the community. The worst thing is that a lot of senior police officers know this is the case and the ordinary policeman on the beat is being railroaded into a sort of policing he doesn't want. It is insidiously creeping into the police force.

Superintendent Webb claims that his network of 'community intervenors' went to work so effectively in 1981 that Handsworth escaped the possibility of a riot when other inner cities were suffering theirs. The Chief Constable at the time, Sir Philip Knights, has confirmed this view: 'We had considerable support from the community in dealing with their young people and getting them off the streets. That is much more important than driving them off with plastic bullets.'

The approach is modelled on successful ventures in some cities of the United States in the late sixties. In Atlanta, Georgia, for example, rioting was narrowly avoided in 1967 by the Mayor's timely action in calling community leaders to his office, including 'Daddy King', Martin Luther King Senior, and persuading them to go to the ghetto with police loudhailers and call for residents to remain calm. Their appeals were heeded and Atlanta saw relatively little violence that summer, in spite of the presence of Stokeley Carmichael and H 'Rap' Brown, the black militants, and the existence of the largest Ku Klux Klan membership in the country.

It is, of course, romantic to think that traditional British policing follows the Dock Green model of helping elderly ladies across the street and offering avuncular cheer to passers-by. Even elderly ladies, after all, sometimes get arrested. For police officers, there has always been a forceful side to the job, whether in the kicks, elbows and legendary clips round the ears for miscreants or in the plain brutality used in the thirties against hunger marches and demonstrations of unemployed workers. What worries some in ACPO today is that public tolerance of this violence is dependent on the image people have of the police. They may accept the odd disciplinary cuff from a policeman they see as one of their own – like an older brother, perhaps, or a strict uncle. Yet they can balk at the mere presence of the same officer dressed up like a member of the SAS. The *Public Order Manual*'s constant attention to the image of police officers reflects this. Its authors recognize that by ordering changes in the way officers look, such as dressing them in riot gear, and in the way they behave, ACPO could change the way people regard the police as a whole.

If the police come to appear generally intimidating or repressive in the eyes of ordinary citizens, they may find it harder to win public consent to their authority. The public may also withdraw co-operation from all manner of police actions. The scale of difficulty this would present to the force is unlimited. Those few parts of Britain which are already very hard to police, the inner cities, tend to be the areas where public consent and co-operation are already lowest. If such attitudes were to become common in towns and cities throughout the country, the task of policing would begin to outstrip the labours of Hercules. In this respect, ACPO's paramilitary policy already has an unsettling effect without a shot being fired. At Orgreave, Wapping, Stonehenge,

Tottenham, Brixton and Handsworth, the public face of the
police altered radically, with unknowable repercussions in the
long term on public attitudes.

PC 2000 – a split personality

Paramilitary policing has brought a sense of confusion to the
training of police recruits. Before 1981, training was a clear
enough process involving several months of rote-learning,
memorizing long passages of Acts Of Parliament, interspersed
with character-building bouts of physical exercise and drill. Once
it was over, the real business of education could begin on the beat
and in the panda car with older officers. Lord Scarman's report
on the Brixton riots came as a body-blow to this arrangement,
criticizing its effects in, for example, 'the ill-considered, imma-
ture and racially prejudiced actions of some officers in their
dealings on the streets with young black people'. The Metropolitan Police began a revision of training at Hendon, designed to
sweep away concentration on detailed knowledge of statutes in
favour of developing personal skills the job requires of its
constables. They must be fit and well-disciplined, so the gym-
nasium and the parade-ground have held their places in the
curriculum. But they must also be attentive, sympathetic and calm
in circumstances of great stress, so new classes were introduced
on the skills of communication, personal development and stress
management. They are taught the techniques of self-understand-
ing and quiet assertiveness. Most significantly, the Met realized
that Lord Scarman's criticism was directed at widespread behaviour which had been picked up from police colleagues rather than
learned in the training school. Its hallmarks were a macho stance
coupled with arrogant displays of racism and sexism. Since 1981,
Hendon has tackled this 'canteen culture' directly. Almost half
the Met's serving officers have been trained in the new style,
known as 'policing skills'. The officer commanding Hendon,
Deputy Assistant Commissioner Alan Young, summarizes the
approach in three slogans: 'Macho is out, sexism is out, racism is
out!' He calls those trained in this way 'the disciples', as if he were

controlling a Jesuit seminary which scatters its flock far and wide among the unconverted. Other police forces have begun to follow similar lines themselves, and a steady influence from Hendon may continue to spread as officers leave London in their hundreds for promotion and cheaper housing in provincial forces.

It would be easy to present this initiative as the same old meat with a gravy of psycho-jargon. But a visit to Hendon today makes a deep impression. Wander down one of the corridors in the Peel Centre and you come first upon a class learning how to take statements. Next door is a lesson on making arrests. Nothing suprising so far. Then notice the lesson called 'aggression and emotion', which teaches the tactic of responding to anger with soft words (an option which is not included in the *Public Order Manual*). The recruits are busy role-playing a confrontation, and discovering how very difficult it can be to continue shouting at somebody who insists on speaking quietly and listens to what they say. The instructor, whose personal manner would do credit to St Francis of Assisi, then gives them a little lecture on body language. The gist of it is that if they storm about shouting and throwing their weight around, they will merely serve to raise the emotional temperature of an encounter and waste their most precious resources – time and energy. The trick, he tells them, is to recognize their own responses (as in the 'Self-awareness' classes) and to gain mastery of a situation by lowering their voices.

Back in the corridor, you check that this *is* the police training school and you have not strayed into a convention of Californian therapists. The next room is being used for an exercise simulating a marital dispute revolving around a large and disobedient dog. The police recruit has to find out who has done what, while fending off menaces from all three parties. The instructor has split the rest of the class into six groups for specialist observation:

'Right then Group A, what were you asked to look at?'
'Law and procedure, sergeant.'
'Group B?'
'Empathy skills, sergeant.'
'Group C?'
'Eye-contact and body posture, sergeant.'

Next along the corridor is the class on 'Stress management', with a discussion about the incidence of suicide, alcoholism, divorce and wife-beating among police families. The recruits are asked to suggest reasons for this unhappy trend. They talk vaguely about pressures of the job and long hours. The instructor leads them in deeper, asking them to explain the reluctance of many officers to admit the stresses of their work. They suggest fear of being thought weak, the difficulty of coming to terms with anxiety and failure. He takes them on to the 'empty macho image-building of the John Wayne syndrome' which denies officers the chance to face their own emotions with honesty. The lesson is over and as the recruits leave the room they speculate on how they will fare in their first posting at a real police station. The general conclusion is that older officers will probably regard them as cissies.

The next class is sitting through a frontal assault on 'Racism' as a social evil. Their instructor presents the hard facts of racial attacks and shows them a letterbox with a locking device on the inside. He explains that tens of thousands have been sold to Asian families in London, to protect them from filth being pushed through their front door, or rags soaked in petrol. Ten years ago, he says, when he was a police recruit at Hendon, the force simply refused to recognize the existence of racist attitudes among its own officers. Today that has changed. The Met, he continues, is predominantly a white male organization socialized during the fifties and sixties and carrying the ineradicable marks of British racism. There is little that the recruits, or the force as a whole, can do about these prejudices. But the police establishment will insist that their behaviour be non-racist. They must at all times remember their obligation to protect the weak and vulnerable. In tomorrow's lesson, they will examine ways of countering expressions of racist sentiment from their fellow officers when they leave the training school. At this point, you probably decide to skip the next classroom where a lesson is in progress on the danger of stereotyping, on the ground that your own preconceptions have already been so shaken that you feel you have got the point. But there is more. The knockout punch is waiting round the corner in a double classroom labelled 'Starpower'.

Just before they finish their twenty weeks training, recruits at Hendon spend a morning playing a team game. They are divided into three groups and given coloured counters to trade with. As the game goes on they realize that it has been rigged to favour one group at the expense of the others. The result is that trading serves to increase the wealth of the richest group, while the middle group struggles to hold its ground, and the poorest just keeps on losing. The top team naturally becomes more and more cocky, while the bottom team starts to sulk. Then the WPC instructor who is invigilating the game cheerfully announces that it is based on the operations of capitalist society and awards the top group a special privilege: they may rewrite the rules of trade in any way they wish. They seize their advantage with vigour, and set out a draconian code which guarantees that all wealth will flow to them. Just in case, they invent a rule which says that they can make up new rules at any time. They establish a 'sin bin' for offenders and appoint a few members of the other groups as policemen and gaolers. Then the game resumes for a few moments, but those in the lowest group refuse to play and make a gesture of defiance by putting all their counters in a heap and piling their hands on top of it. A prison is built around them by the appointed officers to prevent further acts of disruption. Meanwhile, the middle group players discover that their only means of advancement is by cheating, and are hauled off one by one to the 'sin bin'. The whole thing ends in an angry stalemate.

Then the instructor asks them to draw conclusions from it, particularly concerning the nature of policing. They begin to talk about the unfairness of the rules of trade and the problem of enforcing them. They observe the equivocal position of police officers who are drawn from the lower groups to serve the interests of the rich and given inducements and social status as a reward.

After they have left for lunch, the instructor lists the lessons she wants them to remember from the game:

1. Social rules must be fair. It is difficult to police unfair or unacceptable rules.
2. The police are usually seen as outsiders by all three social groups.
3. The police often appear to be working on behalf of the rich, who give them power.

She rounds off her summary with a crisp defence of the game's assumption of a class analysis of British society:

We live in a society which is not classless and we are training recruits for the real world, not for a make-believe world which we would all like to see. The game reflects what society is and that is what we must train them for.

Since Lord Scarman's report in 1981, more than 8000 recruits have passed through Hendon and received the new style of policing skills training. An additional 2000 experienced officers in police stations have also had an abbreviated version of the course. Those in charge of the programme talk about the Met as a long ship to turn round and confidently claim that the sheer weight of the force is now beginning to work for them as these 10,000 officers make their presence felt out in divisional stations. The Deputy Assistant Commissioner explains his policy of sending 'disciples' out in batches, so that they will be better prepared to face the unreconstructed attitudes they may meet on the beat and in the canteen.

A day or two at Hendon leaves little doubt that the training wing of the Metropolitan Police has responded to Lord Scarman's critique with considerable imagination. But this is where confusion arises. For training is not confined to Hendon. There is also the public order training ground at Hounslow, an enormous film set which serves as a purpose-built battleground known as 'Riot City'. It is rather like a remote RAF base with Kenneth More in command. Each day, hundreds of recruits and older officers alike are put through their paces in full riot gear, learning the long shield manoeuvres of Section 18 of the tactical options. They run up and down the mock streets in formation, storm into buildings under a hail of bricks and flush out their assailants, then take prisoners and move forward to gain new ground. Bound tightly like a rugby scrum behind their shields, under attack from real petrol bombs, they learn about team spirit and acting as a unit, in an atmosphere which is the very distillation of machismo. They then all go to the canteen for curried chicken and the conversation is high with the exhilaration of adrenalin. They go off together for a communal shower, then down a few pints before bedtime.

The instructors at Hounslow are action men. Slim, muscular figures in their late twenties or early thirties, with short-cropped hair. Several of them have military backgrounds, including service in the SAS. Among them are the specialist gunners trained to fire plastic bullets and CS gas, who were waiting in the background at Broadwater Farm in 1985 and during the Notting Hill carnival in 1987. The psychological distance between riot training at Hounslow and policing skills training at Hendon seems so wide as to be unbridgeable. Even the Deputy Assistant Commissioner has to confess that his slogan 'Macho is out' does not apply at Hounslow: 'There comes a time when macho must definitely be "in".'

How the teenage recruit is supposed to make sense of this contradiction is never explained. For most of their training they are taught to be sensitive, unthreatening individuals with a finely developed faculty for initiative. Then they are bussed out to Hounslow to run about shouting and bundling people out of buildings. The switch between the two involves a comprehensive change of identity. It is, as the former Hong Kong Police Commissioner Roy Henry said, 'a complete volte-face'. Public order policing is as the ACPO manual says, in direct contrast to normal policing. The study notes distributed to recruits at Hendon make the difference clear:

PUBLIC ORDER DEPLOYMENT
(Deployment means 'a spreading out of the troops')
Most of your police duty will be a matter of doing your job as an individual. You will work your beat as you decide (within limits). If you see an offence, you will identify it, review the powers you have and act as you think the situation demands.

However, when you are deployed as a part of a large-scale police operation for public order purposes, your function changes. You will then be acting as a member of a team led by a supervising officer. You will

depend on him for decisions and he will depend on you to be where he
expects and to carry out his orders as well as you can.

This is an almost exact restatement of a distinction made in 1908,
in the report of the Royal Commission on the duties of the
Metropolitan Police, which stressed that the responsibility for
police work must rest on the individual constable not his superior
officers. The report contrasted the position of police officers with
that of soldiers:

Broadly speaking, the force acts by, and through, individual constables.
An army, for the most part, does its work through groups of its units,
through divisions, brigades, regiments and companies, and the responsibility of a private soldier is, in practice, reduced to such a point that he
becomes little more than an automatic part of a machine.
    . . . The position of a constable in a police force differs greatly from
that of the private soldier. A constable is, as a general rule, placed alone
to perform his duty on one or more beats or patrols.
    . . . It follows that a great deal of the most difficult work of the force is
left to the initiative and capacity of the humblest unit in each division.

Eighty years on, the distinction between constables and soldiers
has been so blurred that some officers complain of the stress
induced by switching between their two roles. In the canteen at
Hounslow, two experienced men, one a sergeant, the other a
constable, reflect on their own experience:

I don't find this exciting, I find it a little worrying. I wouldn't like to say
how I would react to policing a public order situation in the area where I
work and then going back to work in the same place.

I might finish dealing with a public order incident at ten o'clock at night
and at six o'clock the next morning be walking the beat again. You have to
change as quickly as that and behave as if nothing's happened. But what
you feel inside is something different and a lot of the time I am very
confused.

The officer commanding training at Hounslow on the streets of
'Riot City', Chief Superintendent George Crawford, has felt this
tension himself. When he joined the police as a young man he
wanted to concentrate on community policing. But he now finds
himself not only training officers in imaginary scenes of public

disorder, but also leading them into real-life confrontations. He was in command of the shield units and baton gunners brought into Notting Hill during the 1987 carnival. Once the battle was over, he faced the task of returning them to normal duties:

It is a stress problem and when you bring them off the streets you have got to be careful. Divisional management has to watch officers for a couple of days after a disorder to ensure that they have found the level of policing that we require for normal circumstances in this country. It is no different from a rugby match in that you have got to bring them off the high again. It is certainly a difficulty.

The Metropolitan Commissioner, Peter Imbert, says that this dual role means that police officers now have a duty to be chameleon-like even 'schizophrenic'. The problem for recruits is how to reconcile these conflicting police personalities when they leave Hendon behind. One WPC, about to take up her first posting at Hornsey, said she found it very difficult to bring two contradictory types of policing together. Policing skills were designed for everyday occurrences, while the riot training at Hounslow represents force met with force. She had no idea how the two could live side by side and had received no guidance during her basic training: 'I can only hope that this will come along. It is something I will have to find within myself.' As the Parliamentary Advisor to the Police Federation, Sir Eldon Griffiths MP, wrote in *Police* magazine: 'Many police officers are getting confused over the job they are supposed to be doing. Are they law enforcement officers, social workers or poor bloody infantrymen?'

Senior officers at Hendon express anxiety that this confusion is affecting the whole force, leaving its future direction in doubt. They have problems enough, they say, trying to make policing skills effective in practice without having to contend with a powerful internal group of paramilitary officers pulling the opposite way. They speak of two schools of thought in competition with one another: the liberal, tolerant approach against the force of confrontation. What worries them is that while their style may hold sway at Hendon, the paramilitary could come to dominate everywhere else. They already see officers creamed off into the public order elite and the special squad for protecting royalty and diplomats, and they fear further drift in this direction.

Peter Imbert said in a *File On 4* interview in September 1987 that his policy as Commissioner would favour the policing skills style:

> I do not see a place for paramilitarism in the police service. The emphasis is on relating to the community and making it a much better place for all of us to live in. Indeed, the emphasis I plan for the future is on reducing the appearance of paramilitarism. The less of it the better.

Those in Hendon hope that he is right, and that London's police will depend in future on the skills of eye contact and empathy rather than plastic bullets and CS gas. But they cannot be confident that this will happen. Some of the current 'top boys' in paramilitary units are, after all, making their way up the ranks and could soon bring a shift of emphasis in the force management. One of them may, before long, become Commissioner.

The idea of taking public order duties away from the police and giving them to a new force as a special assignment is attractive to many Metropolitan officers as a way out of the confusion of roles they suffer at present. It is also promoted by officers from other city forces within ACPO. But there are strong arguments against it. Peter Imbert, for instance, argues that public disorder is so rare in Britain that a third force of this kind would be looking for something to do most of the time. It would also, he fears, lack any rapport with the community. Others in ACPO maintain that their anxiety about 'the ratchet effect', in which public violence and police repression both escalate in response to one another, would only be heightened by the formation of a specialist riot control force. They point to experience in Paris, where the mere presence of the CRS can act as provocation to a crowd.

The prospects for political action to reverse the paramilitary trend of policing seem remote. If any of the opposition parties get into government, they will face a police force which has some years of dependence on the tactical options behind it. Could any Labour or Democrat Home Secretary stand up to pressure from ACPO to leave matters as they stand? It would be a considerable risk to outlaw, for example, plastic bullets. The Home Secretary would be open to the accusation after any future riot that violence could have been contained by the police if only the government had not tied their hands. This would be a powerful charge to answer, especially if it were made by the Chief Constable concerned.

As for the Conservative Party, the possibility of putting a brake on the police was ruled out by Margaret Thatcher in 1985: 'If the police need more men, more equipment, different equipment, they shall have them.' So the future direction of policing in Britain seems to be left in the hands of the police themselves, commanded by the members of ACPO.

When police recruits finish their basic training at Hendon they are given a book of principles for professional behaviour, to guide them in their office of constable. It is commonly called 'the little blue book'. Among its more philosophical passages is a quotation from a bygone era, the mid-seventies, when Sir Robert Mark spoke as Metropolitan Commissioner:

The police function to which you and I are dedicated is perhaps the most worthwhile and most noble function in any free society. For you and I have this in common, that we represent government by consent.

If the drift of policing throughout the eighties goes on unchecked for a further decade, which form of government will Britain's police represent by the start of the next century?

Appendix A

Part 1: Government statement on rioting in Bristol, House of Commons, Wednesday 6 August 1980

Mr William Whitelaw: The review, which I announced in my statement of 28 April on the disturbances at Bristol [Cols. 971–972], has now been completed. In accordance with the undertaking I gave to publish the results, I have placed in the Library of the House a memorandum setting out the broad conclusions which have been reached following consultations with chief officers of police, the police staff associations and representatives of police authorities.

The review has concluded that it would be desirable neither in principle nor in practice to depart from the present broad approach adopted by the police for dealing with disorder. The successful maintenance of public order depends on the consent of those policed. The primary object of the police will continue to be to prevent and defuse disorder through maintaining and developing the close liaison between the police and the local community. At the same time, the public have a clear right to expect police arrangements to be effective if, nevertheless, disorder occurs. Much has been done in recent years to ensure that arrangements are effective but the review has suggested a number of practical ways in which those arrangements could be improved. These include measures which will help to ensure that an appropriate number of officers can be deployed swiftly to any incident, with mutual aid between neighbouring forces where necessary, and that these officers are adequately equipped and trained.

My officials and HM Chief Inspector of Constabulary will, with chief officers of police and others concerned, proceed urgently with the further work that will be necessary to implement the conclusions of the review. I am confident that these provide a sound basis on which the police will be able to carry out their duty to maintain order in a way which will continue to be acceptable to the great majority of people in this country.

Part 2: Review of arrangements for handling spontaneous disorder – Memorandum by the Home Department

Introduction

1. In his statement to the House of Commons on 28 April 1980 on the disturbances at Bristol earlier that month, the Home Secretary announced that he was asking his officials and Her Majesty's Chief Inspector of Constabulary, in conjunction with the Commissioner of Police of the Metropolis and the Association of Chief Police Officers in England and Wales, to examine thoroughly and urgently the arrangements for handling spontaneous public disorder. He undertook to publish the results of the review.

2. The review has now been completed. In the course of it, the Home Office has also consulted the Police Superintendents' Association of England and Wales, the Police Federation, the Association of County Councils and the Association of Metropolitan Authorities. This paper outlines the conclusions reached.

The basis of public order policing

3. The traditional belief that the police must have the consent of the community to do their job underpins the approach to handling disorder, as it does other aspects of police work. That is why the police in Britain have not, hitherto, adopted aggressive riot equipment, such as tear gas or water cannon, to handle disorder. Instead their approach has been to deploy relatively large numbers of officers in ordinary uniform, usually in the passive containment of a crowd. Where force has been used to restore order, this has been on the principle, which the law recognizes, that it should be the minimum which a reasonable man would judge necessary in all the circumstances.

4. Policing by consent and the principle of minimum force reflect not only a fundamental, humanitarian belief, but sound common sense. The effective preservation of order depends in the long term on the consent of the community. While the use of sophisticated riot equipment might be effective in quelling disorder in certain circumstances, it could also lead to the long term alienation of the public from the police. This in turn would make the task of the police in other areas of their work more difficult, quite apart from being undesirable in principle. Similar considerations would apply to the development of paramilitary riot squads within police forces or a paramilitary national reserve force. The police service itself would not welcome any developments along these lines.

5. At the same time, the police service must be able to keep order efficiently. The police have a duty to try to prevent criminal behaviour whatever its context. Present arrangements for maintaining order have to

be made as effective as possible, within our broad police approach. Much has been achieved in recent years and the police are generally well able to maintain order where an event is known of in advance. But there is scope for improving arrangements to cope with disorder which breaks out suddenly.

Policing methods

6. The practical consequence of this basic approach is that the policing of public order in Britain depends on the availability of sizeable numbers of police, and the public order duties of a police force are one of the matters which are taken into account when its establishment is assessed. But forces must be in a position to deploy speedily an effective number of officers to an area when disorder occurs.

7. It might be argued that we should meet this need for rapid deployment, as some other countries have, by creating a mobile reserve of police on a national basis which could be called to any part of the country. But to do so would cut across the local basis of our policing arrangements and risk jeopardizing the relationship between police and public. There would also be problems in finding routine occupation for such a reserve body, and it would be a costly step. The review has therefore concluded that each force should develop suitable arrangements to enable it to respond speedily and effectively to disorder in its area, taking account both of its own resources and of those of neighbouring forces.

Speed of response

8. The key to these arrangements is the rapid assembly of an adequate number of officers in a short time at the place where they are needed. This may mean calling on officers from a number of sources: from patrol officers on duty; from a force support group or task force (where these exist); from officers in other divisions trained in public order duties whether on or off duty; from further partial or even total call-out of the force; and from other forces under mutual aid arrangements. The circumstances of each force vary so much that it would not be sensible to lay down a single and comprehensive national scheme for response plans. Each force will therefore be re-examining its own arrangements, setting up for this purpose a logistics planning team to ensure that a clearly defined command structure and operational plan can be put into effect speedily and efficiently to deal with an incident.

9. The immediate response to disorder is crucial. It will not necessarily always be appropriate to commit a large number of officers at the scene of disorder: it will be for the senior officer on the spot to judge what is the most sensible response to the particular circumstances. But to ensure that the police commander has an effective number of trained officers

readily available to him, chief officers will set a minimum target for the number on which they can call immediately to deal with sudden disorder. This immediate response might be provided from members of force support groups or task forces or from individually assembled officers. Each chief officer will wish to decide what is most appropriate for his force. The setting up of a force support group where one does not exist at present is a matter for judgment in the light of the normal policing commitments of the force. Chief officers will be examining the case for such a group in reviewing their force's response plans.

10. However the immediate response is provided, all the officers concerned will need to be organized to handle public disorder effectively. The most flexible structure will be units of one sergeant and ten constables.

11. In certain circumstances, it will be necessary for the immediate response to disorder to be further augmented with great speed, either from within the force or by mutual aid. Again, the circumstances of each force will vary and each force will set a target figure for the size of this secondary response. Further consideration will be given by chief officers collectively as to whether central guidance to forces on alert and call-out procedures can be formulated.

Mutual aid

12. The system of mutual aid, under which each chief officer is able to call in case of need on other forces to provide him with aid, has worked well, particularly where an event can be planned for in advance.

13. Effective mutual aid arrangements are as essential in coping with spontaneous disorder as with pre-planned events, and they will be an integral part of the development of forces' response plans and chief officers will consider invoking mutual aid at an early stage in an incident.

14. Each force needs to know the speed with which, and the extent to which, additional trained men can be made available by other forces. Arrangements for providing mutual aid will be reviewed by chief officers of police, in conjunction as necessary with the Home Office, to ensure that they enable a swift and flexible response to be made to disorder.

Transport and communications

15. If trained police officers are to be deployed swiftly to handle disorder, suitable vehicles and communications must be available. This is particularly important in the case of mutual aid. There may well be scope for improvement in existing arrangements here. How best these can be improved will be studied urgently by chief officers of police and the Home Office. Communications procedures as well as equipment will be examined.

Protective equipment

16. Police forces have responded to the rising incidence of violence at demonstrations in recent years by introducing a limited amount of personal protective equipment for police officers, chiefly shields and a stronger version of the traditional helmet. This is a step the police have taken with reluctance. However chief officers, and indeed the community as a whole, have a duty to ensure that police officers are adequately protected during disorderly incidents.

17. At the same time, any development which would tend to alter the traditional appearance of the British police officer and distance the police from the public is to be avoided. The Association of Chief Police Officers is conducting a review of protective equipment, in consultation with the Police Superintendents' Association and the Police Federation and with assistance from the Police Scientific Development Branch of the Home Office. That review will consider how best officers can be protected without radically altering the image of the British police.

Training

18. Police officers at present receive training in the public order aspects of their duties, but the nature and extent of this varies. All officers need adequate training in crowd control, including training in the use of protective shields.

19. Every officer should receive similar basic public order training. This should include instruction in the psychology and problems of crowd behaviour, and the community relations aspects of public order policing. Additional training will need to be given to officers who may particularly be called on to police disorder or to supervise others during incidents. Further consideration will be given to the nature of this training and how it can best be provided.

20. In addition to formal training, forces will be arranging regular exercises to test response plans. There will be emphasis on the dissemination among forces of information about tactical planning and the handling of particular incidents, and on the regular analysis of the lessons of incidents.

[There is no para. 21.]

Public and community relations

22. This memorandum has already emphasized that the successful maintenance of public order depends on the consent of those policed. Against that background, the effort put into establishing contact, trust and respect between the police and all sections of the community is a central consideration.

23. This review has been concerned with the handling of spontaneous disorder, and with the response to such disorder rather than how it might

be prevented. But being able to respond swiftly and effectively to disorder is only part of the police approach to disorder: the primary objective must remain prevention, in its widest sense. In this context, it is the day-to-day work of careful and close community liaison by specialist officers and by those on the beat which can minimize future problems. The establishment of effective links with the organizers of protest events and with local community groups and leaders, is particularly important in this context. Where disorder does break out, the involvement of local officers in handling it can be important in helping to minimize any damage to community relations. Good relations with the press and other media can also help to prevent disorder and defuse tension. Chief officers will keep under close review the effectiveness of their arrangements in each of these respects.

24. The main object of public order policing will continue to be to prevent and defuse disorder and to maintain good relations with all sections of the community. Providing they are set firmly in that context, the conclusions reached in this review should enable the police to deal firmly with public disorder without incurring the penalties of fundamentally changing the concept and therefore the acceptability of the police service in this country.

Home Office,
Queen Anne's Gate
6 August 1980

Appendix B

The Public Order Forward Planning Unit

The Public Order Forward Planning Unit is a national unit staffed by officers from a number of different forces, answerable to the ACPO Sub-Committee on Public Order, and is formed thus:

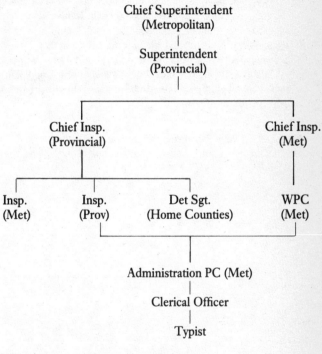

The Unit has national responsibility for:

1. Discovery } methods } for dealing with a breakdown in
   Research   } public disorder.
   Evaluation } equipment }

2. Maintenance and amendments to the Public Order and Tactical Options Manual.

3. Circulating information and suggestions regarding new developments on behalf of the ACPO Public Order Sub-Committee.
4. Production and upkeep of a Public Order Equipment Manual.

   The Unit is based at New Scotland Yard and for day-to-day administration purposes it operates as part of the A8 Branch of the Metropolitan Police. Contact can be made by telephoning (number).

Force Forward Planning Unit Liaison Officer

The Forward Planning Unit will act as a reference point in relation to public order research matters and Chief Officers have been advised to consult the Unit when contemplating any investigation or evaluation of new proposals or equipment connected with the maintenance of public order. In this way unnecessary duplication of effort may be avoided by referring one Force to another which has already considered a proposal, *or*

by giving reasons why such a proposal has already been rejected.

To assist in this respect every Force in the UK has appointed a Force Public Order Liaison Officer, through whom you should direct your inquiries. However, in an emergency or when your Liaison Officer is not available, direct contact may be made.

REMEMBER

In order for the Public Order Forward Planning Unit to function properly it needs to receive and disseminate new ideas, concepts and items of equipment, for the benefit of the police service as a whole.

Appendix c

Extracts from the ACPO *Public Order Manual*

The following extracts were placed in the House of Commons library after being read into court during the Orgreave 'riot' trials:

Long Shields

1. *Introduction*

Long shields have been successfully used since 1977 in England and Wales to protect police officers in public order situations from attack by missiles. Having initially been regarded in some quarters as being an over-reactive and aggressive tactic, the deployment of long shields is now generally acknowledged by the public as being the norm when the disorder has reached unacceptable levels. All forces now possess long shields and train officers in their use.

2. *Objectives*

When shields are deployed they tend to be regarded as provocative and encourage and attract missiles. Understandably, commanders generally deploy shield protected officers only when missiles have already been thrown and then to achieve one or more of the following objectives:

(a) To demonstrate to the crowd a strong presence of protected officers and thereby discourage riotous behaviour;
(b) To provide protection for deployed police lines under attack;
(c) To confine rioters to a defined area;
(d) To enable the police line to advance and gain ground;
(e) To disperse and arrest a hostile crowd;
(f) To enter buildings used by rioters as a refuge;
(g) To recover injured persons.

3. *Formations*
(a) *The Shield Serial or PSU*
The shield serial or PSU comprises one inspector, two sergeants and twenty constables.
(b) *Shield serial*
The shield 'serial' is a formation used by the Metropolitan Police. The serial is formed into *three* 'five man shield units', with a sergeant and six

constables forming a reserve/arrest team. The second sergeant is a member of the centre 'shield unit' and the inspector (with a short shield) is in command. The centre shield man on each unit is the team leader. It is advisable that at least 2 serials work in conjunction. This formation has the advantage of a built in arrest team of a sergeant and six constables (in addition to the six 'link men' from the shield units) and these men are also readily available to replace injured shield carriers.

(c) *Shield-protected PSU*

The shield-protected PSU is divided into two 'sections' each of one sergeant and ten constables. The 'sections' are further divided into sub-sections of five constables each with a team leader. This formation has the advantage of providing *four* shield teams instead of three, but it has no reserve capacity.

(d) *The Long Shield Sub-Section or Unit (Metropolitan)*

The basic sub-section or unit comprises five members: three shield carriers and two link men. The three shield carriers are the front line and they link shields by the two outer shields interlocking behind the centre shield. The centre shield is pulled back and the outer shields pushed forward to maintain a locking seal. The two link men form a 'rugby-type scrum' behind the shields and knit the team together. This is a strong disciplined team with link men able to act as arresting officers. It does, however, tend to be slow moving and restricted in manoeuvrability.

4. *Deleted from the copies.*

5. *Tactical manoeuvres*

(a) A number of existing tactical manoeuvres are set out below designed to achieve the above stated objectives.

(b) The manoeuvres have been grouped according to the required objective.

(c) The manoeuvres stated can by no means be regarded as the only ones that exist, but they form the basis of others which can and have been developed to suit the local needs of forces according to manpower, equipment and other resources available. This is to be encouraged but it should always be remembered that the simplest tactics are often the most effective and need only minimum training and instructions.

6. *Group One – display of strength*

To provide protection for police officers. They are also an indication to a hostile crowd that police intend to enforce the law and have the potential to carry out that objective. In certain circumstances, the mere display of shields will be an indication to the less aggressive members of the crowd that it is time to disperse before the violence escalates.

7. *Manoeuvre 1*
(a) *Brief description* – show of force
(b) *Detailed description*

To use the 'show of force' to the greatest advantage, officers should make a formidable appearance. Officers should assemble at some point beyond the sight of the crowd. This point should be as near the crowd as practical to save time and to conserve energy, and yet far enough from the scene to ensure security. When the unit is in formation, it should be marched smartly into view at a reasonably safe distance from the crowd, thus giving the impression of being well organized and highly disciplined. When confronting the crowd the unit should be in the cordon formation (as described at 10(a) and 11(a)) with shields at their sides in a standby position. This show of force must convince the crowd that the police are determined to control the situation and are in a position to do so.

8. *Group Two – protection for deployed officers*

There is a strong school of thought that shields must always be used to advance the police on the crowd. That is, of course, the ultimate aim when there is serious disorder and peace must be restored. However, it is not always possible and certainly inadvisable if there is not sufficient police strength to achieve the objectives. Action precipitated without regard to the capabilities of the available manpower may result in serious injury to police and require the police commander to withdraw his forces.

9. With the above factors in mind shield units may be deployed statically to:

 (a) Provide a controlled method of filter for non-hostile members of the crowd wishing to leave the area.
 (b) Confine a hostile crowd to a geographical area advantageous to police strategy.
 (c) Distract the attention of the crowd from unprotected officers – in other words to act literally as 'Aunt Sally's' and draw fire.
 (d) Act as a decoy and draw the crowd whilst other police units are strategically positioned.
 (e) Afford protection to police officers who are operating search lights, conducting searches.
 (f) NOTE: This is X'ed through in the original: Protect officers engaged on other duties in searches, operating search lights, etc.
 (f) Protect officers already deployed whilst reserves are brought in.
 (g) Protect emergency services.

10. *Manoeuvre 2*
(a) *Brief description* – unit shield cordon

(b) *Detailed description*
Any number of long shield subsections are uniformly spaced across
the road facing the hostile crowd in the position described at 3(d).
There is a gap between each shield unit.

11. *Manoeuvre 3*
(a) *Brief description* – shield cordon base line
(b) *Detailed description*
The shield units form a cordon as described at 10(b). Instead of
there being a gap between each subsection, they all link together to
form a continuous shield line across the road with the link men in
their normal position. On the command 'open order' the units split
again into the position described at 10(b).

12. *Manoeuvre 4*
(a) *Brief description* – individual shield cordon
(b) *Detailed description*
Officers each carrying a long shield are uniformly spread across the
road in line abreast either in 'loose' formation – a gap between each
shield, or in 'tight' formation – the shields linked together.

13. *Group Three* – *advancing the police line in order to gain ground and
effect dispersal or arrest*
Once the police commander has had time to consolidate his resources
and to decide his strategy he may consider that it is necessary to advance
the police line in stages to:
(a) Positions where it is tactically beneficial to him;
(b) Force a crowd back to facilitate the operation of other emergency
    services, i.e. fire brigade and ambulance;
(c) Secure and protect key buildings;
(d) Recover injured personnel;
(e) Give protection to arresting officers;
(f) Effect crowd dispersal.

14. Having determined and achieved his police line the commander
must try to disperse the crowd and arrest offenders. It is difficult if not
impossible for officers carrying long shields to make arrests, but they can
effectively be used to disperse crowds and to provide protection for
arrest squads of non-shield and short shield carrying officers.

15. To position arrest squads advantageously the commander will have
to consider the terrain and bring units forward under the protection of
the shield serials in manoeuvres described in this group. These

manoeuvres can also be used to bring in units around the flanks and behind the crowd so as to confine them in order to facilitate arrests.

16. *Manoeuvre 5*
(a) *Brief description* – advancing cordon
(b) *Detailed description*
   The shields units as described at 10(a) are uniformly spaced in formation across the width of the road. Gaps are left between each unit, to facilitate return of stranded officers, etc., see 10(a). The units advance on the command in a controlled manner until they have achieved their objective and secured the ground. The back-up men in the unit and following reserves of short shield or non-shield carrying officers run forward when the opportunity arises and make arrests.

17. *Manoeuvre 6*
(a) *Brief description* – long shielded wedge
(b) *Detailed description*
   A wedge is formed from 12 shield officers, with 2 shield officers at the head, standing close but not linking shields. The other shield officers of the unit stand to the rear and slightly to the left and right respectively. The sergeants position themselves at the end of either arm of the wedge. The Inspector takes up his command position in the wedge and is joined by the link men. They obtain their protection from the wedge. The wedge advances at speed through a shield cordon and into the crowd for an agreed distance (never more than 10 yards). At the agreed point the wedge thereby establishes a new secure line. Then, operating a split cordon movement, the 5-men shield sub-section pushes the crowd into side streets. In the event of the crowd running away from this advance, the link men and other reserves with or without short shields run through the line of long shields and make arrests. It is important however that the arrest squads do not advance more than about 20–30 yards to achieve their objectives.

18. *Manoeuvre 7*
(a) *Brief description* – free running line
(b) *Detailed description*
   All officers are equipped with long shields and sufficient numbers are issued to fill the width of the road. The officers are spread uniformly so as to facilitate independent movement. Officers work in teams of 10 under the supervision of a sergeant who is positioned at the rear of the shield group. The line of shield officers advances on

the crowd at a jogging pace. Within the capacity of the officers, the dressing being taken from a central point in the line, the supervising officer at the rear can dictate the speed of advance. The shields are held so that the bottom is tilted away from the carrier. The cordon is given a fixed objective, e.g. a road junction, but it should never be more than a distance of 30–40 yards at a time. Arrest squads of short shield and/or non-shield carrying officers follow up and make arrests under the protection of the long shields.

Short Shields

1. *Introduction*
Long shields have proved to be ideal for protecting officers against missiles, however they tend to be large and heavy and not really suitable for supervisors who whilst obviously needing some degree of protection don't require it to the same degree as the front-line men. The short shield was therefore originally developed for use by supervising officers in charge of long shield units and has in that respect proved to be quite successful. Officers using long shields can't move rapidly and find it difficult to make arrests. Disorderly crowds have recognized that fact, in consequence of which long shields have tended to attract missiles. Obviously a method is needed to advance on the crowd at speed to make arrests but at the same time to give a degree of protection to the officers so deployed.

2. *Objectives*
When missiles are being thrown short shields can be effectively used to achieve one or more of the following objectives:
(a) To protect supervising officers in charge of long shield units and allow them to operate with those units without losing operational control;
(b) To provide protection for fast moving arrest squads;
(c) To provide protection for fast moving dispersal squads.

3. *Tactical manoeuvres*
(a) A number of tactical manoeuvres are set out below designed to achieve the above objectives;
(b) The manoeuvres have been grouped according to required objectives;
(c) The manoeuvres stated are not exhaustive but form the basis upon which others could be developed to satisfy local needs. Long-shield and short-shield units should be predetermined prior to deployment. Where possible both long and short shields should be carried

in personnel carriers. Ideally, however, when actually deployed as a shield unit members of that unit should all carry only either long or short shields and not a combination of both. It is recognized that smaller forces may have insufficient reserves of manpower to permit such a degree of selection. Officers with short shields should not be deployed on defensive cordons and generally may need initial protection of long shields, water cannon or buildings, etc. When they are deployed it should be for a rapid action with very clear objectives.

Group 2 – Protection of four-man arrest squads

Manoeuvre 2
(a) *Brief description* – four-man arrest squads operating outside cover of long shield cordons
(b) *Detailed description*
Personnel are grouped into teams of 4, comprising 2 officers. With short shields in front and 2 back-up men. The teams take initial protection behind the cordons of long shields and on command will run forward towards an identifiable offender in an effort to arrest him. The two short-shield men protect the non-shield men whilst they make this arrest and take their prisoner back to the police lines. The team should not run forward more than 30 yards. They must stop after that distance and return behind the long-shield cordon cover area even if they have not made an arrest. Whilst the short-shield teams are making arrests the long-shield cordon should be moving forward in an effort either to pass the short shield teams to give them protection or to reduce the distance that the short-shield men have to return with their prisoners.

Manoeuvre 3
(a) *Brief description* – Two-man arrest squads allowing one man to operate without a shield
(b) *Detailed description*
Officers working in pairs are deployed behind a cordon of long shields. One has a short shield with or without a baton and the other acts as the back-up. The back-up man holds on to the belt of the short shield man and on the given command they run forward into the crowd either through or around the flank of the long shields, or following up the 'free running line' (see *Long Shields*). The pairs run a maximum distance of 30 yards for the non-shield man to make an arrest under the protection of the short shield. In the meantime the long shield cordon advances in an effort either to pass the short-

shield pairs to give them protection or to reduce the distance that the pairs have to return with prisoner.

Manoeuvre 4
(a) *Brief description* – Four-man arrest squads operating with wedge formations
(b) *Detailed description*
Officers with short shields are positioned inside a wedge of long shields as described in *Long Shields*. Once the long shields have penetrated the crowd they will form into a shield cordon with the arrest teams of 2 short-shield and 2 non-shield carriers behind them. On the command the arrest team run either through or around the flank of the long shields to make arrests. The short shields should not advance more than about 20–30 yards and the long-shield cordon should advance to give added protection.

Manoeuvre 5
(a) *Brief description* – Baton charge to disperse crowd
(b) *Detailed description*
All officers are issued with a short shield and short baton. The unit forms with 2 single files comprising 10 men each under the command of a sergeant, behind the long-shield cordon. When it is relatively safe to do so the files march forward either through or around the flanks of the long-shield cordons. On the command they form a cordon 2 deep across the road ensuring that the rear line have a clear view and path ahead of them. The cordon march forward on the crowd and if missiles are thrown, charge with batons drawn in an effort to disperse. Objectives must be given and the charge should not be for more than about 30 yards. Meantime the long-shield cordon should advance to gain ground and provide protection for retreating short-shield officers.

Manoeuvre 6
(a) *Brief description* – Short-shield baton carrying team deployed into crowd
(b) *Detailed description*
Long-shield officers deployed into crowd and deployed across the road. Behind long-shields, units are deployed all with short and round shields and carrying batons. On the command the short-shield officers run forward either through or round the flanks of long-shields into the crowd for not more than 30 yards. They disperse the crowd and incapacitate missile throwers and ring leaders by striking in a controlled manner with batons about the

arms, legs or torso so as not to cause serious injury. Immediately following the short-shield units the long-shield units advance quickly beyond the short shields to provide additional protection. Link men from long-shield units move in and take prisoners.

Manoeuvre 7
(a) *Brief description* – Short-shield teams deployed into crowd
(b) *Detailed description*
   Officers carrying short shields with or without batons are formed into 2 double 5-men files with a Sergeant at the back of each file and the Inspector between the 2 files. This unit will initially be protected by long shields or personnel carriers and on the command will run at the crowd in pairs to disperse and/or incapacitate. The long shields will follow on to gain ground and give additional protection for arresting officers.

Mounted police
Mounted branch officers may be employed in the public disorder context to achieve one or some of the following objectives:
(a) Confronting a hostile crowd with a display of strength to discourage riotous behaviour; this may be merely 'within view' or at 'close quarters' with the crowd;
(b) Applying pressure at close quarters to hold or ease back a solidly packed crowd, preserving the police line or gaining ground;
(c) Protecting buildings from a hostile crowd;
(d) Opening gaps in a crowd or separating sections of the crowd by the measured weight of horses;
(e) Dispersing a crowd using impetus to create fear and a scatter effect;
(f) Dispersing a crowd using impetus and weight to physically push back a crowd;
(g) 'Sweeping' streets and parklands of mobile groups and individuals;
(h) Combining with other officers on foot (they employ varied tactics) to achieve any of the above objectives.

Group four – Crowd dispersal
When officers are deployed in close contact with crowds there is always the option of gradually pushing the crowds back thereby achieving a slow dispersal. The dispersal manoeuvres discussed below, however, provide for a more rapid dispersal based on fear created by the impetus of horses. A generalization can be made about dispersal tactics of this nature; that they are only a viable option when the hostile crowd has somewhere to

disperse to rapidly. It would be quite inappropriate to use such a manoeuvre against a densely packed crowd.

Manoeuvre 10
(a) *Brief description* – Mounted officers advance on a crowd in a way indicating that they do not intend to stop.
(b) *Detailed description*
     This manoeuvre can be applied whether there are foot police in close contact with the crowd in a 'stand-off' position or no foot police at all. The mounted police officers form in a double rank, line abreast facing the crowd and advance together at a smart pace (i.e. fast walk or steady trot) towards the crowd. Foot officers stand well aside to let them through and re-form behind following at the double. The horses stop at a predetermined spot, foot officers forming up behind. If missiles are thrown protected officers are brought through the horses, which are then in a position to repeat the manoeuvre.

Manoeuvre 11
Description
This manoeuvre is identical to number 10 except that the advance is made towards the crowd at a canter. The same considerations as regards foot police and halting the horses at a predetermined place apply.

Manoeuvre 12
Description
Combining a rapid advance of mounted police with foot police. Mounted officers with their horses formed in line abreast advance on the crowd followed by shield units jogging behind the mounted formation. When the horses make contact with the crowd the foot officers, with shields, are in a position to make any necessary arrests.

   A warning to the crowd should always be given before adopting mounted dispersal tactics.

Appendix D

From the report of the Home Office working party on the police use of firearms, 3 February 1987.

GUIDELINES FOR THE POLICE ON THE ISSUE AND USE OF FIRE-ARMS

Principles governing issue
Firearms are to be issued only where there is reason to believe that a police officer may have to face a person who is armed or otherwise so dangerous that he could not safely be restrained without the use of firearms; they may also be issued for protection purposes or for the destruction of dangerous animals.

Principles governing use
1. Firearms are to be fired by police officers only as a last resort when conventional methods have been tried and failed, or must, from the nature of the circumstances obtaining, be unlikely to succeed if tried. They may be fired, for example, when it is apparent that a police officer cannot achieve the lawful purpose of preventing loss, or further loss, of life by any other means.
[There is no para. 2.]

Authority to issue
3. Authority to issue firearms should be given by an officer of ACPO rank, save where a delay in getting in touch with such an officer could result in loss of life or serious injury, in which case a Chief Superintendent or Superintendent may authorize issue. In such circumstances an officer of ACPO rank should be informed as soon as possible. Special arrangements may apply where firearms are issued regularly for protection purposes, but these should be authorized by an officer of ACPO rank in the first instance.

Conditions of issue and use
4. The ACPO *Manual of Guidance on the Police Use of Firearms* is the single authoritative source of guidance on tactical and operational matters relating to the use of firearms by the police.
5. Firearms should be issued only to officers who have been trained and authorized in a particular class of weapon. Officers authorized to use

firearms must attend regular refresher courses and those failing to do so or to reach the qualifying standard will lose their authorization and must not thereafter be issued with firearms. Authorized firearms officers must hold an authorization card showing the type(s) of weapon that may be issued to them. The authorization card must be produced before a weapon is issued and must always be carried when the officer is armed. The card holder's signature in the issue register should be verified against the signature on the officer's warrant card. The card should be issued without alteration and should have an expiry date.

6. Records of issue and operational use must be maintained. All occasions on which shots are fired by police officers other than to destroy animals must be thoroughly investigated by a senior officer and a full written report prepared.

Briefing

7. In any armed operation briefing by senior officers is of paramount importance and must include both authorized firearms officers and non-firearms personnel involved in the operation. Senior officers must stress the objective of the operation including specifically the individual responsibility of authorized firearms officers. Particular attention must be paid to the possible presence of innocent parties.

Use of minimum force

8. Nothing in these guide-lines affects the principle, to which Section 3 of the Criminal Law Act 1967 gives effect, that only such force as is reasonable in the circumstances may be used. The degree of force justified will vary according to the circumstances of each case. Responsibility for firing a weapon rests with the individual officer and a decision to do so may have to be justified in legal proceedings.

Warning

9. If it is reasonable to do so an oral warning is to be given before opening fire.

10. Urgent steps are to be taken to ensure that early medical attention is provided for any casualties.

Summary

11. A brief summary of the most important points for an individual officer is attached. It is suggested that this summary be placed on the reverse side of each authorization card so that officers will have it with them whenever they are armed.

AUTHORIZED FIREARMS OFFICERS
GUIDELINES ON USE OF MINIMUM FORCE

The Law
Section 3 of the Criminal Law Act 1967 reads:

A person may use such force as is reasonable in the circumstances in the
prevention of crime, or in the effecting or assisting in the lawful arrest of
offenders or suspected offenders or of persons unlawfully at large.

Strict reminder
A firearm is to be fired only as a last resort. Other methods must have
been tried and failed, or must – because of the circumstances – be
unlikely to succeed if tried. For example, a firearm may be fired when it is
apparent that the police cannot achieve their lawful purpose of preventing loss, or further loss, of life by any other means. If it is reasonable to do
so an oral warning is to be given before opening fire.

Individual responsibility
The responsibility for the *use* of the firearm is an *individual* decision
which may have to be justified in legal proceedings.
REMEMBER THE LAW. REMEMBER YOUR TRAINING.

Index

Adie, Kate, 121
Alderson, John, 44, 47–50, 56–7, 59–
    60, 63, 124, 132–3, 144, 156
ambulance service, 118
Anderton, C. James, 47, 115, 132, 140,
    144, 147
Assisi, St Francis of, 165
Association of Chief Police Officers
    (ACPO), 1, 23, 27, 38–47, 49–52,
    55, 57–62, 65–6, 74, 77–8, 82,
    84–5, 89, 91, 93–4, 97–103,
    106–7, 109, 111–12, 115–18,
    120–1, 124, 127, 131, 134–7,
    139–41, 144–6, 148, 150, 152,
    156–7, 161, 163, 169, 172–3,
    176, 179, 183–93
    – ACPO Rank, 43, 46–7, 56, 58,
    65, 84, 89, 97–100, 103, 106, 193
    – Annual conference 1981, 38–41,
    47, 49, 77, 134
    – Community Disorder Tactical
    Options Inter-Force Working
    Group, 40, 42–3, 45
    – Joint Standing Committee on
    police use of firearms, 115–6
    – Public Order Forward Planning
    Unit, 44–5, 73, 125, 152, 181–2
    – Public Order sub-committee, 41,
    44–5, 182
Association of County Councils, 176
Association of Metropolitan
    Authorities, 176
Atlanta, Georgia, 162–3

Bangkok, 133
barricade removal, 22–4, 70, 89
barriers, 70, 88–9
Bath, University of, 147
baton (truncheon), 40, 53, 57, 59, 95,
    97, 131, 136, 153, 189–91
    – baton charge, 70, 93, 101–3, 190
    – drumming on shield, 57, 89
    – long baton, 70, 103
    – use in colonies, 130
baton round, see plastic bullet
battle cries, 57, 89–90
BBC TV News, 121

Belfast, 128
Benn, Tony, 58
Bingley Hall, Stafford, 114
Birmingham, 2, 5–6, 21, 58, 61, 157
    – West Midlands Police, 27, 36, 41,
    60, 157, 159
    – Handsworth/Lozells, 21, 26,
    61–2, 139, 157–9, 164
Blakelock, Keith, 29, 62, 124
Blick, David, 33–4
Borneo, 135
Bramshill, Police Staff College, 46–7,
    55
Brass Tacks, 55–7, 60, 92, 144–5, 157
Bristol, 2, 26, 31, 36–7, 175–6
    – Avon & Somerset Police, 36, 154
    – St Paul's, 26, 36
Brittan, Leon, 29, 153–5
Brixton, 26, 31, 49–50, 61, 91, 116,
    139, 159, 164
    – 'Swamp 81', 37
Broadwater Farm, Tottenham, 7, 26,
    29, 31, 62, 63, 137, 139, 159,
    164, 169
Brodie, Peter, 133
Brooke, Henry, 142, 146
Brown, H 'Rap', 163
Byford, Sir Lawrence, 62, 63

Capper, Sir Derek, 133
Carmichael, Stokeley, 163
Carroll, Lewis, 122
'Carruthers Estate', Sandford, Ch. 1,
    (map p.8), 46, 62, 80
casualty bureaux, 117
Chalmers, James, 41
checkpoints, 70, 88
Chelsea, 1, 4, 6
Chidley, Richard, 21–5
CID, 18, 20, 33, 66, 80
Cirencester, 38
civil defence, 85, 118
Clement, Tony, 57
CND, 88
community intervenors, 7, 70–1, 73,
    75, 162, 180
computerization, 78

Conservative Party, 173
cordons, 70, 87–8, 100
Coventry, 33
Crawford, George, 170–1
Crowe, Eric, 16–20
CS gas (tear gas), 26, 30, 34, 42, 46,
    49, 62–3, 70, 73, 93, 100, 104–5,
    109–6, 136, 148, 151, 153, 156–
    7, 161, 172, 176
 – thrown at boxing match, 114
 – use in colonies, 130–1
 – use in Hong Kong, 40
 – use in Toxteth, 48, 110
Cumberland Lodge, Windsor, 121
Cyprus, 135

Dear, Geoffrey, 27–8, 41, 60, 159–60
Democrats, (SLD party), 172
Denning, Lord, 143, 145
Detroit, Michigan, 27
Devon & Cornwall Police, 47, 49, 115
District Supportr Unit, see Police
    Support Unit
district training centres, 46
Dixon, George, 63
dogs, 3, 53, 70, 93, 100
Dublin, 127–8
Dudley, West Midlands, 20

education, see local government
evacuation, 22

FBI, 61, 140
Fiji, 133, 135
File On 4, 33–4, 172
firearms, 30, 35, 42, 46, 68, 70, 73, 87,
    93, 98, 115–16, 153, 193–5
 – use against police, 25, 61, 109,
    157–60
 – use in colonies, 40, 130
fire brigade, 7, 11, 15–18, 20, 118
Foreign Office, 129, 133
Foster, Michael, 20–1, 25
Freemasons, 124

General Strike, 59
Gill, George, 149–50
Gold Coast, 133
Griffiths, Sir Eldon, 171
Grosvenor Square, London, 34, 50,
    56, 88
Grunwick, 139
Guardian, 53

Hall, David, 41
Hammond, George, 124
hand signals, 117
Harlem, New York City, 27
Henry, Roy, 39, 77, 101, 134–6, 138,
    169
Home Office/Home Secretary, 35, 44,
    49, 52, 62, 63, 85, 94, 112, 121,
    140–2, 144–6, 148–51, 175–80,
    193–5
 – HM Inspectorate of Constabulary,
    62–3, 115, 132, 134, 145, 151,
    175–6
 – link with ACPO, 39, 41, 43–6, 58,
    66, 109, 139, 145–6, 161
 – Public Order Liaison Group, 45
 – supplies plastic bullets/CS gas, 81,
    148–51
 – Working Party on police use of
    firearms, 115–16, 193–5
Hornsey, 171
horses (Mounted Police), 53–4, 56–8,
    70, 93, 98–100, 191–2
Hurd, Douglas, 29, 115, 148

Imbert, Peter, 60, 140, 171–2
Independent, 122
India, 126, 132
informants, 80
information management, 70, 75–6
intelligence-gathering, 10, 20–1, 77–
    81, 103, 136
 – Central Intelligence Unit, 81
 – tension indicators, 78–9
intensive foot patrols, 70, 76

Jeavons, David, 6–7, 10–16
Johnson, Lyndon B., 27, 61, 131
 – National Commission on riots, 26,
    48, 60–1, 131
journalists, see media

Kent, 26, 54
Kenya, 135
KGB, 141
King, Martin Luther, Sen., 162
Knights, Lord (Sir Philip), 34, 38, 85,
    92, 151–2, 161–2
Ku Klux Klan, 163

Labour Party, 172
Land Rover, 84, 130
lighting (artificial), 70, 87

Liverpool, 2, 37, 150
 – Merseyside Police, 42, 110, 115
 – Toxteth, 26, 110, 139, 159
 – use of CS gas, 48, 110
local government, 22, 118, Ch.9
 – education service, 17, 19, 105,
   118–21, 142
London, 2
long shield, 13, 23–4, 34, 41, 46, 53,
   58–9, 70, 91–2, 96, 108, 168,
   179, 183–92
 – Manoeuvres, 183–8

Macoun, Michael, 111, 129–33, 135
Malaya, 135
Manchester, 2, 37, 56, 132, 150
 – Greater Manchester Police, 35–6,
   47, 115, 154–5
 – Greater Manchester Police
   Authority, 147
 – Moss Side, 37
 – university students, 29, 154
Manilow, Barry, 91
Manpower Services Commission, 157
Mansfield, Michael, 57
Mark, Sir Robert, 173
media, 19, 75, 118, 121–4
Merrick, Ronald, 126
Metropolitan Police, 27, 36, 39, 41, 47,
   83, 115, 127–9, 140, 176, 182,
   184
 – at Broadwater farm, 7, 137
 – firearms squad, 64
 – Hendon, 52, 116, 138, 164–9,
   171–2
 – Hounslow, 46, 138, 168–70
 – New Scotland Yard, 35, 44, 125,
   137, 182
 – Royal and Diplomatic Protection
   Group, 124
Moynihan, Colin, 114
mutual aid, 6, 17, 25, 42, 80, 175, 178
 – Inter-force liaison, 118, 152
 – National Reporting Centre, 35, 55

National Coal Board, 26
National Union of Mineworkers, 25,
   52, 81 (see also Orgreave)
New Statesman, 110
Newark, New Jersey, 27
Newcastle-upon-Tyne, 132
 – Northumbria Police Authority,
   148–51

Newman, Sir Kenneth, 27, 63
Nicholl, Jeremy, 122
normal policing, 70, 73–4, 77, 136–8,
   169–71
Notting Hill Carnival (1987), 169, 171
Nuremberg, 107

observation posts (spotters), 6, 7, 10,
   22, 80
Olds, Philip, 124
Orgreave, 52–9, 99, 139, 163
 – 'riot' trials, 53, 89, 91–2, 96–9
 – video, 53, 55–7, 59, 124
Out of Court, 154
Oxford, Kenneth, 42–3, 110, 115

Paris, 116, 172
Parliament, 37, 42, 52, 60, 175
 – House of Commons library, 57,
   91, 183
Payne, Christopher, 41, 44
Peirce, Gareth, 53–4, 56, 59
Peterloo, 59
Philippines, 132
plastic bullets, (baton rounds), 26, 30,
   42, 46, 49, 62–4, 70, 73, 93,
   98–100, 106–9, 112, 114–16,
   125, 136, 148–51, 153, 156–62,
   172
 – at Broadwater Farm, 7, 63, 137
Police Act of 1964, 143, 148–51
Police Authorities, 7, Ch. 9, 175
 – no consultation, 42, 44, 52, 59,
   141, 144
 – plastic bullets, 62, 148–51
Police Complaints Authority, 115, 122,
   154
Police Federation, 29, 45, 60, 94, 115,
   117, 122, 171, 176, 179
 – Police, 29, 45, 60, 122, 171
Police Field Force, see Riot Control
   Unit
Police Mobile Unit, see Riot Control
   Unit
Police Motorised Company, see Riot
   Control Unit
Police National Computer, 35
police observers, 117
Police Review, 35, 63, 116, 123, 135,
   151
 – Public Order and the Police, 35
Police Superintendents' Association,
   115, 117, 176, 179

Police Support Unit (PSU), 5, 10, 15–17, 22, 25, 41, 52, 70, 84–7, 95, 125, 183–4
– like platoon, 52, 138
– like riot control unit, 84
– Orgreave, 55
Polkinghorne, David, 137
Preston, 38, 49
propaganda, anti-police, 10, 76, 96, 114, 123, 125
protected vehicles, 70, 73, 84, 86, 103–4
protective equipment (riot gear), 1, 4–5, 12–17, 24, 34, 46, 52, 55, 63, 70, 73, 76, 82–3, 179, 182
– Scarman report, 50

Quine, Richard, 39–40, 134

Radley, John, 41
Riot Control Unit (colonies), 84, 130–1, 138, 153
– Hong Kong Police Tactical Unit, 40
– like PSU, 84, 138
– riot squad, 37, 59, 176
Rohrer, Rob, 110
Rome, 95, 132
Royal Commissions on police,
– 1908, 170
– 1929, 141, 143
– 1962, 142–3, 146
Royal Hong Kong Police, 23, 39–42, 59, 86, 101, 106, 131, 133–8, 169
– ACPO conference, 39–42, 77, 134
– baton round, 131
– British police visit, 132–4
Royal Irish Constabulary, 127–9
Royal Ulster Constabulary, 29–30, 39, 92, 125, 128–9, 155

Saltley Coke Depot, 35, 59, 85
'Sandford', Ch.1
Sarawak, 135
saturation policing, 70, 86–7
Scarborough, 29
Scarman, Lord, 26–7, 37, 50–2, 110, 164, 168
Scott, Paul, 126
Secret Society, 140, 144
Sheffield, 55
short shield (also round shield), 13, 22–4, 46, 53–4, 57–9, 70, 95–7,

102, 136, 188–92
– like gladiator, 95
– like riot squad, 59, 95, 136
Sierra Leone, 132
Sloan, Kenneth, 35
smoke, 70, 91, 104–6
sound, 70, 89–91
South Africa, 111, 157–9
Special Air Service, 157–8, 163, 169
Special Branch, 77, 80, 122
Special Constables, 12, 117
Special Patrol Group (SPG), 5, 30, 33–4, 70, 83–4
– Territorial Support Group, 83, 137
– see also Police Support Unit
Stalker, John, 155
'Starpower', 167–8
Stonehenge, 88, 154, 163
Strathclyde Police, 36
stress, operational, 117
Sun, 114
Sunday Telegraph, 47–9

Tanganyika, 129
tear gas, see CS gas
Territorial Support Group, see Special Patrol Group
Terry, George, 49–50
Thatcher, Margaret, 58, 114, 142, 158, 173
– the Enemy Within, 32, 52, 147
Third Force, 63, 172, 177
Thompson, Sir Kenneth, 146
Tonypandy, 59
traffic department, 117
Transit vans, 4–5, 83–4
transport, public/private, 70, 83–4
truncheon, see baton
Tunbridge Wells, 38

Uganda, 129
United States of America, 27, 48, 60–1, 119, 131, 162–3

Wapping, 121–2, 139, 163
warnings (police), 23–4, 46–7, 70, 72, 97–8, 131, 192, 194
Warrington, 139
watch and ward, see normal policing
water cannon, 26, 34, 48, 71, 98, 115–16, 161, 176
Watts, Los Angeles, 27

Wayne, John, 166
Webb, David, 159, 162
Weigh, Brian, 36–7
whistles and flags, 117
Whitelaw, Lord, 35, 37, 41, 141, 175–
    6
Williams, Derek, 3, 7, 25–6

women and children, 118, 124–5
Wood Green, 137
Wright, Alan, 29–30
Wright, Peter, 54

Yorkshire, 26
Young, Alan, 164, 168–9